Meet Me At Fir Tree Lodge

RACHEL DOVE

ONE PLACE. MANY STORIES.

HQ
An imprint of HarperCollins*Publishers* Ltd
1 London Bridge Street
London SE1 9GF

www.harpercollins.co.uk
HarperCollins *Publishers*
1st Floor, Watermarque Building, Ringsend Road
Dublin 4, Ireland

First published in Great Britain by
HQ, an imprint of HarperCollins*Publishers* Ltd 2020

ISBN: 9780008375843

To Peter
Ten years of marriage, two boys, and I still love you fiercely
(and your scrumptious bum)
Love George

Prologue

Giggling, Frank almost dropped his breakfast on the pavement as he exited the shop. A passing pigeon looked elated at the prospect, before it was snatched away, and the bird was left cooing crossly. Back to the discarded wrappers and food scraps it went as Frank sang down the street, his knees bouncing with every movement.

'You only want me for my baps,' she'd said. Frank was still chuckling at their little in-joke as he started up his car. Every weekday morning, she said the same to him, passing him his order with a happy smile that he'd grown accustomed to seeing. He looked forward to it. Marilyn always smiled, and she always set him up for the day. Even now, he was still grinning at her saucy humour.

The sun was shining in the suburbs of York as the silver BMW sprang to life, the occupant ready to get on with his regular journey. Pulling out of the side street, Frank took one hand off the wheel and waved at the woman in the shop window he'd just vacated. She saw him and waved back, and he drove off with a smile. It was Wednesday, which in Frank's world meant driving to get a paper and a couple of soft bacon butties from Marilyn's shop, before going to get his hair cut at Tony's later in the afternoon.

With the fragrant smell of bacon and fresh bread in his nostrils, he pulled onto the main road, driving away from the small rows of shops that ran along the streets of Pocklington. Nearing the local primary school, he stopped for Audrey Shingles, the lollipop lady, as she brandished her huge stick and walked into the middle of the busy road. Frank nodded at her and watched the boys and girls all walk past, book bags and PE kits swinging from their hands as they were led across the road like baby ducklings. St Thomas's was where his own son once went, and Frank felt a wave of nostalgia flow through him. Seeing a little boy with brown hair crossing the road, his bag almost as big as him, Frank made a mental note to call his own offspring when he got home.

He drove past the school, grinning at Audrey as she thanked him for stopping for the children. Audrey went to return his smile, but her face dropped a little as he drove by. *Odd*, he thought. *Not her usual cheery self today.* He drove past the school, easing out of the congestion. Away from the chatter at the school gates, the car grew quiet. Too quiet. He could hear a faint buzzing noise in his head, as though he'd just walked out of a Def Leppard concert feeling a little numb between the ears. Frank went to click on the radio, but his arm didn't connect with the button. He tried again, but his left arm barely moved. Panic hit him like a wave of icy cold water, making his right arm wobble on the steering wheel. He pulled the car straight, his heart pumping in his chest. What was happening? He felt like he was tied to his seat. His heart beat faster. *Boom boom boom* in his ears. The pulsing made his head hurt. Feel woolly even.

'What the . . .' Frank spoke out loud, but it came out like a muffled waaa-faaaa sound. He tried again, his panic building as he used his good arm to slowly move to the side of the road. This wasn't as easy as it sounded, given that his whole body was now leaning over to the middle of the car. Frank just couldn't right himself, every movement was awkward, and tiring. Terrifying.

I have to stop this car.

The traffic had dropped off past the school gates, but rounding the corner in the direction of the church, Frank could see a queue forming from the traffic lights further down. He could see harassed school mums trying to get to work, bored-looking people heading to their jobs the shops or breakfast with a friend. Life lay before him, but he couldn't interact with any of it. Couldn't warn them. He was going to crash, and he couldn't do a thing. He tried to shout for help, to stop the car. He jammed the foot that was still working down on the brake as hard as he could, trying and failing to wrench the handbrake up with hands that now refused to obey him. Even his own thoughts were jumbled, chaotic. Frank thought of Luke, and his Debra, and shoved his limp hands down on the horn. Beep. Again. Beep. Again. Closer now. Crashing. Beep. *Help me.* Beep. *I can't, I'm going to . . .*

The silver BMW slammed side on into a row of three parked cars outside the Bella Donna Care Home, sending care workers and relatives scurrying outside to see what the commotion was, and then racing to help, shouting to each other to bring towels, blankets. Call for help. The horn, held down by Frank's bleeding skull, continued to sound, cutting through the noise of everything else. Frank, feeling now like he could barely move at all, tried to reach his mobile phone, which was in his coat pocket. He fumbled with the fabric, trying and failing to push his fingers into the space. His door was opened at the side of him, and people were talking to him. Asking him questions, telling him not to move, that help was coming. He wanted to speak, to tell them that something was wrong, so very wrong, but the words eluded him. They floated like mischievous pixies in his head. Every time he reached for one, they flew off and nothing that came from his lips made sense. Frank was lost and utterly terrified. He thought of the little boy in the backpack, and a tear fell from his slack cheek.

'Don't move, okay Mr Sommersby?' Marilyn's son. Frank couldn't answer him. He didn't know how. When he felt Jamie's hand on his, he squeezed it as hard as he could. 'Over here! He's touching my hand! Quickly!' Jamie's voice sounded strangled, panicked, and Frank wanted to tell him to shush. Not to make a fuss. It was okay. It wasn't, but he felt so very confused. So very weary. 'Mam, have you called for help?'

He could sense someone else there now, and he felt something on his arm. Warm. It pervaded his numbness somehow, and he tried to turn his head towards the warmth.

'No, don't move Frank. It's okay, we're here. Help is on the way. You hang in there, you hear me?' Frank recognised the female voice, but he couldn't conjure up the name or the face in his head. Just the feeling of the voice. The way it made his body respond. It kept the fear at bay, a little at least. He tried to focus, to flex his fingers. He had no way of knowing if his digits had responded, and the voices didn't comment. They weren't silent though, and he could hear other noises too. The toot of a car . . . thingy, and the loud herald of sirens. Help. That's what that sound meant. He didn't remember what a horn was, or the name of the woman holding his hand and whispering pleas to cling on, but he knew that help was here. The sad thing was, Frank's life had already flashed before his eyes, and what he had seen had made him want to let go. Give in. His eyelids fluttered closed, but a voice shrieked at the side of him, waking him up.

'That's it!' the voice said, shakily strong. 'No more baps from me if you leave Frank, so hang on in there.'

'Mam,' another voice. 'Mam, is he answering?'

'No son,' the first voice scolded. 'He knows what to do though. He'll be fine. That's the end of it.' The sirens grew closer, the noise of the commotion growing ever louder still. Frank would have hated all the fuss normally, all the people put out because of him. He'd have apologised, had he been able to, but he was stuck with one image in his head. The little brown-haired boy in the backpack, that made his tired heart clench. He could still hear voices now, but he couldn't make sense of them. They were so loud, and he was in so much pain. He went to say something, but his body was no longer his to control. Trying one last time to squeeze the hand that was holding his, he gave a long sigh, and gave in.

Chapter 1

Sometimes, when everyone is seemingly out there in the world, being happy, joyful, and full of life, a woman just wants to tell them all to sod off and die in a pit of fire. That was the first thought that entered Rebecca's head that morning, and it was probably the most upbeat thought she'd had since she awoke. The twinge in her lower back always made her a little grumpy first thing on a morning. Sometimes she would still wake in an odd position, wracked with a sudden spasm. As though her muscle memory had stored that feeling of horrendous pain. As though it wanted to remind her what could go wrong when you reached for the stars. Falling from the heavens wasn't without injury. Pieces breaking off. It wasn't so much the pain anymore. It was the memory that haunted her the most. The feeling of falling, tumbling, breaking. Hearing her own bones snap. It was enough to make anyone a little bit jaded about the world. Her nan used to call her arthritic early morning pain the 'crabby hour'. Now, reflecting on her current early morning mood, she understood just what her old nan meant. Why she'd been so snarky on so many occasions.

Turning over in bed, registering the current pain-free state of her lower half, she slowly opened her eyes, using her covers as a shield against the bright light coming from the curtained window. She was wrapped up like a mountain Sherpa, with only tiny slits for her to see through exposed to the cold of the room. Turning the heat off on a night saved the pennies, but it meant waking up in a brilliant white icebox. The glamping equivalent of an igloo. It made her even less inclined to jump out of bed with glee.

'Jesus!' She shrieked as her bare feet finally plucked up the courage to leave the comfort of her 13.5-tog duvet. Padding across the wooden floor, she looked at the view from her bedroom window. The same view she'd looked at for the past year, since she'd moved into the master bedroom. On the other side of the thick glass, the French Alps lay glistening before her. The snow-topped mountains were a dazzling white, the powder fresh and untouched yet by man. No tell-tale sweeping scars left from skis in the snow. It looked like a picture postcard. Something to make a person marvel at the wonder of the world they inhabited. Reaching for the curtains, which were thin and utterly useless white voiles anyway, she swished them closed and dived straight back under the covers. Shivering, she pushed out a hand and grabbed her mobile phone from its charging pod.

15 MESSAGES
2 MISSED CALLS

All from one person: Mum. Unbidden, an image of the woman who gave her life popped up in her head. Crying by Rebecca's hospital bedside when she thought her daughter was sleeping off the powerful pain meds she was dosed up on. Medicine to keep her still, to let her body heal, recover. The whispered phone calls, her mother's desperate voice as she tried to field the questions from the press. She could still remember her mother standing there, in the doorway of the private room. Rebecca had woken with the pain, and her mother's anguished hushed tones from the other side of the room had filtered into her foggy head. Her mother was in the doorway, her back to the room. The stark white glow from the artificially lit corridor made her mother's complexion look a little grey, her pale white pallor highlighted more by the trademark bright colours she wore. The woman had never met a Laura Ashley design she didn't love.

'Rebecca will be fine, and your headline is damn right wrong, Bruce. After all the years of professional competing, I think you know the calibre of the skier that we are talking about. The Ice Rebel is down, but she's not bloody well out.' Her mother pushed the last of her words out with a fiery flourish, her voice almost cracking with the effort. As the tinny voice of Bruce, editor of the latest tabloid to latch on to her very public accident on the slopes, nattered back into her mother's delicate ear on the phone, Rebecca watched her mother. The fight had left her with those words, as she watched her mother sink into the visitor's chair and lean her head against a wall. Right there and then, she made the decision that she'd been thrashing round in her head since . . .

The phone rang in her hand, and 'MUM' flashed on the screen. Rebecca let it ring off. It was far too early to deal with speaking to her right now. Not that her phone was blowing up these days.

The thought depressed her every time. Rebecca's mum, and Hans, her boss and once flatmate, were the only people to ever call. And even that was mostly about work. Since Hans had moved out of his flat, leaving Rebecca as a sole tenant, he'd stayed close, checking on the café below. And his friend, of course. Alpine Bites was still his baby, and although his wife Holly grew larger with their first child every time Rebecca saw her, Hans was keen to keep an eye on his business. She flicked through the messages on her screen, each one firmer in tone than the last.

DARLING, CALL ME. MUM

HELLO?

JUST READ AN ARTICLE IN THE GUARDIAN ABOUT CHILDLESS WOMEN OVER 30. DIVORCE RATES TRIPLE!

This was her latest area of interest. A grandchild. Rebecca blamed Holly being pregnant for that one. Baby fever. Not that she resented Holly and Hans for being happy, for taking the next step to add to their family. She was happy for them and couldn't wait to be an aunt. It just didn't mean that *her* clock had started ticking yet. Besides which, she'd only just recovered from a shattered pelvis. Pushing an eight-pound baby out of her hoo-haa didn't sound like a great idea at this time in her life. And since her split with Robbie, she hadn't exactly been surrounded by sperm donor candidates anyway.

She shook her head in disbelief and read on.

COMPETITIONS MUST BE STARTING UP NOW. HAVE YOU ENTERED?

Rebecca rolled her eyes, her gaze falling on the stack of competition entry forms that had mysteriously arrived in the post. No postmark though. Funny that. Hans really had a soft spot for her mother, and she played him like a kazoo. Rebecca could only hope she didn't ask him to drop off a jam jar of his finest, get the ball rolling. *Grow your own grandchild from the comfort of your armchair. Wi-Fi connection required.*

Not feeling up to reading the rest, she was about to delete the lot when she saw the next entry. Clicking on the screen to bring up the full text, her jaw hit the floor.

DARLING, DON'T FORGET. IF YOU WON'T COMPETE, THEN OTHER OPPORTUNITIES MIGHT ARISE TO THE RIGHT YOUNG PROFESSIONAL. YOU COULD DO TV!

An image of herself with a microphone in hand came to mind, watching everybody else have fun and fulfil their dreams, whilst she stood on the sidelines grinning like a Playboy bunny and freezing her norks off. Rebecca gritted her teeth and started to type out a reply. She could feel herself getting so irritated. Why did her mother always just seem to strive to get her back up, every time they connected?

Mother, can you at least let me have a coffee before you regret my existence?

delete

New phone, who dis?

delete

Sorry Mother dearest, was straddling the hot new contender, Javier! Text you back when I'm with child!

delete

Yes Mum, all fine here. Was up late practising, sorry. Competition entries going in soon. Love you. Got to get to work. x

She added a cupcake emoji for good measure. Something jaunty to placate her mother, who was probably already on the phone to Sky Sports, trying to blag her a job.

Looking at the screen, Rebecca sagged back into her quilt barrier and sighed heavily. The time was coming when she'd have to tell her mum that she hadn't entered again, and her matriarch-induced stress headache was already playing the bongo drums on her temples at the thought. She wasn't exactly scared of her mother, but she was weary of feeling like the disappointment in the family. She'd never understood the term 'black sheep' really, but she got the gist now. She put the phone back on her bedside table and dragged herself once more onto the floorboards of icy death.

Twenty minutes later, she was downstairs in her uniform of black slacks and matching black short-sleeved T-shirt, both bearing the Alpine Bites logo, where a happy cartoon mountain took a bite out of a doughnut, all embroidered in a hot pink against the pitch black material. She'd tied her hair up as usual, tight to her raven-haired head. She'd even bothered with a little make-up too. Her mother's influence across the miles leaving her feeling just a little bit shit and in need of a bit of war paint to face the day. One red slick of lipstick daubed across her face felt like a shield of armour against the gauntlet of daily reality. Praise be to the goddesses of the concealer stick.

Unlocking the connecting door that stood at the bottom of the lodge stairs, she closed it behind her and walked out into the huge open plan space that was Alpine Bites café. Or as Hans called it, the jewel of Alpe d'Huez. The lodge upstairs, her home with the icy floors, was called Fir Tree Lodge. It suited the place too, it was cosy. Hans loved his business babies, and he named them well. Rebecca did feel at home here, and oddly territorial. For the first time that morning, she smiled to herself as she looked at the expanse of tables and chairs, sofa areas surrounding little nooks and coffee tables, and glass and light wood walls all around. The walls were mostly thick panels of highly polished glass that ran from floor to ceiling, with thin but solid beams in between, making it look like an ultra-modern lodge against the backdrop of the ski slopes around them.

This café had some of the best views of the slopes, and a birds-eye view of the main arena, the largest slope that Alpe d'Huez had to offer. Rebecca loved it, and not just for the views, or the hit of adrenalin that she passively smoked all day long. People talking about their days on the slopes, dissecting their errors and achievements. Laughing at the one who ate the most snow as they lost their balance falling in the fresh powder. She loved it because it kept her tethered to the edge of what was once her reason for living. At least here, she got a hit of the 'old days' now and again. She used it to confirm to herself that she hadn't always been one of the most miserable people on the face of the universe. That once upon a time, she'd been just like them. One of the gang. Ish. She still lived like a hermit outside of work, but then she had cake.

Locking the door to her apartment, she tucked the key in an apron hanging on a nearby hook and wrapping it around her, she stepped down a couple of further steps and was immediately in the baking and serving area. It ran along one long wall, an oval shape that left the front of the café open for seating in front of those big wide windows. In this little egg, Rebecca spent her days serving, baking . . . and people watching. She could almost smell the holidaymakers as she got to work opening up the café for the day. She preferred to blend in these days; with her new hairstyle and the fact that she was a bit of a recluse from the media in the first place, it wasn't hard to work behind the counter and serve customers without them so much as batting an eye about her previous life. If she'd been Kim Kardashian, and her face was known everywhere, she'd have had to move to a deserted island and would have done willingly. No doubt her mother would be parachuting in supplies and eligible bachelors every month. Well she was through with that. Robbie was the ultimate eligible bachelor, and she didn't like the cut of his bloody jib these days. She was a lot of things, but willing arsehole magnet was not one of them. She shook off the memories that tried to settle around her and got to work.

Being an early riser had its perks, once she had shaken off her righteous indignation at waking up as she did every morning, alone but henpecked from home, in the dazzling white of the French resort. It had gone seven now, and she needed to get the display cases filled with her creations. Ready for the families, the professionals, and the thrill-seekers. It was Monday morning, the middle of the competition season, and today would be no different to the past few months. The resort would spring to life as soon as the sun was up with the babble and bustle of the thousands of people who visited every single day. She could smell the adrenalin and excitement in the alpine air already, but it wasn't just the competition hopefuls she looked forward to seeing. It was the snarky couples, the over-the-top proposals, and the full-on family fights. The minutiae of life laid bare whilst they guzzled coffee and cake in her little hideaway. Little goldfish for her to observe, only she was on the same side of the glass. If life was all around you, it meant you were still part of it, right? A bystander maybe, but that suited Rebecca just fine. Who needed to be in the spotlight, when all that did was expose the chinks, the ugly cracks and flaws? She was much better in the shadows of life.

Scars don't show in the shadows. It was one of the first things Hans had said to her after the accident. He didn't mean her to take it so much to heart, but at the time, it saved her. She took the café job he offered, with no experience or inclination. It was a lifeline. A moment of anonymity in the place she still wanted to be a part of. A reason to stay. They'd had some laughs along the way too, it hadn't all been doom and gloom.

Checking the calendar on the wall behind the large till, she smiled once more. This time a far broader grin, one that Alice in Wonderland might baulk at on sight.

'Croissant Death Day,' she declared to herself excitedly. 'Oh Hans, my friend, you are in for a treat.' Reaching for one of the files on her recipe bookshelf, she thumbed through her scribblings, looking for something special.

The very fact that she owned a book full of recipes would have been unheard of half a decade ago, but now it felt like home as she flicked through the handwritten pages. An occasional mark from a bit of dropped batter punctuated the pages of cut-outs from magazines and little photos of Rebecca's handiwork; on some of them, Hans and Holly had rated them *Bake Off* style. That was back in the early days, when Hans lived here and he was showing her the waitress ropes. She had recovered enough to go home, but the ticket for the flight had been stuck in her bag since her mother had sent it. Hans and Holly gave her the means to stay, and she had fallen right into the gig without really thinking about her next move in life. *Little did I know I'd end up running the place.* Rebecca smiled at Holly's moist rating on one of them. Her strawberry tart design had gained the coveted five tongues for supreme moistness, and it still made her laugh every time she saw it. Not today's chosen recipe though. Today she knew exactly what she was looking for. One of her first creations. The one that made Hans and Holly shudder at the thought of. After the pressure of her morning, she was ready to have a little fun with her friends. Get her routine right back into its happy little rut.

* * *

12

Luke ruffled his hand through his sandy-brown hair with an un-gloved hand, the index finger of the thick material dangling from his mouth as he looked up at the gorgeous wood and glass café in front of him. His footwear was now as much use as a chocolate fireguard, and his feet felt like blocks of ice. Or more like concrete, truth be told. He couldn't feel anything below the waist, so even seeing his boot-clad feet still attached to his legs gave him a flooding sense of relief. Squinting against the bright glare of the snow, he took off his black-rimmed glasses and peered once more at the screen on the phone in his frozen hand. This was the place, and it looked even better than the pictures he'd been poring over in the taxi. This was something that he was discovering more and more in recent days. Luke's learning curve was not really a curve, but rather more of a vertical incline. He still had nausea from the last-minute white-knuckle plane dash across the world. He wasn't exactly an experienced flyer, in fact, he'd never really been anywhere before this. Work had always offered him the opportunity to travel, see more of the world, but he'd never pulled the trigger. He'd been busy enough staying close to home.

His phone hadn't stopped bonging at him since he'd landed either. His clients were in some kind of meltdown, it seemed, and standing there, he could jolly well relate to how they felt. He felt like he could throw up or pass out, or an eye-boggling combination of the two. Right now, he didn't just wish for better boots, he wished for sparkly red shoes. Christ, he would bang those things together three times before anyone could even utter the word wimp. No wonder his dad hadn't wanted him around. Luke had called again the second he landed but the news was still the same.

He's comfortable. No, he's not talking yet. No, he still doesn't want to speak to you.

He sighed to himself, putting his glove back on and heading for the entrance. He wouldn't have the heels anyway. If this was Oz, he'd have the paws of a cowardly lion. Following some crazy dream his parents had before he was born was uncharacteristic, sure, he was crapping his pants at the prospect of actually following it through. But the memory of watching his old man in that hospital bed spurred him on, Luke could see in his withdrawn expression that he had given up on life, and now it was his responsibility to show his dad that he still had something to live for.

Standing right outside the entrance to the café, he gathered himself, taking a breath.

'Well, old man,' he muttered. 'Here goes nothing.'

He grappled to open the door with his numb, thick, sausage-like gloved fingers, before yanking it open and promptly pitching forward. He ended up hanging half in, half out, dangling there like a puppet with a string caught. Pulling his glove free of the thick metallic door handle, he straightened himself up and stepped over the threshold. Looking around, it seemed for once his rather less than elegant entrance had been missed. No one was looking, and that left him free to let his own eyes roam.

What struck him immediately was the smell of the place. His friend had told him about the food, but it wasn't the same as inhaling it firsthand. A metaphor for his life up to that point, he supposed. The warm air enveloped him, stopping his body from shaking quite as vigorously as before, and drugging him into feeling sugary-safe. He found himself stopping dead in the doorway, closing his eyes and taking a deep, long sniff of the heavenly scent into his lungs. Coffee, warm air, and baked goods. Wafts of fruit flavours that made his mouth water. He hadn't exactly been fine dining lately, and his stomach had started to revolt against him. He just wanted a moment to just be here, to relish in the fact that, he alone, took this trip an—

'Are you going to order, or just stand there gawping all day?'

'Huh?'

'Did you ski into a tree or something? The medical centre is back down there.' The woman speaking to him was standing behind the corner, hands on her hips. She looked familiar somehow, but he couldn't quite place the deep brown eyes and raised eyebrows. She was dressed in black, and it made her look a little scary. Witchy even. Hot witch. More Morticia Addams than hag, but still.

A woman came into the café, walking around him after a moment of confusion and smiling at the witch. *Err, woman.*

'Hot chocolate and a croissant please, and do you have any apple squares?' The customer gave her order with a big smile, and the woman behind the counter gave Luke another long look and got to work on the order. The customer, all long blonde hair in a tight pink skiing outfit, started chatting away.

'Been fun on the slopes today, you ever get out there?'

The woman behind the counter gave a little snort. 'Nah, not my thing.' Luke noticed a name tag, pink with black lettering. REBECCA.

'Oh, well that's a shame. You're missing out.'

Rebecca passed over her order with a smile.

'I'm really not, but thanks. Have a good day now, and take our card.' She beamed at the blonde, passing over a black and pink piece of card. 'We'd love to see you again.'

The blonde opened her mouth to say something, but then smiled back, taking the card.

'These smell amazing, I will. Thanks!'

She twirled around, almost knocking into Luke, who jumped out of the way like a dancing monkey. He whirled the whole way around like a carousel, stopping in front of Rebecca as the woman opened the door and headed out into the great outdoors. The blast of icy air she brought with her was enough to make his leg muscles contract, till he was bent like a pretzel in front of the counter. He was still trying to slap some heat back into his body when Rebecca spoke again.

'Look, can I help you?' She leaned closer, till they were at eye level. 'I feel like you just fell out of a plane.' Looking at his suitcase behind him, abandoned at one side, and his jerky body, she narrowed her eyes. 'Or a spaceship. Where are you booked in?'

He knew he was gawping at her again, but he couldn't find his words.

'Hello? Do you need assistance?' She was openly staring at him now. *Luke, speak mate.* She was tapping her foot and looking around the café nervously.

'Are you always so . . . edgy?'

Her head snapped back a little, and he shrank his own head back into the comfort of his body. Worked for tortoises.

'Edgy?' She echoed. He opened half an eye out of his shell, and she was still glaring at him. 'Are you always so articulate with your words, or is it just the mountain air inspiring you?'

Luke cleared his throat, pushing his glasses back up the bridge of his nose. *That's it. Insult her* and *rock the nerd look. Great start, Lukey boy.* 'Sorry, I'm not explaining myself very well, am I? I'm here about a room.'

Dammit. Such a shame that people don't research their trips properly before swiping the plastic at the airport. He had left it far too late, everything would be booked up well in advance. Even the townsfolk who rented rooms out would be taken by now.

'Sorry, I don't know of any spare rooms. You'll be hard pressed to find accommodation anywhere now. Packages are usually the way to go.' He shivered, just at that moment, and her eyes jumped to his chest area. He didn't look scruffy as such. A little harassed and scatty maybe. His clothes were nice. He had a designer jumper on, but it was far too thin for the resort's weather. He looked as though he'd walked onto the wrong plane and just never realised. He looked a little lost. *The guy must be freezing*, she thought to herself. She felt a little bad that she'd been short with him, but she didn't take kindly to people hanging around her like that. It was then she realised he was speaking again, and she didn't like what she heard.

'I'm sorry?' she said, dumbly. 'Did you say you were staying round here? Where?'

A couple walked in at that moment, heading straight for one of the empty tables. Rebecca nodded distractedly at him, before passing another table a menu and grabbing her pad. Taking the couple's orders quickly, she headed back to the counter to get it ready. Luke gave her an 'I'll let you get on' look and took a seat near the counter. The man of the party complimented her on the café, and she beamed with pride. She did love the place. She would never deny that.

She got to work, chatting to the customers, making sure the tables were happy, checking on her baking, but all the while she found herself peeking at one particular new face. He looked at odds with the landscape she was used to. He looked like he was having some sort of crisis for one. His hair was dishevelled and he was tapping away at his phone, swiping screens on his iPad, and stuffing bits of paper back into his bag, which was filled with little notes. She smiled to herself, thinking that he looked a bit like a student about to take his final exams on five hours' sleep and a ton of energy drinks. Still studying the menu, taking his time, he placed his fingers near his chin, and she noticed the light stubble running across it. As he was reading the list of dishes for the twentieth time, the glasses on his nose steamed up. He needed little wipers for his Clark Kents. Rebecca found herself wondering what the guy's deal was, but that wasn't part of her day. She had a plan, and helping weirdos wasn't one of them. Distracting herself, she gave a couple their orders, and started to clean the empty tables on her way back, stacking the dishes in the dishwasher ready to go. After the weird morning with her mother, she needed the guy to leave so she could switch her brain off once more. Thinking too much about things was never good.

'Nice place, it smells amazing walking in here.'

He was looking right at her now.

'Thanks. It's not mine actually. My friend Hans owns it, I'm just the live-in manager.' She turned her back to him to clean a tabletop, hoping he would get the message and return

17

to the note-strewn workspace he was currently creating in her sacred, neat café.

'Well, it's nice,' he added, looking at her intently now. 'Hans, eh?'

Rebecca nodded at him. 'Yep, he's the boss. You want anything?' She raised the order pad, tapping on it with her pen in a determined manner. She didn't look at him, keeping her eyes on her pad.

'I'll just have an Americano for now. I think I need to thaw out a little before I get some food. I didn't mean the edgy comment, by the way. I just meant that you had a bit of an edge to you.' He continued the conversation like they'd never missed a beat, and it was then that she realised what had been irking her so much. He was really annoying, sure but the thing that irked her was that she wanted to know more about him.

She passed him his coffee, taking the money and trying not to react as his hand brushed hers. She felt a push and pull towards him that was getting a little bit weird now. She wished he had a label, like a trinket on a shelf. She wanted to find out more about him, what his deal was, but she also wanted him to go away and never return so she could get on with her day. Hans would be here later, and she had stuff to do. He'd taken a high seat at the counter, taking his satchel type bag off the seat next to him and taking out a newspaper. *Great, he's really staying. Close too. Shurrup, Rebecca. He's a person, remember? A customer.* Feeling like she needed a distraction, Rebecca returned to her baking. She was soon back to her old self, though her eyes were a little busier than usual. Mr Scruffy, as she had now nicknamed him in her head, was reading the paper, she was doing her thing, and the other café-goers were all happy in their own little caffeinated bubbles. After looking at the perfect creations on her tray, she loaded them into the oven and started to clean up again to set up for the next rush.

'Can I ask,' Mr Scruffy began in a broad accent. It was gruff, deep and Northern, she noticed now. A thick accent from back home. She could barely make it out at first. Her Yorkshire radar was a little rusty, given the setting she lived in and the multicultural clientèle she crossed paths with daily. 'What did you just make?'

'Croissants, with my own twist.' He looked at her, an eyebrow raised in question, and she gave him a knowing look. 'You'll see, if you're still here when they get out of the oven.'

He drained his coffee cup, putting it back onto its saucer and pushing it towards her.

'Well, better have a refill then.'

Rebecca, you great, big-mouthed tit. He won't leave now! Never mention baked goods to a man if you want him to leave. Rule 101 of baking. Although, with Robbie, she wouldn't have been able to coax him in the first place. Her ex-boyfriend wasn't a carb-lover. Cake was an alien foodstuff to him. If she'd offered to whip him up a Victoria sponge when they were together, he'd have laughed in her face and skied for two hours to work off even the thought of the calories. She laughed to herself, before she remembered that she wasn't that person back then. She wouldn't have been baking. She'd have been on the snow with him, giving him a run for his money. If Robbie saw her now, he'd probably be relieved he got out when he did. She pulled the hem of her top down, suddenly aware that she was flashing her muffin top to the room. Robbie would have laughed at that too.

She filled the man's cup up from the coffee pot, trying to turn her brain back onto autopilot. She had all the feelings today for some reason. About her mother, about the competitions she was avoiding yet again. About Robbie, the man she once knew so well, and now didn't understand one iota. Things changed, she knew that only too well. She didn't even trust her own body anymore. Mr Scruffy started tapping away on his tablet screen again, in between taking deep, appreciative sips of his coffee. The man was making love to the cup! It was like watching an alien meet the world. He just looked so . . . she came back to the word lost again. He looked out of place there, driven. Definitely not a holidaymaker.. It had made her think, and she didn't do that anymore. She lived day to day, and that was just bloody fine. She topped his coffee up again.

The man thanked her, taking the cup between his hands and holding it to his mouth a moment. His glasses steamed up again, and he didn't even seem to notice. He was too busy enjoying his drink like a man who had never seen a coffee bean before. God help whoever had to accommodate him. It wasn't *her* problem though. She had the next batch to get on with and people to serve. Same as every day.

'So, you live here year-round?' She could feel his green eyes on her, and suddenly she found herself wishing she was more like her old self. Just for a second, she wanted to be more. She hadn't felt like that for a long while, and it was very unsettling. *I've been out of the race for a long time, but now, I regret that I don't have anything to say to this man. Which is fine, because soon he'll be gone. He'll be gone and I'll be back in my little flour-coated bubble. The old me would have chatted away, no paranoia about who he was. Who I was. I miss just feeling normal.*

'Yep,' was all she said in the end. He nodded at her, but didn't look away.

'So, the café isn't open year-round, right? What do you do then?'

She answered him without looking, keeping her focus on her work. If she bored him quick, he would leave quick. Worst-case scenario, she could throw a bun at him. Shut him up.

'I read, hang out, there's plenty of work in town, so I tend to do that. Bit of cleaning, baking gigs. I don't need much. Hans needs a sitter here, so the rent's pretty cheap.'

Or free, truth be told. Rebecca did pay him something each month, when he let her, but it was a token rent really. She paid her own utility and phone bills, and bought her own food, so he wasn't fussed. She found out a while ago that she didn't need a lot. Sometimes she looked through old bank statements to laugh at herself, and how the old Rebecca used to live. It seemed like she'd had it all at the time. How odd it is that things change so much.

The man's nodding at me as though he's really listening to what I'm saying. Weirdo. It's my turn.

'So,' she said as cheerfully as she could, getting on with the baking, 'what brings you here?'

I'm a supreme master at changing the subject. Especially when someone is asking about my life. I don't tend to talk about that.

He opened his mouth to speak, to finally, hopefully tell her what he was doing there, and more importantly, when he was leaving. Rebecca held her breath as he started to speak, but the door was suddenly flung open, a blast of cold air billowing through the café from the force.

'Good morning Alpine adventurers!' Hans strode in, bellowing, his beard full of ice, encased in his usual Day-Glo warm weather gear. He kicked the door shut behind him, his arms full with a huge cardboard box. He came over to the counter, nodding and saying hello to customers as he went. Leaning forward to look at Rebecca's handiwork, he took a deep sniff.

'Nice,' he said jovially, his iced eyebrow raised in her direction. 'Croissant Death Day rolls around once more.'

'Yep,' she agreed, trying not to grin at him. This was what she'd been waiting for. After all, what made a girl feel better more than taking the mick out of her friends? 'I just wanted to mark the day, you know, so you wouldn't forget.'

'I'll never forget what day it is.' He nodded to the calendar, his face grave. 'The follicles on my forearms still scream when you get near.' Rebecca chuckled, making Hans cover his arms in reflex.

'I know, I know. Your arm hair's safe. Newbie error. The treats will be worth the trauma.'

He came around the side of the counter and dropped the box at her feet, and then his gaze slid to the man in the corner. He banged his hand on the counter hard, making a couple of the customers jump.

'Luke! Luke! My friend! You came! I can't believe it!' Rebecca was looking at the door, at the diners, wondering who Luke was and why Hans was so excited. He was a bounding puppy on his lowest days, so this was extra-excitable behaviour.

'Can you believe this, Becca? Luke!' Hans tapped her on the arm excitedly, before striding back over to the man he called Luke. The very man Rebecca herself had been obsessing over all morning. He grabbed him in a big hug, lifting him clean off his feet. Luke was quite a tall lad, but Hans was a huge, craggy rock face of a man. The first time Rebecca had met him, she'd half expected a Sherpa to be herding goats across his back.

'Hans, dude, have you been eating ski lifts or something? Jesus, you're bigger than the mountains!' Luke, aka Mr Scruffy, was perched in his arms like a giddy puppy, his gangly legs dangling down. Hans just clung on for dear life, laughing his head off. It was like watching a bear hugging a salmon. A rather gleeful salmon, that seemed happy to be caught. And, in the right light, Luke did have a rather Clark-Kent-cum-Superman thing going on about him. She'd been too irritated by him to notice earlier, but now Hans was in effect crushing the life out of him, she could admit to herself that he was a tiny bit cute. In certain lights. Maybe. *And now I'm fantasising about sexy fish wearing glasses. I need help. I bet David Attenborough doesn't have these problems.*

'So,' Hans says, releasing him just enough to enable him to draw breath, 'what are you doing here? I never thought you'd . . .' He made a plane movement with his hand, complete with whooshing sound. 'I mean, I'm just so—'

'I'm here to do this, let's just leave it at that.' Luke rubbed the back of his neck with his left hand, and Rebecca realised, he was uncomfortable with the question. 'Work's been a bit mental, I guess . . .' Hans clocked the messy workspace, and raised a brow in surprise. Rebecca glared at the mess at Luke, but he was too busy avoiding Hans's eye. She knew shifty when she saw it.

'But anyway, I made it! Are we . . .' He paused and shot a quick look at Rebecca, then back up to Hans. '. . . all set?'

He said it jovially, but there was something in his voice. Rebecca noticed the way he and Hans nodded at each other. *I'm intrigued, but realistically, it can't be good, and I want nothing to do with drama. I have had enough of that to last a lifetime.* Baking the next batch of croissants was something she could do. She could make coffee, serve customers, clean tables. There was routine in that, a regularity to the mundane that she needed to keep herself steady. Present, and not on that mountain top, about to shove off the snow and screw up the life she knew and dearly loved. At the time, anyway. She'd had her eyes opened on some things with the rose tint of time. Robbie, for example. That was another disaster she'd skied right into.

She folded the next set of croissants, laying them out on trays so that she could pop them in the oven. The two men kept chatting quietly together all the while, and Rebecca found herself relaxing once more into her work. But she didn't miss Hans shooting her looks from time to time, which was odd. Even for him. Probably checking the fire extinguisher was still on the wall, ready to go. The poor man had PTSD from their 'Hans School of Baking' time. It wasn't every man who could take a broken, slightly bitter, ex-professional skier and turn her into not only a decent waitress, but a bloody good baker to boot. Hans had done a good job, Holly too. They'd held her together till she could stand on her own feet once more. One of them had even sacrificed a forearm to the cause, and a fair bit of man pride.

The men still had their heads together when her chicken timer clucked loudly. Another gem from her mother under the guise of career development, but at least this one had a good use. The biographies of influential female athletes she sometimes posted were still firmly in the bottom drawer. Taking the special batch of croissants out of the oven, Rebecca beamed as she looked at her work. She might have zero interest in . . . well, anything, but these moments, seeing what she had made, they helped her drag herself out of her frosty pit every morning.

'Are these what all the fuss is about? They smell lovely, but what is that flavour?' Luke was suddenly there in front of her, bent double, looking enraptured by the tray of golden loveliness.

'It's my own creation actually, I like to try new combinations.' *Shut up, mouth.* She pursed her lips together tight.

Hans was standing behind him, huge hands on his hips, an odd look on his face. A look Rebecca knew well.

'Well, they smell lush.' Luke looked up at her, well, into her breasts. It had been a while since a bloke had done that. Even if it was just an eyeline faux pas on his part. *I wish I had worn my better bra. I bobbed my comfortable one on this morning. Lets the ladies do their thang. It had to be a man who invented the underwired bra, I tell you. Those babies take out washers and dryers with a single errant wire, so why the hell do we shove our breasts into them, scaffolded and bound like captives? No thanks. I'll let my puppies fly free, ta.* Still, given the way that Luke was looking at her relaxed little uniboob, maybe Victoria's Secret had a point.

'Thanks,' she said, folding her arms over her chest, removing his viewpoint. He looked up at her, and she could see he was blushing. Which made her blush, and when recognition hit that he had been caught out, his face exploded into a tomato-like hue. It was endearing in a way. She found that she didn't mind him looking. The feminist in her shuddered, but allowed it.

'So Luke,' Hans boomed from behind, making them both jump. 'I have somewhere you can stay, for a few days at least. I'd put you up myself, but things are hectic at mine.' *Hans is the least hectic person I know. What's going on?*

'That's okay, I wouldn't want to impose.' Luke waved him off, looking ever more awkward by the minute. 'Nonsense!' Hans stepped forward, slapping him on the back hard. Luke took a stumbling step forward and coughed a little. 'You can't impose on us, right Becks?'

24

Shit. I think I know what's coming. Nah . . . he wouldn't do that. I know he won't. Surely he won't . . .

'Miss Atkins here would be honoured to put you up, wouldn't you, Becks?'

'Er . . .'

'No!'

'Brilliant!'

Luke and Rebecca both spoke in unison, but Hans was by far the biggest, loudest windbag. *Damn him.*

'It's settled then! The lodge has a guest room, it's pretty big, there's a desk there, Wi-Fi is a bit patchy sometimes, but it works. Rebecca will be glad of the company, I'm sure!'

He looked at her cheerily, and she made an 'I'll murder you in your sleep' face at him, complete with throat-cutting action. His grin only got wider, and she even spied a little Swedish twinkle in his eye. *What an utter berk. I wish I'd burned his other arm bald too now.*

'I don't think Luke here wants to stay with a stranger, Hans! You have room at yours, surely? It's just the two of you in that big place.' She threw her arms behind her head wildly, gesturing to the upstairs. 'Better than this pokey little hole, I'm sure!'

At that very moment, the thin clouds in the sky parted, and the sun shone bright through the windows, making the whole place look like a holiday postcard. Hans's face was pinched, and he was straining with the effort of not laughing at her. She could see it. She wanted to headbutt him, to Morse code her distress to him with the anxious tapping of her feet on the solid wood floor.

A-b-o-r-t.

N-o w-a-y-H-a-n-s.

Hans looked her in the eye and his face spread into a slow, smug smile.

'It's settled then! He'll stay here.' Hans spoke as though Luke wasn't standing at the side of him, looking back at his case as if he were wishing it was big enough to sleep in, and he could avoid the game of pass the stranger. 'I tried to get him a room, I looked as soon as Luke said he might visit. It's all booked up.'

'Right,' Rebecca muttered. She knew he was telling the truth, but it didn't make him less of a git to speak it. She waited till Luke wasn't looking and made an angry face at her boss and one-time good pal. 'Err . . .' Luke was pulling a face himself, but looking at Rebecca expectantly. 'It would only be for a few nights, just till I find somewhere . . .'

He trailed off, and they all knew that it was highly unlikely. Hotels and B&Bs around here all had waiting lists, and cancellations not snapped up in seconds were few and far between.

'It's fine,' some cheery woman said. Rebecca looked behind her, but saw nothing but the wall of the kitchen area. *Great, it was me. Stupid, helpful, cheerful me.*

'Are you sure?' Luke checked, and she found herself feeling a little bit sorry for him. He did look a little pathetic, a tad waif and stray.

'Of course!' Hans cut in, throwing his arms wide theatrically. 'Not a problem, my friend.'

Rebecca looked at Hans in a last-ditch attempt to get out from under this mess, hoping she could project her inner feelings from her eyeballs to his brain. He ignored her at first, standing there like a waxwork. She tried to grab his attention, to glare into him the fact that she didn't want some old friend of his shacking up under her roof. She had things to do, real, serious things. She was halfway through her *Midsomer Murders* boxset for a start, and she wasn't stopping that for anyone. She didn't want Luke there, in her life. She just wanted to bake and forget, and be left the ruddy hell alone. She hadn't shared a space with a member of the opposite sex since Robbie. She didn't count Hans. He was Holly's, and they didn't see each other that way. Never had. They had bonded over the sport, and then over their love for the resort. Baking had been an unexpected bonus for both of them. She was still staring at him, Luke busying himself with tidying some of his papers now.

26

'So we're doing this?' she asked, trying not to plead. 'Like, really doing this?'

Hans flashed his gaze her way then, and she knew she'd lost. He had the same look in his eye many times, and it only ever ended one way. His. *Eugh, chirpy people are so relentless. I'm pretty sure he knows just how much I will hate this, but his shit-eating grin just tells me that I lost. Rats.* Luke was back now, looking like the Danny DeVito of the *Twins* duo at the side of Hans.

'And you're sure it's okay with you, Rebecca? I feel awful just turning up and messing your day up.'

'I'm sure, Luke. I would be happy to put you up.' *Put up with you, more like.* 'Would you like a croissant?' Ignoring her shaking hand, she picked up her tongs, knuckles white on the handles, and placed one onto a plate. Hans stepped forward too, but she passed the plate to Luke and started tonging the others into the display cabinet swiftly, ready to sell.

'Sorry Hans, but you're allergic to these.' She gave him her very best, friendliest smile. The one she reserved for the worst of the customers, those who ground her gears to the max. The one that looked like it said, 'I understand, I am here to serve you,' but really meant 'Leave now, and I'll let you live.'

Hans looked confused as he pushed his huge hand through his hair, sticking his thick hat back on his stupid broad head.

'I don't have any allerg—'

Rebecca closed the back of the glass cabinet and looked straight at him. He shuddered, and Rebecca's eyes narrowed.

'Yes Hans, I'm afraid, if you eat one of these, it will definitely kill you.'

Have that, boss. You fill my spare room, I don't feed your belly.

Chapter 2

Okay, so the day didn't really get any better from there. In fact, Rebecca was half expecting Arnold Schwarzenegger to come running in, talking about the end of the world. Either that, or she was going to have to kill Hans and bury him in the ice. The competitions were thick on the social calendar, and the season was just getting going, ramping up more and more each day. The big one was a full two months away, but the buzz was starting already, and they would soon be descending in droves to take part in the competitions that ran here. This year though, it was going to be different. The organisers, Ski Scene Scream, had really topped themselves, bagging a huge sponsor, Bowness Whisky, who were launching their signature line of new drinks, headed by the mint-flavoured gin they were launching as part of the event. It was a pretty impressive label, and the company had lots of clout. It was going to be big, and to mark the event, they were launching a new competition: the Ultimate Alpine Ski Challenge, sponsored by Alpine Gins. She'd read up on them obviously, studied the companies and their competition rules and regulations, if only to know what sort of people were going to be rocking up to her mountain café. She wasn't the most social person these days, and she had the added pressure of having people to avoid. Plus, now a random Yorkshire man in her spare room.

All day, Luke had been in the café. He'd installed himself right in the corner, near taking windows at the front, directly next to her favourite counter. She liked to work there in the afternoon, so she could see out of the windows without being noticed herself, chat to the regulars who came in, and now she had her lodger displayed in her window. He'd been clacking away on his laptop, taking phone calls outside, walking left and right, outside the window. She spent half the day working, and the other half stalking him. *What? Watching! I mean, watching him. At one point, he even took a selfie with the mountain. Who does that?* She wondered where he had uploaded it to. Who he might have sent it to. She was still on social media herself, she just didn't update any of her profiles. Ever. She was an occasional lurker. She would have deleted them all entirely, but she did like to check in on people from time to time. She almost always regretted it, but that was how regrets worked in the first place.

In between calls and frantic tip-tapping on the laptop, he'd eaten half the menu. He followed his croissant with a bacon sandwich, a large coffee, and then started tasting some of her other baked goods. She found herself wondering how much money he would take to feed, before she realised that it wasn't her problem. She would feed him in here, for cash, but upstairs he was on his own. If he so much as breathed near her Rocky Road, it was his funeral.

Half an hour till closing time, and Rebecca was tired. She started to put things away, clearing the dirty tables and setting things up for the morning. She was almost done when she noticed Luke had his camera phone going. He was aiming at her glass cabinet. She cleared the final table in a hurry, putting the things into the kitchen and getting her cleaning supplies out to #hinch the cafe. *Yep, social media lurker. I like to have things clean and squared away, so I can sleep easy. This café is my oasis. If it does well, so do I. Some ding-a-ling taking photos in here doesn't sit right.*

'What are you doing?' she asked him finally, when she couldn't stand holding the question back another moment. Spraying one of the vacant chairs with cleaning spray, enjoying the hit of pine fresh smell it created, she looked at him for an answer. He snapped another photo, and she felt her fists tighten around the cloth. 'Luke?'

He looked across at her, a shy little smile on his face.

'I wanted to photograph some of your stuff, it looks so good. Do you make all your own recipes, or do you use other people's?'

She shook her head before she answered. The cheek of it!

'No, I use the basic recipes but then tweak them. I like to add my own ideas.'

He nodded at her, looking right at her. She could almost feel him, but she kept working, not wanting him to linger too much. *I have to share my lodge with him, and I can't even stand in the same café as him without feeling annoyed that he's here. Asking me questions.*

To make it even more awkward, the last customer waved goodbye and left. Closing time. Just the two of them. For the whole night. Alone. Rebecca gulped at the prospect and faffed with some napkins in a dispenser.

'But where did you study?' he persisted, as she headed over to the front door and locked up for the evening.

'I studied here, Hans taught me.'

She could feel him again, watching her movements, and she turned her body to face him. Hand on hip, she stared right back at him. His eyes narrowed a little.

'I know you.'

Shit. She hadn't expected him to say that.

'What's your name again? Atkins, right?'

She looked back at him, nodding slowly. Hans had used her real name. He usually left it out, or used the code word. Dammit. He must trust Luke. Did he . . . did he know? Rebecca felt like her jaw had locked shut.

'Yep. You finished?' She tried her 'leave it' look on him, but he just frowned, making his glasses move further up his big nose. Well, it wasn't big exactly, more button-like. It wasn't a *bad* nose, it just seemed to like inserting itself into things that were none of its beeswax.

'You okay? You got a headache or something?' She raised her brows in his direction.

'No,' he said after a moment, before looking away. 'I'll let you get on.'

Moment gone. Thank Christ for that. She put her face straight and started putting the chairs up on the tables. He followed her lead without being asked and started putting them up with her. The two of them worked in silence, till the only table left was the one where his stuff was still laid out. He muttered 'terribly sorry' in a faux posh tone under his breath, starting to put things away, chucking pens into a case he produced from his bag.

'Really, *Star Wars*? How old are you? And what's with the telephone voice?'

He looked at her and in his best Yoda voice said, 'Doesn't matter, age. Always cool, *Star Wars* is. Work tone, voice is.' After a moment, when she was still scowling at him, he laughed sheepishly. 'When I get nervous, I go all hoorah Henry in the voice department. I don't know why. My dad does it.'

She groaned, but it trickled into a giggle despite her best efforts. He laughed too, his deep voice chuckling along as he put his things away, throwing his bag over his shoulder.

'I do know you from somewhere, it'll come to me.' Rebecca ignored him, quickly cleaning his table down and getting it ready for the next day. Taking her time till he went away. Then she realised he wasn't going anywhere.

'Right, well I'll be off,' he surprised her by saying. 'Okay if I leave my bags with you? I only need my wallet, Hans is taking me out for a pint.'

Rebecca mentally took out some of the pins from Hans's

voodoo doll in her head. Not the good ones like the goolies, just the boring ones, like an elbow.

'Oh, that's nice,' she replied, as though bored. Really, she was thanking the god of pubs for giving her a little bit of time to come round to the idea of having this man in her personal quarters. 'Well, have a nice time.' Cloth in hand, she was waiting for him to say goodbye, see you later, and leave. He just stood there gawping back.

'So,' he says, looking from his feet to her face to back to his feet, which were encased in very unsuitable shoes. *I'm surprised his toes haven't dropped off yet.*

'So,' she repeated, looking pointedly at the door.

'Er, a key?' he ventured. *Oh dear Lord.*

'Hans wants to give you a key?'

Luke ran his hand through his hair, a nervous gesture. *Good. You need to be nervous, asking me for a bloody key.*

'Er yes, he said you kept a spare for er . . . guests.'

'Great. That doesn't make me sound like a hooker at all.'

His face fell. 'I didn't mean—'

'It's fine,' she retorted, smiling through tight gritted teeth, taking a key out of the drawer next to the till. 'Here's the key. You'll have to come through the shop, so please don't forget to lock up properly.'

He still didn't move, so she went to him and held the key out, taking care to hold it by the string it was attached to. She didn't trust herself to touch him flesh to flesh. He stood there a beat too long, staring.

'What are you looking at?'

'Nothing, sorry.' He seemed to mentally shake himself together, before taking the key gently from her grasp. She could feel the heat from his skin. 'I'll lock up, don't worry. Just leave my bags there, I'll bring them up when I get back.'

She nodded at him dumbly, having had no intention of carrying them up anyway. Who was she, Jeeves?

'Fine, see you later then.' She turned to leave to go upstairs, eager to wash the day off and frantically clean up the guest room.

'Rebecca? Thanks again for putting me up. I really appreciate it, and I'll make it up to you, I promise.'

She turned to say something to him, acknowledge him, but he was already on the other side of the door, locking up. She watched him put the key into a zipped pocket, and when he looked up, their eyes locked. She raised a hand and softly waggled her fingers at him. He did the same with a gloved hand. It looked more like a lobster claw, but it still made her heart beat that bit faster for some reason. It was probably just the fact that she had given a total stranger a key to her castle. As he walked away in the snow, giving her another long look over his shoulder, she had one thought in her head.

That man is going to be trouble.

Hours later, after a night of emergency cleaning, leg shaving, and hiding of personal information around the lodge, Rebecca turned off the radio and headed to bed. She did think about delving into her bedroom drawers for that slip she knew she still had kicking about, just in case they happened to cross paths in the middle in the night going to the bathroom, or getting a midnight snack. She soon talked herself out of it, seeing sense in favour of PJs and fluffy unicorn slippers, which were shrugged off at the side of the bed. She shouldn't be embarrassed of her comfy clothes, he was the invader, after all. It was her home. Besides, he might think she was trying it on with him, all nipply from the cold floor and groggy from sleep. That would be far worse than him laughing at her oversized Disney nighties. Snuggling under the covers with a satisfied sigh, she finally felt herself relax a little. She had been thinking about waiting up for Luke, to check he locked up properly, but decided it would be better to get some sleep and get out of the way. *What would I say to him anyway? It's not like I even want him here.*

She'd closed her own bedroom door, leaving the guest room wide open to avoid any confusion when he got home. Picking up her Kindle, she thumbed through the covers to find her next read, and settled in, switching off her bedside lamp and snuggling into the pillows in the dark, the screen the only light in the room. Peace and quiet, just how she liked it. She sped through the first chapter of the book, where a dashing hero sidled up to a coquettish woman in a bar.

Then she found herself wondering if Hans was having a good night. He'd seemed very excited to see Luke. Did Holly know him too? Rebecca herself didn't recall a Luke in any of Hans's ski stories. He wasn't one of the scene, she knew that much. Even without seeing him trip over his own feet every fifteen minutes since she'd met him. The man walked like a newborn fawn. She read on, and the hero waggled his eyebrows, saying something charming and funny and making the woman in the book hang on his every word. *Luke wouldn't be able to do that. Hah! The man is awkward with a big fat capital 'A'. I wonder what he looks like without his glasses on . . .*

Rebecca shut the screen down and punched the pillows beside her. Romance novels late at night were not always good for a woman who had . . . gone without for a while. A long while. Years. No wonder she was fantasising about what her squatter looked like without his bins on. He wasn't exactly built like Dean Cain. More sugar cane.

She turned her head to her window, looking through the ineffectual curtains at the mountains around her. They looked blue tinted in the dim light, beautiful. It made her long to get back out there, but after the accident, it was done. She'd never just be a hobby skier. It would be like licking the frosting and not eating the cake.

Robbie had said the same, before they'd parted. How different she was now, how much she needed to get back out there. Back to reality. Easier said than done when you'd had as much time

34

to sit and think as Rebecca had. Nothing but time to pore over the moments in your life where a decision led to something else. Another life entirely. Another person. Whoever she was that day, up there taking her next shot at the top, she'd left her up there. A piece of herself that she would never get back. What was the point in trying, when the last time almost broke you? Career, relationship. Both shattered. She wasn't some old vase, the cracks in her body and soul were not fused with gold. They were creaky, chalky, jagged pieces. If she moved too fast, it would all crumble. Taking a last look, she turned her back on the mountain, flicked her book back on and waited for sleep to claim her.

Chapter 3

'Smug lil' git, arent ya! I'll get you, you . . . buffoon! Next time, you's can fix your own ruddy dongle!'

Rebecca was jolted awake by a deep voice, and a large crash. Her kindle, propped up on a pillow, pitched forward and smacked her straight in the face. Cursing, she flung it to the side, her back against the pillows, heart hammering, listening for whatever it was that woke her.

'Awww shit!' Her startled ears could make out the Yorkshire twang in the voice this time, and her heart started pumping again as realisation set in. *It's just my unwanted lodge guest.* She squinted at her bedside clock. *It's 3.45 a.m. I have to be up in a few hours, and this gobshite is just rolling in. Not a good start to our enforced living arrangement.*

'Bloody Hans.' She grumbled her way out of bed, shuffling around the room. She'd sent him a text earlier, basically asking him why he hated her and wanted to destroy her, but the big lump had never replied. Too busy with his new little bestie, probably. She heard an odd series of knocks. It sounded like someone was knocking on the interior door. *Great.*

She headed straight down the stairs, only stopping to put her slippers on, and opened the door slowly. It opened inward, and as soon as she pulled down the latch, the door swung towards her, bringing with it a huge lump of something that smelled like it had been marinated in alcohol. He dropped backwards onto the stairs like a sack of potatoes.

'Eugh, you stink!' She pinched her nose, stepping over him gently. She was feeling a little drunk on the fumes, and felt an icy blast. *I knew it, he's left the flipping door open. I can see the snow falling outside, the door wide open, the key still in the lock. What a total twonk.* She padded over in her slippers, cupping her boobs to prevent her nipples from shrivelling up and blowing away like tiny frozen peas. Getting to the door, she looked outside, but saw nothing except staggered footprints and tracks heading towards the scene of crime. Hans's handiwork no doubt. If he wasn't a first-time expectant father, he would be in a whole heap of rolling pin related revenge right now. 'What did you drink, besides everything?'

'I'll get him, you know. He won't get the better of Luke Sommersby. Lukey boy will win!' He raised his hand in the air, managing to half punch himself in the face and not even noticing. 'For Frank!'

Rebecca looked down at the body that was currently sprawled out on the stairs up to the lodge. He was singing to himself now, a garbled version of 'Eye of the Tiger', with punching movements. *At least, I think they're pretend punches. He could be having some sort of dance party by himself.* He turned his head and looked up at her, eyes bloodshot, a lazy, slow grin spreading across his face languidly.

'Hey! Re-bakie! There you are. Got any of them croissants?' He slurred out croissants like quix-sants, and then started talking about all the flavours of the food he'd scoffed that afternoon. 'You should do cakes! Big cakes, with—' he raised one hand and made a sprinkling motion with it '—stuff on it, you know?'

Rebecca was already thoroughly fed up, knackered and freezing. Planting her feet closer to him to get a good grip of his arm, she got ready to pull the stupid dolt up. He looked down at her feet, which was when she belatedly realised they were clad in her unicorn slippers. He laughed, bopping one of them on the horn with his finger. Or trying to anyway. He more jabbed her leg.

'Ha ha! Cute. Can you help me stand up? I need to pee.'

'Lovely. Of course that's something I want to be involved in.'

He looked at her again, his eyes unfocused, his head tilting further back to the stairs behind him as he tried to focus on well, one of her, at least. Rebecca was pretty sure he was staring at more than one of her with his beer googles on.

'Come on.' She grabbed his arms as best she could whilst he was still waving them around and gave him a gentle tug. He didn't move, just lay there, laughing to himself. Rebecca rolled her eyes and planted her feet firmly on the ground again, digging her toes into her slippers like little diggers.

'Come . . . nnggggg . . . on!' Heaving with all her might, she still only just managed to lift his back off the stairs.

'For God's sake, what did you drink? You're like a ton of lead!' Trying again, she went to plant her feet a bit further apart, only to be kicked in the knee by him trying to get up, taking her off balance. Not surprising really when he was flailing like a tortoise on its back.

'Lead! You can't drink l . . . oooo, saucy!' He giggled again, catching her as she crashed into his body, headbutting him for good measure. His head was flung back onto the corner of the stair, making a small thud against the carpet. 'Oww, I'm sorry! I didn't mean to do that!' He grabbed at her to steady them both, and before Rebecca could even process what was happening, her face was inches from his, and his arms were around her tight, his grip now as solid as a rock. His hands were also however, planted squarely on her bottom. *He literally has my butt cheeks in his hands. I can feel the heat coming through the flannel material.*

He lay back again, wincing at the pain no doubt caused by her collapsing onto him, but then he looked right at her, his piercing green eyes flicking all over the features of her face, his hands squeezing the globes of her backside still.

'Shall we try this again?' she asked reluctantly. She knew she should be mortified, angry even, but in all honesty, it was the most action she'd had in a while that wasn't either a dream or a romantic scene from one of her favourite books. The thought was so depressing. She motioned to lift herself off him, but he held her firm.

'Just give me a minute, okay? Ev'finks spinnning. Feel a bit sick. You're really pretty, you'snow that?' His eyelids were fluttering now, his dark lashes longer and more noticeable than Rebecca had first realised. He sighed heavily, treating her to a good dose of spirit-laden breath. Wow, a girl could get drunk just off the fumes he was expelling. 'I want to make fings alright, you know? These things have to be sorted, they has to be, don't they? Sometimes you just have to try, right? When things are bad, and the frozen chips are gone.' Rebecca had no idea what he was spouting on about, but he was looking intently at her. Waiting for an answer to a question he hadn't even asked, or at least, not in a coherent way. She'd half suspected when he'd arrived that his chips were down, but she didn't want a drunken confessional dragging her into it. She looked down at him, and realised that she could do one of two things. She could utterly crush him and tell him that there was no point in trying anything or bothering with anyone. People went away when everything fell apart anyway, no one wants to see the ugly aftermath. Love doesn't conquer all, it buggers off and pleases itself. There was no meaning of life, it was just a case of survival.

Or, she could cut the poor super dork a break, and maybe even get some more sleep. Looking down at him, she smiled at him kindly, speaking to him in her nicest voice. The real one, not the customer version.

'You do, you're right. You should absolutely go do all of that, but not tonight, eh? It's been a long day for you. A good night's sleep is just the ticket.' She reached back and slowly tugged his hands off her behind, placing them in her hands. 'Now come on, upppp!'

She pulled back with all her batter-whipping strength, standing up and finally bringing Luke to a standing position with her. He teetered a little, Rebecca pushing gently on his chest to steady him. Huh, she felt a muscle. Maybe his office had a gym. She turned him around, pushing him gently towards the stairs. She daren't put his arm over her shoulders – one wrong move and they would both be down them arse over tit. Instead she opted for half pushing him, half dragging him up the stairs. All the while he was muttering about somebody being stubborn, and how he was going to help. Seemingly whether they wanted it or not. Another poor sod who was having their life meddled with. All this was whilst he was singing a medley of various testosterone-soaked hits from the 1980s. Mostly the high-pitched ones, naturally. She managed to get him up to her place, quickly closing the door at the top to prevent any further tumbles. Turning round, she started to talk to him, but he'd gone.

'Luke?' she called out, feeling weird shouting a man's name in her home. Nothing. She was about to call again when she heard the clang of a belt buckle, a zip, and then the distinct tinkle of running water. In desperate hope, she ran past the empty guest room to the bathroom, but flicking the light on, she found the room empty.

'Luke!' She shouted again, louder and more frantic this time, running from room to room to find them all empty.

'If I lay heeerreee, if I just llllaaayy hereeee, would you lie with meeee and just forget the worlddddd!'

Oh my Lord, what the hell is he doing? I love that song too. Drunken berk. She ran, racing to the sound of him butchering one of her favourite tunes, and she found him. In her bedroom. More importantly, in her bed. He was lying across her duvet, in a pair of black boxer shorts, trying to pull her hand stitched comforter over him. Another smell hit her too, and her nose slowly turned her head in horror, till she saw the bin next to her desk. Right next to his discarded trousers.

'Luke! What the holy hell are you doing! You pee'd in my bin, and this is my bed!' Stomping over to him, she leaned forward and gave him a hard shove. He rolled a little, and she got a flash of bulge as he tried to right himself. 'You stupid drunken git! Get out!'

'Get out, get out whilst you still cannnnn!' He immediately started to sing again, pretending to play the drums whilst he did his best James Bay crooning expression. 'Oooo oooo oooo!'

'Luke!' She tried again, fists balled at her sides now, her face feeling flushed and hot. *Bulge.* Her brain was so angry, it was just firing random words at her. *Nice. Angry. Urine. Eugh, moment gone.* He flumped down under her comforter again, exhausted from flailing around, and looked across at her bleary eyed.

'What . . .?' His eyelids were drooping now, and in another second, it was clear he was out for the count. A loud snore erupted from him as his body relaxed visibly before her. She hoped to heaven the man had no pee left in him. Looking at him, almost peaceful in sleep, lying amongst her belongings, looking a bit familiar in them himself, she wondered for a moment . . . which scatter cushion she was going to use to smother him to death with. If she used the sequined one, it would leave a trace, but the bowed one . . .

'I'll make it better, promise. Hang in there. For me.' For a man unconscious and full of drink that he obviously wasn't used to, those words came out as clear as a bell. She looked down as his face, handsome in sleep but obviously troubled. Maybe she could put up with him for a little bit. At that moment, Luke turned onto his side, farted loudly, and started to snore like a baby piglet. *Maybe not.*

'Thanks Hans, mate. Just peachy dude, cheers. Bloody hell.' She looked gingerly at her bin, but made no move to clean it up. *No way am I touching a bucket full of pee.* Suddenly glad that her bin was solid plastic, rather than the wicker pee fountain it could have been, she checked on Luke. His head was off to one side, still looking her way as she stood at the side of the bed. *I just know he's going to wake up with a cricked neck, and as much as that pleases me, I can't leave him like that.* Kneeling on the bed, she gently turned his head and rolled his body towards her, so that he didn't choke on his vomit if he yacked, or pull his neck muscles. Reaching behind him, she moved a little closer to put a pillow under his head and cover him over properly. His clothes and hair were damp from the snowfall, and she didn't want him to catch cold. When she finally pulled back, his eyes were open, and he was watching her.

'Sorry,' she said softly, though quite why she was apologising she had no idea. She should have left him to fart himself into oblivion. 'I was just tucking you in.'

He smiled, a luscious, happy, smile, with just a hint of sadness in his eyes. Basically, he looked like Clark Kent in puppy form. *Sheesh.* She smiled back, despite her best efforts to stay being a snarky cow. *It actually feels nice to look after someone else.*

'Thanks.' His face dropped into a comical frown, his lip jutting out in a childlike way. 'You's fink we can do it, don't you?'

'Your big plan?' she guessed wildly, and he nodded once. 'Of course you can. Now get some sleep, and I'll see you in the morning. Okay?'

He nodded, and was almost asleep by the time she left the room. Almost, but he said something first that stopped her in her tracks.

'I know you. I don't know where from, but I'll remember. I remember your face.' Rebecca could feel her heart pause in her chest, as though it held its own breath, waiting to hear what he said. *Does he know? Did Hans tell him? Surely not.*

She stood there, frozen in time, waiting for him to say something, say anything, just so she could take a breath again. 'Luke?' All she got in reply were soft snores, accompanied by the beating drums in her ears, and the tingle in her feet, urging her to run. *I can't stay now. I can't be here. It's been five years, and I finally thought I was okay. As okay as I can manage, as scarred as I am.*

Baking was easy for Rebecca. The principles of it, anyway. The love and talent she had for it now was down to the usual formula too, in part. Work hard at something, love it, and you will get better. Do it once. Do it again. Fail. Get. Back. Up. Adjust, adapt and try again. Keep on trucking. It's the human race at its best. We humans find something we love, and we surround ourselves in it. We sacrifice, we push ourselves to achieve, and we cheer others on as they hit their goal. It didn't all have to be trail blazing. It didn't have to be anything special. Something as simple as a cup of coffee, a cupcake could turn a bad day around. People needed the little things. Good food, a great book that felt like a shot of romance in the arm, a hug from someone you love. All little things that added up to those feelings of connection, of being part of something bigger than a simple batch of sweet goods. Rebecca knew that now, working here. Baking was her solace, her way of still feeling useful. Detached, but still there. Hans said it was hiding, but what did he know? He hadn't failed. Not many were in Rebecca's league of big fat fails.

Baking was safe and always there. It expected nothing from her. You put the oven on, sourced the best raw ingredients, followed the recipe, it ended the same way every time. Routine, with an expected outcome. Like a tick list. You made a list of goals, and then worked towards them. Worked till the day was completed, and you could tick that box, cross the item off that list. It sounded a little hollow even in her own head that morning. All she wanted to do was go into the café, keep busy.

She'd been up for hours, not even trying to sleep after the first hour of tossing and turning on the sofa. She felt sick to her stomach at the thought of facing Luke and his questions. Hans must have known it would be like this. Adding the final egg to

43

the mixture, she mixed it together by hand, the bowl balanced on one hip. She didn't even need any more cupcakes, but she couldn't stop her hands from making more. It helped to distract her from the massive urge to flee. She added peppermint extract and folded it into the mixture, gnawing on the insides of her lip as she tried to calm herself down.

Her mother had taught her how to bake, years ago. Before the obsession with success had taken hold of Rebecca – and her mother. Rebecca could still remember dragging her little stool to the countertop to help her, her little cherry-patterned pinafore apron matching her mother's. This was her favourite recipe, peppermint cupcakes with mojito frosting. They'd designed it together, adding the mojito when she got older and baking was one thing they still enjoyed together; she made them whenever something bad happened. Now, she was making them because she knew something bad was coming, and she couldn't do a thing to stop it. She stirred a little faster.

Last night. Her old friend anxiety whispered in her ear softly, provoking a reaction like being slapped in the face with a breeze block. *What am I going to say to him when he wakes up? Will he bring it up?* Hans had a lot to answer for, the brave little bastard. What was he thinking, saddling her with a stranger, and a geeky, all-knowing, all-seeing man child at that? Luke was going to keep digging, she could see the frustration in his cute drunken expression last night as he struggled to place her face. She worked that bit faster at the mixture, to shake the anxiety off and try to focus on her task again.

'Bec . . . Rebecca?' A weak little voice limped into her awareness, and she jumped, ditching the bowl on the countertop and raising her wooden spoon in front of her, like a wizard wielding a wand. A gob of batter fell to the floor, making a loud 'splat' sound. Luke was in the doorway, or rather, was lying against it pathetically, his knuckles white as they gripped the corner of the door. 'What are you doing down here?' It came out as a little whine, and Rebecca found herself feeling a bit sorry for him. Before she remembered. He had to go. She ventured forward to look closer at her uninvited houseguest.

He looked rough. As in bear's arse rough. His stubble was quite dark now, casting a deep shadow on his face. He had dark circles under his eyes, and his hair had that tousled look, as though someone had grabbed him by the shoulders and shook him hard. It reminded her of a toy she had as a kid, a little hairy gonk thing that said 'yabber yabber' when you shook it. Same annoying whine too.

'I'm baking, I couldn't sleep.' She didn't ask what he was doing up. His liver probably woke him up in protest. *I just want you to go.*

'You bake a lot, don't you? Did I wake you?' *Did you wake me? Are you kidding?* She rolled her eyes and started to spoon the mixture into the cupcake cases, working methodically as she tried to stop her hands from shaking.

'I think you know the answer to that,' she started, trying to ignore the butterflies kickboxing in her stomach. 'I don't know what you think you know about me, but—'

'I get it, you don't want houseguests coming home late, it was a one-off. It's way out of character for me, I can assure you of that. I apologise. It won't happen again.' He stumbled over and very gently lowered himself onto one of the stools, moving forward at a sloth like leisurely pace till his left cheek touched the tabletop. 'Ohhh, that's nice and cold. Mmmmm.'

Rebecca threw a tea towel over his head and put the trays of cupcakes into the oven, flicking the timer on.

'Ow, that hurt,' he moaned from under the towel, his voice muffled and dull.

'Aww poor baby,' she pouted before she could stop herself. *I can't bring myself to look at him, even with the tea towel covering his knowing face.*

He lifted his head up, looking like a drooling shepherd in a pub nativity play nightmare.

'Sorry for waking you. Hans and I kind of tied one on, you know?' Putting the cupcakes in the oven, she set her chicken timer and waited, listening to the ticking in the silence. He squinted a little as he looked right at her.

'I know, I had to put you to bed.' Signalling the end of the conversation, she sprayed the surfaces down and started scrubbing. She concentrated on the monotonous motion to steady her. She always got like this, when someone noticed, spoke about the competition or looked at her a beat too long. Just thinking about it made her feel exhausted once more, and yearning for the sanctity of her duvet. *Once the cupcakes are out cooling, I intend to get some sleep, frost them in the morning. The normal person's definition of morning, anyway. Duvet. Damn.* She got a flashback of the bin and winced. 'Also, you will have to get my room cleaned. Sheets, and the bin, of course. I was happy to take the sofa yesterday, but tonight, I am back in one of the beds, either way.'

One flick of her eyes towards him, and she could tell. He had no idea what she was going on about. He looked bewildered.

'The bin?' she ventured. Nothing. Just a gormless, rather scary-looking shepherd with stubble stared back. 'You came into my room, peed in my bin and then passed out on my bed.'

His face went slack, his jaw practically swinging loose. Relief washed over her. If he didn't remember that . . . He knew less than Jon Snow. Luke didn't know her, or her past. Either that, or Hans *had* told him with beer-lubricated lips, and then he pickled that knowledge with alcohol.

'I didn't,' he said eventually, feebly from his sloth position on the countertop. 'Did I?' His Yorkshire accent grew thicker as he started to mutter and curse under his breath. If her mother were here, she'd be mortified. The last time Rebecca had said 'nowt' to her mother when she had asked what was wrong, it had been hell. All week her irate mother had sent her interviews of sporting people having ridiculous accent meltdowns on TV. To be fair, the French Joey Barton clip had creased her, Hans, and Holly up for weeks.

'I am so sorry. I don't drink that much, as a rule.' It took a minute for her to realise the tea towel was still mumbling.

'Good rule,' she quipped grumpily, thinking of the pee bucket in her room, next to her lovely, warm and usually man-free bed. 'You had a good night though?' She kept it light, but really she wished she could take her wooden spoon and go digging in his hungover brain. Hopefully one of the brain cells he had killed last night contained Hans's little Rebecca bulletin.

He nodded feebly at her, his brows furrowing and un-furrowing like aerobic caterpillars. 'From what I can remember. I am sorry, I won't do that again. I do appreciate you putting me up. I'll go clean.'

Ready for him, Rebecca reached under the countertop, grabbing a roll of bin bags and some gloves. 'Here.'

His face softened as he looked at her, and she couldn't help but smile at him. *Damn it. This is piss in a bin guy, Becks. Knock it off.* 'I'll be coming back up in ten. I need some shut eye before we open.' *Oh crap. I dropped a 'we' then myself accidentally, but I can't take it back now. Too obvious. I can see it though, floating in the air between us. I need to pluck it out of the air, stuff it back in and force out an I. I will open. This is temporary, having 00-drunkie under this roof.* She made a mental note to call Hans as soon as the hour was suitable for ringing a friend, to bollock him. *Holly's pregnant and bored too, so I bet she'll give him a good ribbing for me.*

Luke, moving for the first time as though he was human, came towards her around the countertop, reaching for the items she was offering him. She felt his fingers close around her hand, just for a second, before he withdrew. Slowly, like his fingers were saying hello to hers. She didn't totally pull hers away either. Sleep deprivation was making her cuckoo.

'I am sorry, for last night. And this morning, I suppose. I know it must have been a lot for Hans to ask, you putting up with me and everything. I do appreciate it though. It was a bit of a spur

of the moment thing. I didn't even realise what it involved, really.'
He looked around him and out of the window. The view was
looking rather spectacular this morning, with the light trickling
over the mountains, showing the fresh, untouched powder. He
stopped talking, transfixed. Rebecca found herself looking at that
powder, remembering how it felt the first time she had been the
one to ski through that pure white canvas.

'Living here must be amazing,' he said, almost wistfully. She
nodded, but couldn't bring herself to answer. The chicken timer
went off, and the moment was broken. He jumped as though a
grenade had gone off behind him, his knees bending in reflex.
Rebecca had never been more grateful to an inanimate object in
her life. Well, nearly. She was a single girl after all. The nights
were long, lonely, and full of battery-powered distractions. She
didn't answer, and after a moment she could see his shadow move
towards the interior stairs. She took her phone out of her apron
pocket and went to tap out an expletive-filled text to Hans, but
he'd beaten her to it. She put the phone on the counter as she
read the first few words.

**I know you don't like any of this, but he's a friend. He needs
help, and I know you understand that. Please try to remember
that. Don't hate me. Holly is typing this for me, because I am a
drunken dickhead who tried to call you with the remote control.
I am in big trouble.**

She didn't need to read anymore. *I don't want to know anything
else. Denial is a powerful bedfellow, and I fancy snuggling up with
it just that little bit longer.* She knew what Hans was like. He was
the biggest lug with the loudest voice, and the biggest heart too.
As unlikely as his friendship was with Luke, who looked like Kevin
Hart beside the Rock when the two friends were stood together,
she knew it mattered to him. Hans made a family around him,
and you were in it whether you wanted to be or not. She would
just have to put up with it. Once they were ready, she left the cakes
on the cooling trays, closed everything down, and headed upstairs,

where she faceplanted straight onto the couch and promptly fell asleep, exhausted. Her phone stayed right where it was, abandoned on the countertop.

Hans and the Yorkshire pee fountain stayed clear of the café all day, leaving Rebecca alone to process the recent events, and the feelings it was pushing out of her usually cold, cold heart. Her bedroom alarm clock had awoken her for work from across the hall a few hours later. Next to her, Luke had written a note, telling her he was taking himself into town to see Hans for the day. Her sheets were gone from her bed, and she didn't see anything in the washer but his clothes, whirling around and making themselves at home. She checked her laundry basket in a panic, but thankfully he hadn't thought to wash her smalls with his. The bin was missing, and the carpet had been cleaned, the windows opened for ventilation. Looking around her room, she was relieved that nothing gave her away. None of this place did, the only photos she had up here were of her, Hans, and Holly, and some of the other crew from town. Rare nights out that she got dragged on over the years. The opposite of her old self. Six years ago, she was a different person. Everyone said that, it wasn't unusual. The human body grows new cells over years, so the body changes. People are all different, changed when age and gravity start to take hold, and their life choices leave the consequences for all to see on their faces. It ran a little deeper than that for Rebecca though.

Six short years ago, Rebecca was at the top of her game, happy and in love with her life. Her mother was proud of her. She told all the neighbours, the church, the Costa crew of ladies she lunched with about Rebecca's achievements. 'My daughter,' she'd say, a smile beaming from her face. Now she said it in hushed tones, as though being a baker and café manager was the worst thing in the world. Anyone would think Rebecca was robbing old folks' handbags for a living the way her mother behaved.

She'd texted already that day – a Facebook memory she insisted on torturing Rebecca with. Why did people do that? Send people photos of good times, dogs long dead, neighbours they don't speak to anymore?

This memory was a real humdinger, Rebecca beaming at the camera, her mother clapping her in the background, bright eyed and wrapped in splendour. The screenshot of the article the photo was attached to swam before her eyes as she thought of that day. *Mother, why the hell did you send me this, today of all days.* The caption underneath said it all. *This year, baby. This year.*

Rebecca shoved her phone in the drawer beside her and got on with her day. She didn't need to answer. She'd already told her mother that she was entering the competition. She wouldn't find out for a while that it was a lie. Her annual disappointment would be right on schedule.

Rebecca managed to have a good day, making it to closing time without any more annoying housemates, customers or messages from her mother. The resort was coming to life, and having something to do really helped her to switch off her brain and engage with the stuff she could control. She was just heading to the doors to lock up, when Luke appeared at the other side. He peered in through the glass like a wary zoo visitor approaches a dark glass cage.

'What's wrong?' she asked as he entered, shopping bags in his hands, closing the door behind him with his foot. 'You think I might bite?' He looked at her, puzzled. 'You looked like you were trying to suss out what mood I was in.'

He smiled, but it was tight, and he didn't make eye contact. *Fine with me.*

'I just thought I'd give you a little space, after my behaviour.'

'It's fine, we've all gotten drunk and urinated in strange places.' She knew she had to think of Hans and put up with him, but she couldn't resist the little quip.

He raised one eyebrow, but she didn't elaborate. A girl needed her secrets, and telling him about her own lightweight ways wasn't going to happen. He pulled a dark grey backpack off his back, taking off his coat straight after. His cheeks were flushed from coming into the warmth of the café, and it made his eyes sparkle. Even she had to admit, although her houseguest was the worst possible person to share her home with, he was quite easy on the eyes on closer inspection.

'You finished for the night?' he asked, looking around at all the empty tables, chairs stacked on top.

'Yep.' Clicking off the lights, she plunged them into the dim glow from the lighting outside. 'Lights out.' Inside the café, it was all wood and high ceilings. She loved this café like it was her very own. One day, maybe it would be, or she could buy one somewhere else. Her mother would kill her, but still . . . It would mean she could live in the Alps forever, or on some other corner of the earth, just her. 'You have any plans for tonight?' she added, curious.

He gave her a sheepish look, and took a bottle of wine and a wrapped plastic bag out of one of his bags.

'Well . . .' He wiggled the bottle at her. 'I thought we could have a meal. I'll cook, to say sorry for last night and to thank you for putting me up. I do appreciate it, I know you like to be alone.'

His presumption wasn't wrong, but it still irked her. She felt a little judged, and that automatically brought out her snark.

'It's only temporary, so I'm sure I can endure it. The toilet training needs to improve though, or all bets are off.'

He reached back into the backpack, and pulled out a baby's nappy. 'Got it covered. Hans gave me one.'

'Bollocks,' she said, starting to laugh. 'I was going to rib you myself later.' He visibly relaxed in front of her and put the nappy back into the bag. 'Okay Marco Pierre White, you go and make a start. I'll lock up.'

She took her time cleaning down the rest of the work surfaces, enjoying the silence of the space. Once she was done, she headed to the bottom of the stairs, listening in on what Luke was up to.

She checked herself out in the oven door, pulling a face at her red cheeks and slightly dishevelled hair. She gave up and scraping the worst clumps of hair back into her bobble, she listened in again, trying to time her entrance. Luke was murdering some song off the radio, and she could hear things being banged around in the kitchen. Taking out her phone, she kept one ear on the door and logged into Facebook.

Her page loaded, and she suddenly felt overwhelmed by how different she was to the person that originally set up this profile. Her photo looked like a different person altogether, living a different life. *I want to give her a huge shake, and tell her to wise up. To do better, do things differently.* She brought up her friends list, and scrolled through for what she was looking for. Hans, and *his* friends list.

'Rebecca?' Luke called from upstairs. 'Where's the pepper?'

She jumped, almost dropping her phone. She felt guilty, but he didn't know, did he? It was what people did these days, checked people out online. She was hardly hacking MI6.

'It's on the top of the microwave! In a pink pot!'

Further shuffling from upstairs. She could hear him walk across the kitchen, his steps coming to a soft halt. It felt strange to hear someone moving about. It felt like forever since Hans and Holly had left.

'Do you know that these are breasts?' he shouted down, amusement curling his words. 'The pots?'

Does he think I walk around in the dark?

'Yes, I bought them. Cute, aren't they!' She'd bought her mother a matching 'pair'. Suffice to say, she'd never seen them in the background anywhere when she FaceTimed her parents. Logging back out of Facebook after deleting her search from the history to stop herself being tempted again, she headed up the stairs to the flat.

'Cute, sure,' he drawled as she entered. He was shaking a boob-shaped pepper pot over a huge pair of steaks that were sizzling in her favourite griddle pan. It smelled amazing, and Rebecca's treacherous stomach started to get a bit vocal. 'Just surprised me. Would you like some wine?'

Throwing a raised brow in his direction as she headed to the cabinet where her last two crappy wine glasses sat, she grabbed them and headed over to him.

'Does a bear do his business in the woods?' She held out the glasses to him, grateful that they were actually clean and streak-free. He probably already thought she was a bit mad but she found herself caring, just a little, about what he might think about her living arrangements. He laughed and filled both of their glasses up.

'I set us up to eat in the lounge, if that's okay?' He took a slow, deep sip of his wine, closing his eyes and letting his head roll back. 'Ah, better now.' He tapped his chest once, twice gently with an open palm. Rebecca drank from her own glass, trying not to laugh. She failed and he turned to look at her.

'What?'

'Did you really need that wine? What's with the little taps?'

His cheeks went bright red, which was both a dead giveaway and almost adorable.

'Oh, that. It's just a thing I do sometimes.'

'Crack cocaine is a thing people do sometimes, doesn't mean it's a good thing. Looks like a therapy move to me.' She didn't wait to hear his answer, taking her wine through into her small, neat living room and plonking herself down on her crappy little sofa.

'Maybe it is,' he called from the kitchen, in between the sound of a knife scraping the chopping board and his humming along to the latest song she'd never heard. 'Maybe not. You ready for this culinary delight?'

He came in, a tea towel hanging off his trousers like a waiter, two plates full of food in his arms. 'The French have nothing on this. Feast your eyes!'

He put the plates down on the coffee table, which he had thrown a clean white bath towel over, and looked at her like a child with a crayon drawing to his adoring parent. Full of excitement and nervous energy. Anyone would think he was serving the Royals afternoon tea, not steak, chips, and salad to a fed-up baker with a sarcasm problem. He was openly grinning at her, waiting for a gold star. She smiled back as best she could, feeling awkward, and sat forward in her seat to fully appreciate the meal. It did look lovely, and her stomach was gurgling in anticipation, rather loudly. Her body betrayed her once again on the food front.

'Thanks, this looks amazing.' His grin widened even further, taking it to Joker proportions, and he passed her one of the plates. The one without the chip in it. She looked across, and he was eating his meal from it, taking a seat on the other side of the couch. It wasn't very big in the first place, and they were practically sitting on top of each other, but it wasn't totally awful. Rebecca flicked the TV on and he grabbed the remote from her, flicking the channel over.

'Hey!' She jabbed him in the hand with the fork. 'Off the clicker!'

'Clicker? Loser.' He laughed in her face, easily holding the remote control out of her reach whilst shovelling a chunky piece of fresh tomato into his smug mouth. 'These,' he waggled them at her, 'are called buttons.'

She snorted, almost coughing up a piece of lettuce in the process. 'Buttons! Oooo, where's Cinders? It's a clicker mate, you press the button, it clicks.'

'Yes! Button, you said it yourself. Buttons you press. Not click.'

'Yeah, well, button off Yoda, and give me it back. It's my TV.'

He pulled a face at her and scrolled through the channels.

'It says "property of Hans" on the back of the TV. It's labelled. A few bits are, actually. What's that about?'

Rebecca rolled her eyes. 'I used to label my stuff with one of those machine labellers, fridge stuff, my shampoo. He's a hairy dude, he used to cost me a fiver every time he had a shower. He bought the cheap stuff and used mine.' She lunged for the remote again, almost losing her plate in the process. He swerved her and sat back, tucking into his food.

'That explains that then. Still, Hans said that there's a good film on, I thought we could watch it.' He looked across at her. 'Unless you have plans?' He looked around him, as though a suitor was going to ride up the stairs any second on a tall white steed.

'Er no,' she said to her steak, 'no plans tonight.' That would cover her for now, but what about the next night? 'Truth is, it's a busy time here so my social calendar takes a hit.' Too far. 'I still go out, obviously.'

'Ah yes, we have that dinner, don't we, Saturday night?'

He was focused back on the television now, but Rebecca hadn't moved.

'Dinner?'

'Yeah,' he said, munching away as he made himself at home. They sounded like a bloody married couple now. 'Holly and Hans's place, they're having a few friends over. After the baby shower.'

Fuuuddgggeeeee nuggets. The baby shower. Arghhh! She'd forgotten, and she hadn't been shopping yet, or got them a baby gift. And she didn't know about the dinner after either.

'Oh, that. Yeah, of course.' She flapped her hand nonchalantly. It was her day off tomorrow, Hans was coming in to work. She could escape into town and get what she needed. Ring Holly and get the skinny on what Saturday was all about, and why she needed to be tied to the train track too. The baby shower was fine, she loved Holly, but a dinner? What for? Would she and Luke have to arrive together?

'Yeah, I figured we could go together, share a ride?' She could feel his eyes on her, and she nodded, forcing her fork to pick up more food. 'Great, I'm glad. I hate these things normally. I avoid them, if I'm honest.'

Rebecca groaned gratefully. 'God, me too. I mean, I love them both obviously, but their friends and everyone? It's a lot.' She reached for her wine, taking a gulp to push down the tide of social dread she felt wash over her. Glugging it down noisily, she took a breath, and he rushed into the silence.

'It is a lot! When he invited me here for the shower, well – I mean I was never going to come. I never do when he invites me over, but then I saw the invitation on the fridge, and I just went for it. Booked a ticket, packed a bag. I mean, I never do that. If you knew me . . .' He flicked the remote control around in his hand, gesturing wildly. 'I mean, really knew me, you'd laugh. You really would. Dad . . .' He deflated, and his conversation tapered off to a whisper. 'It's just not me, that's all. So, I'm just glad that we're going together, we can brave it and then come back here and drink enough wine to recover.' He blushed then, pushing his glasses back up his nose. 'I mean, if you want to drink wine. You might have plans for after.'

There it was again, the plans thing.

'You have a lot of plans, back home?' Deflection was a woman's best weapon. That and her brain.

He winced, sitting back before answering her. The TV was on, but the volume was low. The menu screen listed some movies Rebecca had never seen before. Now they were facing each other, their legs tucked up beneath them, plates in their laps. Their knees touched, but neither made a move to pull back. Not wanting to drop the steak in their laps, probably. She was enjoying it a lot more than she thought she would; given his murdering of the top ten and level of noise coming from the kitchen, she'd half expected an inedible mess. He swallowed a mouthful of food, and Rebecca watched his jaw flex with the movements. The more she looked at him, the hotter he looked. He licked his lips, and she found herself copying him. She tried to squint at the wine bottle on the coffee table in front of them, to check the proof. She must be getting squiffy.

'No, not really. I worked a lot.' The blood drained from his face. 'Oh shit, work. I haven't even checked my emails yet today.'

He went to get his phone out of his pocket, tipping the wine in his hand straight over himself, and his mostly empty plate. When it hit the ceramic, it bounced up, all over Rebecca, and her food. Squealing like a pair of schoolgirls high on sugar, the two of them jumped up, dropping everything they still held to the floor and leaving the pair of them standing on the sofa, wet through and smelling like steak.

'You idiot!'

'Jesus, I'm sorry! I was reaching for my phone!'

'Yeah, well, I didn't think you were reaching for Excalibur, did I, you total klutz!' She looked down at her fabric sofa, the one Hans had bought her one Christmas by way of a bonus. It was grey fabric, plain but nice enough. She'd bought some mustard-yellow cushions in town, to jazz it up, but now everything was ruined. 'Look at my sofa.' She reached down and pulled a piece of meat from one of the cushions. 'And my tea. That steak was lovely.'

'Really?'

'Not the thing to focus on, furniture bomber. What are we going to do now?'

Looking down around him, a piece of lettuce astride his socked foot, he winced. 'I'm going to get my credit card out, and pay for this fixing.'

Rebecca looked at him, one hand on her hip and one hand on the back of her couch to steady herself. 'Credit card? For who, the cleaning fairies? Last time I checked, they dealt in cash or toddler teeth. Go look in the long cupboard in the kitchen, there's a mop bucket and a dustpan and brush in there. I'll get some cleaner for the couch.' It was red wine, so she didn't hold out that much hope, but she wanted to get out of her clothes. Looking at him, she realised he probably felt the same. 'Sorry, we should probably go shower first.'

His eyes widened, and she pressed her lips together. 'I mean separately, of course. You go first, I'll wait till you've done.' He looked like he wanted to argue, so she moved first. Which wasn't that easy, given that she was standing on cushions, covered in junk and bits. Taking a small step forward, she toppled a little, and his arm was around her middle in an instant, pulling her tight to him and squashing a piece of tomato that was hanging out on his top between them.

'Careful,' he said, close to her cheek. 'The glass. Stay there, till I get it cleaned up. Don't move. You go shower first, okay?' He was oddly masculine, and for a second she thought he was going to ask her to braid her hair and head to the Red Room. His knitted tank top ruined the daydream a little, but she went with it. He steadied her, and not letting go, he stood down, avoiding the shards. Leaning forward slightly, he looked around him, mentally and audibly mapping out his path. Turning back to her to give her an all clear, he then leaned forward a bit more. His head was hovering near her stomach, poised. 'You ready?' he asked.

'Yes,' she said, and before she got so much as a pinkie off the fabric, he hoisted her right up over one shoulder, and crab walked to the hall. He didn't stop there either, heading straight to her bedroom, her slightly panicked hands grabbing at his bottom to try and stop her head from moving like a windscreen wiper. 'Hey! I can walk now, thanks.' He opened her bedroom door, and when they were both inside, he whirled her around in his arms, and put her gently to her feet. She couldn't see him very well, since her hair had come loose and was now around her head like a lion's mane. Scraping it back behind her ears, she puffed a bit of fringe out of her eyeline.

'I'm so sorry,' he started. 'I'm sorry that I'm saying sorry, yet again. I must be your worst nightmare. I swear, in my flat, I have a nice place. I've lived there a year now, and only had one minor house fire. Well . . .' He was still holding her around the waist, and seemed oblivious to the fact. She didn't know why she hadn't brought it up either. Trauma perhaps? Shock? She'd felt something. It was probably her stomach mourning the loss of that meal. 'It was *pretty* minor. There was a singed rug over the balcony incident.'

'Really? What happened?' She could feel her lips twitching. He really was a geek. He was adorable with his glasses on, his face all pinched up at the memory.

'Well, I pulled my tea out of the oven, and it was on fire, so I dropped it on the rug. Then the rug caught fire, and I just grabbed it and, well, I ran out onto the balcony and threw it over the side.'

He moved a hand away from her waist to illustrate his story, imitating himself throwing a flaming rug out into the night. She laughed, but it stopped in her throat when he put his hand back where it was. She could feel the heat from him. He seemed to notice it too, because he looked down at his hand.

'The thing was, the neighbour had a lot of pots out, and some clean washing. The whole lot went up, she ended up moving out for a while, it was a whole thing.'

He squeezed his hand tighter, just for a second, and then released her. Looking into her eyes, he gave her a shy little smile. 'Anyway, no fires here. I'll go clean up, shout me when you've done.'

He left the room, leaving her standing there staring after him. A moment later, the radio started playing again, and she half smiled as he started to sing. Heading for the shower, she realised that she hadn't thought about competitions or failures for a few hours. It felt pretty good. Maybe Saturday wouldn't be so bad after all. Bearable even.

Chapter 4

There was a pretty pot of daffodils on the windowsill, but they couldn't be real. Wrong time of year, he was sure. As sure as he was about anything these days. He'd have a look, ask someone usually. Offer to cut some fresh blooms from his own garden. Stuck here, in this squeaky-wheeled bed, he couldn't do a thing but stare at them. Was the water in the bottom real? If he knew that, he could figure it out. He squinted his eyes, but his face still felt odd. He wasn't sure he even had control.

'Morning Frank, time to get up and shaking lad. Come on, your friend is here to see you again. I wouldn't keep her waiting either if I were you.'

She was here again, the woman from that place. *Oh, where was it, please, just remember. Everything's so foggy, and I just feel so tired. I'm glad my son didn't stay. I couldn't bear for him to waste any more time. Especially not on me. I've already wasted enough of his.* It was all too late, he saw that now. *I don't want him here, seeing this. What's the point in . . . what's the point in . . .*

Dante came into view, kneeling a little to get to Frank's level. 'Come on Mr Sommersby,' he said kindly, patting his huge, dark hand over the top of Frank's rather pale-looking counterpart on the bed sheet. 'We've been through this. Stroke is all about fast action and hard work. You got medical treatment fast, your body just needs a little help, is all.' His voice was deep but rich, soothing. Frank could almost feel it wash over him. The man cared, but he didn't realise that it was all a bit too late. Such a waste, really. Frank didn't like to disappoint people. He never had.

'Anything, Dante?' A voice came from the doorway. Dante turned half to the door, patted Frank's hand once more, and stood up.

'Not yet, but it's early days. The son coming today?'

Frank refocused on the flowers on the sill, resting his head back on the huge stack of pillows behind him. He needed to be kept upright, wanted to see out. He hated being laid down, his body uncooperative and clumsy. He hated this bed altogether, hated hospitals. He'd avoided the place like the plague for years. Now here he was. And so was she.

'No, he's . . . dealing with something at the moment, bit of a project, I think.' She looked at Frank from the corner of her eye, and smiled when she saw that he'd turned his head to her. 'Yes, I know you're listening.' She winked at him, and he felt a stir of something in him. Recognition? Annoyance? Frank puffed out his lips, a cavernous sigh erupting from him. It might as well be flatulence. He couldn't even say the word, let alone decipher what his body was trying to tell him.

'Oh, don't be sighing at me. I'd rather have a wink, thanks.' Turning back to Dante, she nibbled at the corner of her mouth, just for a moment. Frank recognised the movement, as though she did that a lot. He wanted to tell her that, to ask her if that was true. That his brain was still working, still remembering the things he wanted it to. Needed it to. He knew he wouldn't be able to get the words out though, not without coming out in a cold sweat from the effort, so screw that. It had taken enough for him to scream at his son to get out, to go, to leave and not come back. He'd screamed at the nurses whenever his progeny showed up, and finally, they all got the message. No point anyway, in trying to articulate what he wanted. They wouldn't listen, and they certainly wouldn't help him. He sighed again, but the woman was there in front of him now. Looking out of the window. Now was his chance. He tried to raise his hand, but he got nothing more than a weak finger wave. He grunted in frustration, and tried again. Nothing. He couldn't lift his own wretched hand from the bed. He wanted to punch something, to hit, to scream out, but nothing. Marilyn had turned to him now, and he tried to direct her back to his desire by opening his eyes wide. An old dog from his memory sprang to mind, eating a lolly on some garden back step. Him, laughing with someone else at the dog's wide open eyes as he licked. The memory hit him so strongly that he could almost feel the fur under his hand, the warmth of the sun on his face. The memory faded, and Frank was left frustrated once more. He jerked his head wildly to the sill, and with one huge burst of anger, he shouted 'Oooooouuuuuwwwtttt!' He pushed the almost feral sound from his lungs with every little bit of strength he had. Marilyn looked at Dante, who grinned, exposing a huge set of white teeth that added a little shine to the rather dull room.

'That's it, Mr Sommersby, you sounded like a lion then! Roar again, go on!'

Frank clenched his fists, or at least tried to send out the signal, and took a breath. Marilyn was bouncing in front of him on the spot, her hair staying the same each time she landed.

'Come on Frank, that's it! Tell us what you want!' She leaned in close, her eyes bright with excitement, the dark circles under her eyes at odds with the rest of her demeanour. He could see Dante, off to one side, ready to help. He felt like a bloody toddler, trying to take his first clumsy steps. He wanted to lash out, punch something. The fact that he couldn't only made him worse.

'Oooouuuutttttt!' He tried again, looking intently at the cheap pot of artificial flowers on the sill. If he was going to sit here and waste away, then he jolly well wasn't going to sit staring at that.

He tried to flick his head, and the woman twirled, looking where he was, and picked up the pot.

'It's this,' she said to Dante, her words coming out in excited whispers. 'He loves his garden.' She eyed Frank, who was staring at her from the bed with a wretched look on his face. 'What's the matter Frank? Is it this?' She waggled it in front of him, and he deepened his scowl as much as he could muster. His face was still being as uncooperative in parts, like his stupid body. Marilyn looked at him, and to Dante, and then she placed the pot on his over bed table. Right in front of him.

He was about to try to grunt at her, to move his face into an expression that would hopefully display his vehement anger, when she looked him right in the eye. Her own eyes were cornflower-blue. Frank looked into them, and she smiled.

'I know you're in there, Frank, but you have to try. They told you, remember? Right hemisphere strokes are hard Frank, but your body can do it. You need to fight like you've never fought before, to come back to us. If you give up, that's it. Your son is worried sick, he's not been eating much. he looks awful! He needs to see you. I can't imagine what he's thinking. You can't let him—' She stopped, the air pushing out of her lungs as she spoke. 'You can't give up Frank, God knows you have enough already.' Dante kissed his teeth behind her, always warning her to stay positive, but she didn't stop. 'I mean it Frank. You have to try. God, I never realised you were this stubborn! I wish I'd said something years ago. What did you want to tell me?'

It was the first time someone had actually asked him that. In all the days since he'd crashed his car, people had been talking. To him, at him. Dante was a man of few words at the best of times, but he was gentle. He had warm hands and a lot of respect, which Frank appreciated. He couldn't tell him, but just seeing him there made him feel so much better. Less alone, less scared. When he thought of his son, his heart lurched. That was the worst thing in all this, the worry on his son's face that day in the hospital. His car was a write off, as were half the parked cars in the street. He knew how worrying that must have been to see. He did nothing but cry when he came, they cried together. It was about the only way they could communicate, even being so close, but Frank knew. He knew he could try harder now. He just wasn't very sure that he wanted to bother. Turning away from her expectant face, he looked back at the now bare windowsill, and closed his eyes. He should have put up more of a fight years ago. When he was young enough and well enough to do something. He'd become a dad, and that had been his life. Till his wife died, and his whole world felt like a hole had been blasted through it. He'd never dealt with that hole. Not really. He'd tiptoed around it for years, too scared to live in case something else happened. He knew back then he wouldn't survive it.

His son didn't have to live that way. He had cut the apron strings now. It was done. He just wanted it all to be done, so he could finally find peace. Maybe see his wife again. Get out of this knackered body. He didn't tell her any of this, he never said a word. He just stared at the pot of flowers.

'Stubborn old fool,' he heard a few moments later. The door to his room closed, and Dante's voice filled Frank's ears.

'Your son looks like you, you know? I saw it, when he came to visit.' Frank didn't move, he didn't want to think of their last meeting. It hadn't gone well. *What I wouldn't give to be able to pick up the phone. Explain it to him properly. Make him understand that it was for his own good.* 'Is he like you, too?' Frank made an odd noise in the back of his throat, and Dante waited.

'Y-yes.'

It was only a little word, but Frank heard it. He'd said it, answered the question. He felt Dante's hand cover his, and give him a slow pat.

'I thought so,' he said eventually. 'You know Frank, people surprise me in this job all the time. I think you're one of those people. Marilyn sure does.' Frank flinched at her name. *Marilyn.*

The woman with the cornflower-blue eyes. The pain in the arse with the flower pot. He didn't try to reply to Dante, it wasn't worth the effort. The fact was, Dante Flores had hit the proverbial nail on the head. Frank's son, the apple of his eye, was just like him. And that was precisely why he'd sent him away.

Chapter 5

The following morning, Rebecca was up early, eager to get a start on her day off. After last night, Luke having cleaned up and made them grilled cheese sandwiches, she felt a little better about not waking up alone in her little oasis. She rolled over in bed, giving the view a glare as she opened the curtains. She dressed in a pair of black trousers, a pink sweater and her usual walking boots, and then she packed her bag with her phone, cash, and a list of stuff she needed to get from the shops. With Hans at the café all day, she wanted to go see Holly too, see how she was coping being cooped up indoors. Bedrest was the worst. She knew from experience what it felt like to spend hours and days staring out of the window, watching everyone get on with their lives. She had to live with Hans too, and was growing his spawn, so the least the woman deserved was a cuppa and a chat.

Heading out of her bedroom door, dressed and boots in hand, she heard a voice in the living room. She wanted to say hello, but she headed to the bathroom instead. It was nearer to the living room, and his voice got louder as she approached.

'He really did that? Why?' Rebecca could hear the confusion in Luke's voice. 'What about the activities coordinator? Did she try like the manager suggested?' A woman's voice came back across the phone line, and whatever she said made Luke gasp. 'No! The middle one? That's not like him, none of this is.' Rebecca found herself venturing around the corner. He didn't sound okay. 'Well, I suppose at least his fingers are working. Did he say anything, ask about me?' Rebecca walked into the room, and he noticed her then. He was sitting on the sofa, which was covered in a couple of her king size duvet covers. His laptop and notebooks were spread out all around him, but he was sitting back on the sofa, one hand running through his dark, messy hair, the other holding his phone to his ear. He smiled at her, and looked her up and down. She was grateful to have scrubbed up that morning for once, for putting some make-up on over her tired eye bags. She'd not been sleeping very well of late. She gave him a little wave, mouthing her apologies, but he beckoned for her to sit down by moving some of the papers next to him. He patted the seat.

'Okay, no problem. Listen, thanks for letting me know. If you need anything, I . . .' The voice was insistent in its refusal, and he rolled his eyes. Whoever the woman was, she was a woman who spoke her mind. 'Okay, okay. Still, anything, okay? And thanks, okay?' He was saying okay a lot, gesturing again for Rebecca to sit down next to him. The man had no boundaries, and after last night, and the heat she'd felt from his touch, she found herself nodding, taking up his invitation to sit down. Tucking her feet under her, hiding her Homer Simpson socks, she waited for him patiently. He was saying goodbye to the woman, and talking about bacon sandwiches for some reason, so she respectfully tried to tune him out. Looking around her, she could see various plans and notes. Technical stuff that looked like it was gobbledy-gook in places.

'App designs, for clients.' He was talking to her now, and his phone was on the coffee table. As it lit up, she saw a familiar image, the café, sitting in front of the mountains looking gorgeous. Just in the window, she could see herself, behind the counter, bowl in hand.

'I like the view,' he nodded at the screen. 'Gorgeous here, isn't it? Hans always sent photos, but it's nothing like the real thing.'

Their eyes met when the screen went dark, and he nodded towards it again.

'Sorry about that, a call from home. I—'

'It's fine, I should have given you more privacy. You working today?'

He looked back at his laptop screen, which was showing a very full inbox with a lot of urgent-sounding headings.

'Yep, my trip here was a tad unscheduled so—'

'Just a tad?' she teased. He blushed, and she felt a bit mean. 'Sorry, go on.'

'I came last minute, as you know, and my clients are just used to me being around. I don't usually travel.'

'I gathered,' she smiled, wanting to leave on a good note. The fact that he was wearing a pair of sweatpants and a white vest was nothing to do with it. Having a man sprawled on her sofa wasn't going to stop her leaving to see her friend. 'So, Hans is coming in today to run the café, I have a waitress coming too at 11, to give him a hand. I'll be back later. If you need anything, he'll be downstairs. You should be able to get some work done up here, it's pretty quiet.'

'You not working today?' he asked, half reaching for her hand but putting it back on his own lap. She noticed a watch on his wrist, an old leather strap around an expensive-looking time piece. It had gone nine.

'Nope,' she said, standing up again and picking up her boots and bag. 'Off into town, got things to do. You need anything?'

He reached into his side pocket, flashing a bit of toned midriff. He might make apps for a living but he clearly made time for the gym too. Pulling out a black leather wallet, he took out some Euros and offered the notes to her. 'Here, for the bin and the sheets.' It was a bit of a wad, more than what was needed.

'It's fine, don't worry about it.'

'No.' He stood now and walked over to her, pushing the notes into her free hand. 'Please, let me. I'll feel better. I'll get on with ordering a sofa too.'

She wanted to protest, but the wine-soaked sofa behind her covered in her now battered sheets silenced her. 'I'll pay half, okay?' She closed her fist around the money, offering him a fist to bump. He laughed, bumping it but dodging her attempt to put the money back into his hand.

'Nice try, now scoot. I have a lot of angry clients to soothe.'

As if on cue, his mobile phone rang again, and his laptop pinged with yet another email notification. She sighed dramatically, putting the money into her bag and waving him goodbye. He flashed her a big smile, his black-rimmed glasses nudging up his nose with the movement. She headed to the hallway, sitting on the little chair to push on her boots. As she laced them up, hearing Luke chatter away to a client, instantly turning him from angry to elated with a few work updates, she felt weird leaving him. Like she wanted to stay around today. Odd.

Lacing up, she grabbed her thick, red coat and headed out to the café. She wanted to avoid running into Hans. The last thing she needed was him to see their rather domestic setup. She was pretty sure she'd just offered to buy a sofa with a man she lived with. That was enough weird behaviour for today.

'It's not funny Holly! You utter shitbag!'

Holly was now on all fours in front of her corner sofa, braying like a donkey, wearing loungewear, laughing her head off. 'Stop then, give me a minute. I'm going to give birth here!' She exploded again into a fit of giggles. Rebecca slurped her tea and waited for her friend to roll herself back onto the sofa. She did it with surprising dignity, followed by a snort that a rhino would have been proud of.

'Oh God, I feel like Shamu the whale on this bloody thing! Don't deprive me of the little bit of enjoyment I get. You have a hot man in your house, and all he does is wreck it!' Another snort. Rebecca eyed her friend over her cup rim. 'You didn't argue when I said he was hot.'

'Ah . . . I mean, he's not really my type, but . . . yeah he's okay. In a Henry from *Ugly Betty* kind of way.'

Holly pulled a face. 'Jesus, get over Henry already. Daniel was the hot one.' She lay back on the white fabric, pushing her swollen ankles out flat and placing both hands on her bump. 'Besides, Luke is hotter than Henry. He's a lovely guy.'

Rebecca looked around the room, which had the same wooden look and design of the café, but with Holly's warmer touches. The little Moses basket in the corner even matched the décor, baby supplies set out in neat little baskets, all labelled up.

'You need to get out more, this place looks like a home interiors magazine, or a *Hello* shoot for a movie star.'

Holly gasped. 'Not the décor, you know you love it. You always get snarky when you don't like the question. Answer me, what do you think of Luke?'

Rebecca thought of the drunk, tormented man who urinated willy-nilly in her flat, and the man who took charge last night and carried her fireman-style to her bedroom. She hadn't told her any of that, about their knees touching and flirting with each other, or about her sniffing his aftershave bottle in the bathroom that morning, like some sniffing weirdo.

'I don't think anything about Luke, I'm doing it as a favour to you and Hans. How does Hans know him anyway?' Deflection. Winning.

Holly patted her bump, giving her a sly look.

'Hey, little one in there, that's your Auntie Rebecca, avoiding the question again. Don't you let her do that to you, little peanut. Just like your mum doesn't.' She pretended to listen to her unborn child, who was visibly kicking now. *Little cherub . . . Auntie Rebecca needs to teach you how bloody pushy your mother is.*

'What's that now? Auntie, cut the shit?' Holly pretended to

listen again, nodding along to nothing. 'Well, the language is something I don't like, but nice work kid.' Holly looked at Rebecca, giving her bump an attaboy pat. 'Spill. What do you think?'

'He's okay. Hot, I'll give you, but he's got stuff going on. He's a bit clumsy too, like a baby lamb.'

'He is a baby lamb! Hans loves him though, he's a great guy. Hans has been trying to get him to come here for years, so it's a big thing for him. For them both, really.' She fell silent then, and given the fact that she hadn't stopped yakking since Rebecca had arrived, she noticed.

'So why did he come?'

'Because Hans invited him, and he needed to get away. He's got a project going on. Your turn.'

Rebecca drained her cup, putting it down on the large glass coffee table in front of her. She noticed that there were little rubber stoppers on the corners already. 'Hans?' she asked, and Holly nodded.

'I almost murdered him with a dessert spoon yesterday. He went to the shops and I couldn't get the ice cream out of the freezer. Child locks! He's going to be a nervous wreck at the birth. You need to be there, I keep telling you.'

Rebecca could tell her lips had pulled back tight, she could feel the breeze around her exposed gums. 'Rebecca! Stop pulling faces, it's childbirth! It's a wonderful thing.'

'It is not,' Rebecca retorted. 'It's noisy and messy and bloody, and scream-filled rooms are not my forte.'

Holly humphed. 'If you don't answer your phone, I will let Hans carry out his placenta tree idea, and make you come watch the planting. When I am ready to pop this huge Swedish baby out, that will probably be the size of a ruddy Viking, I want you there to tell Hans off, and to stop me from showing myself up.'

'Pooping yourself more like,' Rebecca grimaced. 'My mother did, Dad told me. She shat all over the table and the midwife. He used to laugh about it when he was drunk at Christmas.'

A cushion whizzed towards her, clocking her square in the face.

'Stop it, you horrible, horrible friend! Tell me whether you fancy Luke or not!'

'No!'

'Why not? You just told me about your own birth! I have visions of your mother in the throes of pushing now! Tell me!'

'No!'

'You so do.'

'I don't.' Another cushion came to see its mate, clocking her on the cheek this time as she half dodged it. 'Argh, that was the zip, you cow!'

'Aww, zip smip. Admit it, he's more than hot. He's single, a nice guy, has a good job, uses his brain.'

'Wow, take me now. Most people have most of those things, you know. I don't date anyway, so it's irrelevant. What's going on with him anyway? Why does Hans feel the need to help him? He's not a skier, is he? Where did they even meet, if Luke's never been further than the end of his street?'

Holly pulled herself up using the larger back cushions.

'You need some help?'

'Yeah,' she puffed. 'Bit late though. You could have told me copping off with a giant would end up with me birthing what feels like a teenager.' She punched the cushions behind her, settling in again. 'I'm bored, so I'll play. Luke has been Hans's friend for years. Hans went over to the UK on a school exchange, but Luke never came over here to visit. His family situation is a little complicated, so him being here, getting on a plane . . . It's big. It means a lot to Hans, and Luke has something to do here too. He wants to ski, and enter one of the novice competitions.'

Rebecca didn't say anything for a moment. She just sat there, processing the information. 'Ski? Luke? He'll break his blessed neck on the nursery slopes.'

Images of him dancing in the kitchen cooking sprang to mind.

She hadn't caught him yet, but she could tell he wasn't moving around like a normal person would.

'Does Hans know he's a clumsy oaf? He's basically Mr Magoo. Mr Hot Magoo. It's a fool's errand.'

'Care, do you?' Holly waggled her blonde eyebrows, giggling again.

'No. But if he smacks headfirst into a barrier, where will he stay, eh?' She waved her arms around her like a preacher delivering a sermon. 'He can't live here.' She nodded to the coffee table, the art books and the latest thriller of Hans's open on the glass surface. 'You'd have to bubble wrap the place.'

Holly looked around her. 'He won't need to come here. He's got a room, with you. I have a nurse's outfit in the closet. I won't need it for a while. Hans has a doctor outfit too, but I doubt Luke will fit it.'

'Eugh!' Rebecca got up, taking that gross image into the dark depths of her mind and dousing it in acid for good measure. 'That's my cue to leave. I'll speak to Hans myself. You need anything from the shops?'

Holly shook her head. 'Unless you can get me a waistline, I'm good here. Netflix is babysitting me.'

Rebecca squashed her friend in a hug, not letting her get up. She looked tired, and comfy where she was. Pulling a throw off the back of the sofa, she covered her friend's legs and raised her legs up onto a cushion. 'Good, stay put. Love you.'

'Love you,' Holly smiled at her, remote in hand now. 'Now go get that stud muffin.'

Rebecca could hear her friend's laughter even after she closed the front door. The woman was a huge pain in the posterior. Saturday was going to be bloody awful, and she still had to brave the shops. It wasn't till she'd left Holly's that she realised, she hadn't asked Holly about Saturday at all.

Chapter 6

Luke finished the last of his calls and headed to the kitchen to make himself a drink. He'd been talking for so long, his mouth was as dry as the bottom of a parrot's cage. He sounded like James Earl Jones. He was still feeling a bit tired and hungover, and his clients hadn't taken it easy on him. He'd realised over the last few days just how accessible he'd been to them in the past. *Call me any time* was not manageable here, with all the upheaval. Plus, being a houseguest made him hyper aware of all his actions. He'd already trashed most of her gaff, and made a tit of himself more times than he wanted to think about too. Looking around the neat kitchen, he tidied away the dishes from the other night, flicking on some music to work to. Then he made a coffee, put some toast under the grill and hunted in the fridge for the cheese he'd bought. It was still there untouched, amongst the wine, fresh vegetables, and fruit. For a baker, she ate like an athlete. She'd still ripped into his steak though. It was nice to see a fellow carnivore enjoy a meal. Luke always loved his steak and pint nights with his dad down at the pub every Wednesday. The pair of them would never miss a week for the world. Till now. Today was Wednesday, and for the first time in their relationship, they weren't even speaking.

His dad had never pushed him away like that before. The fact that he'd had a stroke at the wheel and survived a car crash barely intact was bad enough. They'd had to cut him out of his car, and he knew how his dad would have felt about that. He hated people hovering around him and never wanted a fuss – he was a proud man. But that moment in the hospital room had tipped Luke over the edge. He could see that he was the cause of his father's distressed state. Although he couldn't so much as utter two coherent words, there was no mistaking the cold look in his eye that shattered Luke's heart into two. He just didn't know why his dad had turned like that. It was the two of them against the world normally. The two Musketeers. All for one and all that.

That first night sleeping in Dad's house alone had been the worst night of his existence. Even losing his mum didn't match it. He was so young when she passed, he just didn't have the same bond that he did with the parent who had raised him single-handed. His mother was a photo in a frame, an abstract idea rather than a tangible person. He and his father had done just fine though. They were the ultimate team, always had been. It was why he'd stayed at home for so long. He was happy with his dad, and his dad lived for him.

When he'd turned his key in the lock of his childhood home, there was no life within. No buzz of the sport on the telly. No Dad shouting 'that you, lad?' like he always did. As though they had loads of visitors. It always made him chuckle, and he missed it now. He might never hear that action again. This family home had no family left in it now. Just memories and the settling dust.

Plodding up towards his dad's office, he opened the door and got to work. His father's care would need to be looked after, and Luke knew his dad had always been a saver. There were no money worries, but he wanted to check his dad's policy, see what healthcare they could get covered without Dad's nest egg being used. One look at the staircase in the hall told Luke that things would need to change around here too. His dad had been pretty much resistant to everything done to help him at the hospital, and not only that, he was mean too. Angry. Frustrated. All things that Luke had never seen in his dad before now. He was . . . well, just Dad. Happy. Cautious. Predictable.

Opening his father's filing cabinet, he was presented with their whole life. It was divided into files, all colour-coordinated with labels like TV LICENCE and CAR PAPERWORK. Luke's heart clenched when he saw his dad's handwriting on the labels. Would he ever sign his name again? Right now, he was so angry and deflated, he wouldn't even try. The doctors had spelled out how hard Frank's fight would be, and how much worse it could have been. How crashing his car brought people running to his side straight away. They'd spotted the signs, got him to hospital. He had every chance of recovering.

That was day one.

When Frank finally came to, the man Luke called Dad looked like a different person. Acted like one too. Luke understood, it was a lot. He'd been struggling with the news himself, but this was different. It was like the light went out in his father that day, and his dad seemed intent on smashing every bulb they tried to turn back on. When he'd kicked him out of the place, the nurses all giving him sympathetic looks as he passed them, Luke had sat in his car in the half empty car park and cried, hidden by the dark of the night around him. He felt like little orphan Annie, adrift without a responsible adult to hand. He needed to get his dad back, and fast.

Looking through the labels, he saw what he was looking for: INSURANCE. He reached for it, but in between the suspension file and the back of the cabinet was another file, hidden away. The label was tatty, faded and not written in his father's scrawl. Luke recognised the style though. The looping S's and Y's. His mother had written SOMEDAY on the label. Pulling out the two files, he went and sat at his dad's desk. He was long retired now, but still sat in here every day. Filing his post, writing to friends, talking to the birds that he fed from his windowsill every day. There were none there now, but he wondered how many mornings the birds would come to the window, looking for Frank. Luke pushed the thicker insurance file to one side, and slowly opened the Someday folder.

In it were clippings of holiday destinations, ideas for family days out in zoos, theme parks, anything that might take a person's fancy. There were gardening ideas too, home décor. Kids games. *Blue Peter* crafting and sticking. Some of the photos Luke recognised, they were replicated from his childhood. He could still remember helping his dad. When he was old enough to hold a hammer, he was eager to be like him, do things together. Cutting all the wood for the sleepers, the pair of them painting them together in the sunshine with large glasses of pop filled with ice. He remembered the zoo days, the aquarium visits, the camping trips they shared. Man and boy, under the stars. He kept flicking through, realising that his mother had made plans for their lives together, their little family, but they never got to do any of it.

But his dad did. The articles and clippings, notes from his mum, notes with his own scrawl on, he'd kept it going. Adding to it, ticking off the ones they had done. He welled up when he saw the next one. His mum had written on one of the photos, a picture of the French Alps. In the sky, in blue pen, she'd written: *Skiing holidays for the whole family! Can't wait to tick this one off!*

A tear slid down Luke's cheek as he read his mother's wishes, over and over. Stuff they had done, and many more they hadn't. The more daring stuff didn't have a tick anywhere. His dad had lost his mojo it seemed when it came to finishing the list. Maybe it was a bit *too* adventurous for Dad. He was a homebody, and he didn't even watch the news anymore because it freaked him out so much. Luke had heard from family members how bubbly his mother was, full of life, daring. She drew the shyness out of her husband, just as much as he was the calm to her storm. And then the storm died out, and the landscape of their lives changed forever.

'Oh Dad,' Luke sobbed, closing the file and tucking both under his arm. The next morning, when he went home to his empty flat, the first thing he noticed was the invite from Hans, his longtime friend. Inviting him to come and stay in the French Alps, to share in the joy of Hans and Holly's first child. He'd never met Holly properly. FaceTime wasn't the same. He'd already bought the card to send with his regrets over not being able to make the trip out there, but looking at it now, something clicked. Rushing to the hallway to grab the files from his bag, he chucked the insurance folder on the kitchen countertop and rummaged in the 'Someday' folder for what he was looking for.

A second later, he was dialling.

'Lukie boy! How are you? Calling to tell me you are snubbing my unborn child for another week sat in front of a screen like a pasty loser, yeah?'

Luke smiled, the first hint of adrenalin running through his veins.

'Not quite, mate. Not quite. Listen, you got a minute? Something's happened, and I need your help.'

Hans had already been up and popped his head around the door like a giant bouncing ginger Tigger. He bounced around for a while, mooned Luke whilst he was on a conference call, and then headed back downstairs to work. No mention of Rebecca, or where she was, but he did raise his eyebrows at the sofa. Luke had almost opened his mouth to tell Hans about the planned joint purchase, but he realised just in time how weird it sounded. It sounded odd, that he would end up owning half a sofa, with a girl who baked in the Alps. It sounded odd to a normal person, let alone someone with Luke's highlight reel. He hadn't exactly been adventurous, prior to this lunacy abroad.

Slicing some cheese to put onto the untoasted sides of his bread, he looked out of the window. This place was amazing. He felt different here, detached. More fun even. It felt nice to share a place with someone too. Since he'd moved out of his parents' house, he'd been well aware of the empty feel of his flat. After the calls had stopped, and everyone else was settling in for the night. It felt nice to be in someone else's space, with someone else for company.

Taking his cheese on toast and cuppa through to the lounge, he sat back on the sheeted sofa and ate in silence, looking around at Rebecca's things. Or lack of them. The furniture was nice, but there wasn't any personal feel to the room. Any of them really. It looked like a holiday cottage, all set up for life, but no evidence of living. She had no photos around, nothing that told him anything real about her.

She liked nice bed sheets, and things kept clean. She read books, he'd seen a few laying around. Notes in the margins of some of them, bookmarks and sticky tabs in others. She liked nice perfume, and good shampoo. She hated most humans, and he didn't know why. He'd always felt awkward around people, but that wasn't it with her. He'd watched her with customers. She was relaxed, open, and unguarded. Around Hans too. She trusted him, but he suspected that even that hadn't come easily. She was a puzzle, and he was already here trying to solve another. He thought of the call earlier, the one she'd overheard. He'd never got the chance to tell her about his dad, but she seemed to be in a hurry. Finishing off his food, he placed the plate back on the coffee table, and noticed something underneath. On the floor, one corner just poking out from under the wood, was a black book. He leaned forward, and pulling it out, he noticed the gilded gold edges, and the title of the book. *Photo Album.* He stared at it for a while, before putting it back underneath the table. Right where he found it. He wanted to know about her, but he didn't fancy pissing her off any more either. His fingers tingled at the thought of what was inside, what made a woman like her hide herself away here, without seeming to need or want anyone. He couldn't really understand that. He couldn't cope without speaking to everyone he wanted to back home. It was killing him being away from his dad, and he'd thought he was going to have to be sedated to even get on the plane to come here. It had felt so terribly wrong to be leaving, especially now. Even if his absence was what his dad wanted. Luke had avoided work trips abroad at all costs before, being a homebody just like his dad, wanting to stay close, and now he felt a little stupid to have only just used his passport.

They were so different, Rebecca and he, and being shoved together had obviously mortified her. Still, he could see glimpses of the real Rebecca coming out, and that's who he wanted to know more about. He just wasn't about to go riffling through her underwear drawer. He had caught himself sniffing her perfume bottle this morning, and that was bad enough. He'd half expected Gillian Anderson to come running in and arrest him. *God, I've watched too much bloody TV for my own good.* He just couldn't resist though, he could smell something around Fir Tree Lodge he couldn't place. A nice smell. Turned out, it was her. It must be sharing with a girl after living in a man only zone with his dad. Even their cleaner had been a man. He'd hardly grown up with a woman's touch, despite the adoring women that his dad had attracted over the years. A single dad was like a baby gazelle to the voracious tiger-like mum set in their little village. He was hot property for many years, but his dad never bothered with any of them. He was already madly in love, with the wife he'd lost. So it had just been the two of them, and now, Luke was alone. Alone, in the French Alps, about to make a very horrendous mistake, and quite possibly break his damn neck. A little perfume sniffing was to be expected, he supposed, in the face of all that. Looking at his phone, he wished that he'd taken Rebecca's number. He could call her, ask her if she was doing okay. If she needed anything maybe. *God, I'm pathetic.* It was gone four now and the café would be closing soon. He tucked his phone into his sweatpants, and making himself look a little more presentable, he headed downstairs to see Hans, and maybe even buy a piece of Becks' cake. *Rebecca. Damn.* He liked the name Becks, it suited her but she seemed to hate it. Rebecca seemed too formal for her. There he was, thinking about her again. Dammit. He needed to get out of here, get some coffee into his addled brain.

The café was busy, people milling around coming in and out, others sat at tables eating, drinking and laughing. There was a real energy in the room, and Luke steeped down into the counter area, closing the door behind him just before Hans barrelled into him, knocking him off his feet and both of them halfway across the opposite counter.

'Ca-can't. Brea-the,' Luke gasped, his torso gripped by what felt like an over-friendly bear, his hips jammed into the countertop as Hans crushed him from above. 'Gerroff. Daft . . .' He managed to take a gasp of air as Hans propped them both up. 'Pillock!' The air rushed out of his lungs all at once, and Luke shouted it loud into the space. The bloody high ceilings and echoey room bounced the word back around them, and the whole café was staring at them. It was then that Luke heard a familiar voice.

'Pillock was just what I was thinking! Hans, put him down, he's squashing my Chelsea buns!' Rebecca strode into the room, bags weighing her down, her nose pink from the cold. Looking around her, she plastered on a smile and addressed the room. 'Anyone need anything?' It was as friendly as you like, to match her angelic-looking face, but it had an edge to it. She basically gave the whole room a 'stop it now, or your baby photos are going on social media' look, as though she was an overworked mother addressing her unruly children. The café-goers all shook their heads politely, the murmur of chatter starting up again. One man raised his hand, but his wife slapped it down and shushed him. The two women nodded at each other appreciatively, and the spell was broken.

Forgotten now, Luke managed to prise Hans's meaty hooks from around his middle and push him off. Well, push was a strong word. He'd need a strong wind to make a dent. He barely moved him. Squeezing himself out from the gap, he tried to make a run for it, but Hans tripped him up as he moved to give him room, and before he knew it, he was on the floor. After screeching like a parrot and flailing his arms and legs around like a wonky windmill.

'Hans!' Rebecca was round the counter in a moment, glaring at any customers who'd dared to laugh. Luke could see her from his position on the floor. He'd twirled like a top before landing on his back. 'What did you do that for!'

'I didn't mean to!' he protested, bellowing like Brian Blessed. A toddler sitting at one of the tables nearby tried in vain to cover her ears, but her snow suit was so thick she just ended up waggling her hands ineffectually before bursting into tears. Hans groaned.

'Oh no, not again. How the hell am I going to be a dad? Sorry Luke.' Hans's face looked wretched, and Luke tried to think of something to say to help his friend. He didn't know much about kids though, apart from being one once upon a time. If he'd been a toddler and had seen Hans, he'd have probably filled his nappy too. The man was big, but that wasn't all he was.

'Hans,' Rebecca jumped in, dropping her bags by her feet and coming to kneel by Luke. 'You are going to be an amazing dad. Your baby will have the best protective parent ever, and that little one is going to love the bones off you. The kid will have its own bodyguard, teacher, and portable climbing frame. Now suck it up, go apologise to the parents, and give them some free cake. Get some practice in. Bribery is basically 85 per cent of parenting anyway from what I hear.' Hans nodded, smiling now and he headed off to the cake counter. Luke tried to get up, but Rebecca placed her hand on his chest.

'Don't move, just for a minute.' He felt weird, down here with her, on their own. He could hear Hans talking to the parents, laughing with them. Cake solved many problems, it seemed. He could hear the café sounds around him, but it all sounded muffled. Distant.

'You had a good day?'

A lame question to ask when you were on the floor after being felled by Chewbacca. Rebecca looked down at him and all over his face, and then she started to run her hands through his hair. 'Not bad.

Don't talk.' He had to stifle a groan, it felt so nice. He did nothing but stare up at her, and she was looking right at him the whole time. She leaned closer, moving her hands to the back of his head now, his neck. The perfume he knew so well now filling his already jangled senses. *Is she going to . . . to . . . she is, she's going to kiss me!*

'Oww!' She poked a sore spot on the back of his head, where his head had clunked to the floor. 'That hurt!'

'Sorry,' Rebecca muttered, still prodding around his scalp and making him follow her finger. 'You're fine.' She didn't look sorry at all. In fact, he was pretty sure he saw a smirk. Either that or the tears in his eyes were blurring his vision. He was pretty embarrassed, even in their little bubble. She went to pull him up, but when her hand touched his he closed his fingers around hers.

'Thanks. I can get up.' He heaved himself up on the counter with his free hand, and when he stood up, the whole café clapped, and Hans whisper whooped along with them with one fatherly eye on the startled toddler, who was looking at him as if Hagrid had popped in for an americano, and she was the only one to see it. 'Ah . . . yes. Thank you, my dear fans. I did enjoy my trip!' He went with it, bowing, and then his hand was being pulled up the stairs, and the clapping began again behind the closed door.

At the top, Rebecca took him into the lounge and deposited him on the sofa.

'Wait one minute.'

She headed back down the stairs, leaving him sitting back on the sofa like a lemon. He heard her tell Hans off again at the bottom of the stairs, the unmistakable wallop of a plastic bag hitting a Swedish pillock. Luke chuckled, and waited for his lodge mate to come back up.

Laden down with the bags, Rebecca had belatedly realised that her bags actually contained some precious things, so she was pretty miffed with herself. If she'd have remembered, she'd have given Hans a swift kick. She could do that now, bar the odd twinge and occasional night spasm in her back. Three words she randomly remembered many times. Often in the dead of night. *Full mobility restored.* Like she was fixed, all shiny and new. As if healing came with a memory wipe bonus. Plus, she could have kicked him in the goolies. Holly wasn't in need of them, it would probably have given her a laugh too. Putting the bags down in the lounge, she went to check on the patient and found him turning on his laptop.

'Your head okay?'

'Yeah, fine. Used to it now.' He rapped his knuckle on the top of his head. 'It's pretty tough. He got me worse than that the first night here. He forgets we're all Borrowers compared to his size.'

She snorted with laughter, shutting the laptop lid. 'Nice try, but I've been felled by Hans before too, he's basically a toddler in a man's body.'

'I know that, when he stayed at mine back home, we always knew he was around. Dad used to hide the good china.'

'I bet, the breakage rate skyrockets on my days off.' She pushed the laptop lid shut again when he attempted to open it. 'Besides, no more work. I have a job for you.' Heading back over to the bags, she lugged them onto the sofa next to him and gave him her sternest look.

'Now before I open these bags, I need you to remember that you owe me.' He put up a hand to protest, but she karate chopped it back down.

'You owe me, despite the fact that you did replace most things . . .' She eyed the sofa with a devastated look. '. . . You do still owe me an apology. So,' she pulled a small plush orange cuddly dinosaur from one of the nearest bags, 'this is how you will pay me back.' The look on his face was worth all the lugging of bags after all. He looked terrified.

'You fancy a cuppa?'

'Now, that's the best thing you've said all day.'

'Ah, come on,' Rebecca teased him. 'You loved every minute of it.' Looking at him dishevelled on the floor next to her, covered in glitter and bits of ribbon, she suppressed a smirk. 'They look great.'

All around him were baby bits, including a rather impressive nappy cake that they had spent half their crafting time putting together. Luke hadn't even heard of one before, and thought they were about to bake. As if that was all she did. It had irked her at the time, but she was getting less and less shocked with every little weird thing he did and said. She realised, the guy was a brainbox, but he didn't have a lot of life skills. Bear Grylls would have left him whimpering in the boat, strapped to an inflatable unicorn. It was cute though. And glitter suited him.

'They do, but the whole experience was definitely a bit weird. Did you have a lot of babies around you, growing up?'

She thought of her childhood. 'Nope, only child. Baby free. I didn't even have time for babysitting to be honest.' She got up to go to the kitchen.

'Really?' Following her in, he swerved around her, taking two mugs from the tree and flicking the kettle on. 'Super nerd, were you? Sat in a corner somewhere, reading comics?'

She popped a tea bag into each mug, him passing the milk to her whilst she reached for the sugar.

'Two, right?' she checked, and he nodded. Spooning two spoons in each one, he grabbed the kettle the second it flicked off and poured the water in. 'And I think you'll find that you were the comic geek.' He blushed, and she knew she'd nailed him. *It. Nailed it.* 'I was the one who hung out near the gym, for fun.' *Oops.*

'Really . . .' he muttered, trying to slowly lift the lid of his laptop again. 'Any photos?'

Her eyes fell below the coffee table before she could stop them. Her heart was thudding in her chest. She'd had her album out before he'd landed in her life, a night filled with wine and regrets. Fuck. Had he looked? Surely not.

'No, sadly not. I hate the camera.'

That was true enough. It had never been about that. Not for

her. They both watched the tea stewing in the mugs, for lack of anything else to say.

'So . . .'

'Anyway?'

They both laughed nervously, their awkwardness made palpable by them removing their tea bags and adding milk in annoying synchronicity.

'What I was—'

'What I meant was—'

'Got any plans for tonight?' he blurted out, dropping his tea bag into the bin as he asked, missing it entirely. They both watched it slowly slide down the side of the bin, leaving a little tea puddle on the floor, and a path down from lid to bottom where the tea had dripped. He shrugged his shoulders nonchalantly. 'I meant to do that. Pa Borrower uses them to fertilise his allotment.' She was about to call him a plonker, when he put his hand over hers.

'What I was trying to say, was that I would really like to get out of this flat for a bit, I was thinking we could go out to eat? I've not had a look around yet. My treat, to say thanks and sorry yet again. To you and your poor bins. Do you have plans?'

She didn't, and if he'd seen her work calendar downstairs, he knew it too.

'No, but you don't have to do that. You already made it up to me.'

'I know, but you've got to eat anyway, right? What were you going to do?'

She looked at him blankly. She had nothing. A family-sized bar of chocolate and a romance book in bed wasn't exactly comparable to going out with a cute guy, to have a free meal. She'd only have to fend her mother off anyway. She'd rung once whilst she was out shopping, but Rebecca ignoring the call wouldn't put her off.

'Nothing really, bit of paperwork.' *Nice save, Rebecca. Cupcake empire boss vibes.* Not reading about a hot vet whilst ignoring the competition entry forms that were now stashed in her bedside drawer, taunting her silently. *You won't enter, and Mum won't listen.* 'Food out sounds nice actually. Dutch, of course.'

Luke rolled his eyes, taking a deep slurp of his tea. 'Fab, pick you up at seven, then. You need a hand with the lounge stuff?' He'd already tidied up, there were only the packages ready for Saturday stacked up. They could wait.

'Pick me up?' She shook her head at his offer of help. She didn't want to cram them all into her room, they could stay there for now. She could get Hans to collect them before the big day, keep them stashed. 'Where did you have in mind?'

'There's a great place on resort apparently. Hans was telling some of the customers about it, have you been? Top notch, he reckons.'

Rebecca was already making a face. She knew exactly where he meant. She'd been there before, many times. Being schmoozed and celebrated. 'I have a place, a better one. Trust me.'

Luke frowned, but he didn't argue.

'Well, that's decided then. See you at seven?' He looked at her for confirmation, and she realised that she was nervous. Her stomach flipped at the thought of going out with him. *This isn't good Rebecca, come on. He's leaving soon. You have to get your life together. Crushing on a passing hot nerd is not part of the plan. Besides, he annoys you, remember?*

'See you then,' she said and he left to go to his room. Minutes later, she heard the bathroom door close, and the shower turn on. He was getting ready. Looking at the bags she had left to unpack, she picked them up and headed to her own room. Holly was right, she couldn't answer the question about whether or not she liked Luke. Not to Holly, but now she couldn't really deny it to herself any longer. He hadn't been here a week, it had been what, three days? She was already interested in what he had to say and why he was here, and she knew it went deeper than just wanting to get the clumsy northerner out of her home, and out of her life. He was growing on her. It's not every man that would sit making up games and favour bags for a baby shower. The fact that he didn't know what a nappy cake was had made her laugh, but before long his technical brain had kicked in and he was designing structure ideas and colour schemes from what she had brought. The man was like a wedding planner, but looked like a GQ model. She'd had so much fun, till she'd realised that unlike everything else in her regimented sheltered life, it was temporary. He would do what he came to do, and leave. Just like everyone else around here. They came to visit and went home. She should be used to it, but right now she couldn't help feeling just a little sense of panic. Closing her bedroom door behind her, she pulled out the outfits she'd splurged on in town. There was a nice little clothing boutique there that didn't treat her any differently than they did when she shopped there before . . . well, just before. They always made her feel welcome. Comfortable. She could try things on there without getting a complex about flashing a scar, or catching someone spotting one of her flaws. She felt like enough of those were on show already.

'Not seen you for a while Rebecca! How's the café?'

Francesca, the owner, had just been seeing a customer out as Rebecca had entered the shop, the tinkle of the bell making her feel instantly at home. It was like a front room, rather than a clothing shop. A sewing machine sat off to one corner, storage boxes full of ribbons, zips, and tiny pearl buttons.

'Not bad,' she said as the customer smiled and left, bags in hand. They were alone. 'Except for my houseguest.'

Fran's eyes bulged, and her smirk was positively devilish. 'I heard. Luke, isn't it? How's that going? You beaten him to death with a hand mixer yet?' Her French accent curled her words beautifully. Even hand mixer sounded sexy when it rolled off her tongue. She was effortlessly chic, but not aware of it at all. She could turn heads as she entered a room, but she would be more interested in checking out the quality of the fabric in the curtains, and how a seam on a dress didn't look right from across the room. Confident in her own skin, like most people were. Even

88

Luke. He knew who he was, but he still wanted to push himself. That was the thing Rebecca missed. The impetus to try again, to care about getting a different outcome.

'Not quite. He's . . . interesting.'

'Interesting? Explain. Oh, and I have a nice little outfit for you in the back. I've been saving it for when you came.' She toddled off, raising a hand behind her at Rebecca. 'Don't worry either, it's not from a designer. It's off the rail. My rail, actually. I have a couple that would look great on you.'

'How did you know I wanted some new clothes?'

Francesca turned around on one heel, like a ballet dancer, and eyed her up close. Rebecca came to a screeching halt, colliding boob to boob with Fran, who didn't flinch. 'You came to me. I've seen him, you know, Holly showed me his photo. It didn't take a genius to work out that your horrible sweatpants were suddenly going to be an issue.'

'Hey! I don't always dress like that.' She totally did. 'I don't *all* the time, anyway.'

'No,' Fran countered. 'The rest of the time you're in your uniform. I'm right, yes?'

'No.'

'Nightwear doesn't count, Rebecca.'

'Oh. Yes then.' She followed her friend over to the rail of clothes, running her hand along the rainbow of different textures and fabrics. 'You don't have to give me a lecture you know. I get it.'

Fran pulled out a long dress from the rail. It was a dark blue colour, but the fabric shimmered in the light. 'This one's for a night out, and I thought this one for Saturday.'

Reaching further along the rail, she held out another dress. This one was cream, neat little blue flowers embroidered along the hems. It looked lovely, fresh and perfect for the shower. She didn't even need to check the sizing. Fran had a hawk-eye for these things.

'You going, on Saturday?'

Fran nodded, taking out another outfit from the very back.

'Yep, here's mine.' It was a lot brighter than the one she'd offered Rebecca, pastel colours giving way to vibrant tropical colours. The female equivalent of a Hawaiian shirt. 'I must say, I am looking forward to meeting this Luke.'

Rebecca blushed, taking the outfits from Fran and heading to the changing rooms to see how they looked. Fran would insist on it anyway, she never let anything leave her shop that looked and felt anything less than perfect. Rebecca thought about her baking and could relate.

'He's okay.' Pulling the curtain shut behind her, she put the hangers on the peg in front of her and sat down for a second on the upholstered chair that sat in one corner of the changing room. Opposite, the full-length mirror looked back at her. She looked at the outfits on the rails, and back at herself. The dress had a little thigh split in the material, that gave it a sexier look. She'd not worn anything like that in such a long time. She wouldn't have thought twice about it before, but now, it was all that she could think about. Once more, Rebecca realised that the life she had was gone forever, and looking back at herself, she brushed back the tears. Standing up, she tried the outfits on facing the wall. She never looked behind her or turned around. By the time she left the changing room, outfits in hand, she was perfectly shut down once more.

Open-mouthed in the mirror, looking like a fish gasping for air, Rebecca ran the wand up her lashes, almost poking herself straight in the retina when there was a loud knock at the door.

'Luke, can you get that please? I'm just putting my shoes on.' She pushed her feet into her favourite heels and grabbed her bag. The knock came again, but no Luke.

'Luke, you here?' She looked into the lounge but it was empty. His room door was closed. 'Luke?'

She headed to the door to the café downstairs, wrapping her

long coat around her tightly and pulling the handle down as she threw her handbag strap over one shoulder. Luke was standing at the other side, flowers in hand.

'Hi.'

'Hi,' she replied, looking from the flowers to him. He looked gorgeous. His glasses were off, his hair freshly washed and shiny. She could smell him, recognising the scent she'd been enveloped in using the bathroom after him. Soap, and his cologne. He hadn't even touched her shampoo. 'You really meant pick me up, didn't you?'

He grinned. 'Yep, all out tonight. I wasn't sure how we were going to get there, so I ordered a cab to be safe. Okay?'

She nodded dumbly. 'It's the west-facing slopes we're heading to. Not far. Nice flowers.' They locked eyes for a moment, and her mouth went dry. He looked so good, so confident now.

'Oh yes, sorry! These are for you,' he said, offering them to her. 'I hope you like them.' They were beautiful, wrapped with ribbon and full of colour. As she leaned to get them, their fingers brushed each other's and the jolt that ran through her confirmed what she already suspected. She was starting to fancy the pants off her dorky clumsy houseguest, and she was going to be spending a whole evening with him, on what looked like a very date-like non-date. 'I just wanted to say thanks, for everything you've put up with. I'm happy to have met you Rebecca, I mean that.' As he spoke, the two of them slowly gravitated closer. Had her hands not been full of flowers, she was pretty sure she would have snogged the lips off him. The butterflies in her stomach had changed into huge bats now, all jumping and flapping their wings off at the thought of her lips touching his. 'I am happy to have been able to get to know you.'

'Me too.'

His eyebrows raised, and he moved closer, pushing the flowers tighter to her own chest, and his.

'Really? Redeemed myself a bit, have I?' She felt too drunk on his proximity to answer him clearly. It was like they were in a little bubble. 'I'm glad. Actually I—'

The toot of a horn broke the silence, and she turned to put the flowers in some water.

'Cab's here,' she said unnecessarily. When she returned to the stairs, she could hear him outside talking to the driver. Smoothing her coat down around her, making sure she was covered, she headed down the stairs. Once more, he'd been cut off from what he wanted to say. It was getting harder to act like she didn't care about what his back story was, why he was really here.

Pulling up at the restaurant, they could hear the people outside, sitting in the outdoor heated seating area, which ran around one side of the restaurant, drinking, eating and laughing. The neon sign lit up the place from above and cast rainbows across the snow around them. She opened the cab door, stepping out and drinking in the great outdoors. Rebecca would normally be holed up in her place right now, tinkering around by herself. She'd missed the adult life. She'd been living like a hermit a bit too long.

'Nice place,' Luke said behind her, pushing his wallet back into his pocket. The cab drove away.

'How much for my half?' She went for her purse, but he took her hand movement as something else and pushed his hand into hers. Linking his fingers over hers, he put his hand down, pulling hers down with it, her body moving closer till her arm brushed his.

'Tonight is on me, no arguments.' He smiled, lifting his hand to drop a kiss on the back of hers. The scratch of his bristle on her skin made her whole body fizz into life. 'Let's go get a drink.'

They got a table pretty quickly. Mina behind the reservation desk smiled and waved them through. Rebecca smiled back, laughing when Mina made a 'who's the guy?' face at her. It felt good to be seen out for a change – have a little banter with people she'd once spent a lot of time around. Mina had been on the circuit too, they'd bonded pretty quickly. She was one of the few people who didn't bring Rebecca out in a cold sweat to socialise with. Not that she'd done much of that lately. As Mina seated them, Rebecca grabbed her hand. Mina drew her closer and wrapped her arms around her.

'Sorry it's been a while,' she murmured, not looking at Luke. She could see in her peripheral that he was looking at the menu. 'I've . . . no excuse.'

Mina squeezed her hand, pulling away and pecking her on the cheek like she always did.

'Er yeah, you do. Nothing to be sorry for. You're here now, with . . .?'

She turned her head to Luke, who put down the menu he was holding.

'Luke Sommersby.' He leaned forward, his dark blue shirt cuff brushing the table as he stood to offer her his hand.

She took it, beaming at him. 'Pleased to meet you Luke, Mina Huang.'

His hand flopped a little, Mina having to lift hers to avoid them clanging to the table. His face paled.

'Good God. You're not, are you?' He looked at her as though she were a microbe under a microscope. 'You are! Pleased to meet you!' He grabbed her hand tighter now, shaking it vigorously. 'My dad loves you, you know.' He turned to look at Rebecca like an excited meerkat. 'Oh . . .' He seemed to remember where they were, and Rebecca waited for it. Mina gave her a sneaky side look and she couldn't help but smirk. 'Sorry. Do forgive me. I do forget my manners sometimes.'

He'd gone all Jane Austen now, brushing up on his etiquette. Rebecca wondered what he would look like in a wet white shirt. Having just jumped into the lake on his grounds to cool his hotness off. Well, more like fell off a horse straight into it. It was Luke, after all. He looked handsome tonight though too. He'd got himself some boots and a decent coat. His black trousers showed off his muscular legs, and the shirt was open at the collar. She could see a peek of chest.

'Don't be silly! I love your dad too, just for that!' Mina put a hand around each of them and hugged them both to her. Rebecca looked across at Luke, and he was looking back at her. The place was lively, people having fun, but he only seemed to notice her. 'Lovely to see you guys!' Mina released them both in front of a table, and whirled off, muttering about letting them have time to look at the menus. They were both still standing melded to each other. Luke recovered first, wrapping one arm around her back and guiding her to her chair. He pulled it back for her, and she realised that she was still wearing her coat. Luke had put his on the back of his chair. Swallowing hard, she unbuttoned it.

She felt his hands take her coat from her, and she took her seat. His fingers brushed her shoulder as he pushed her coat onto the back of the chair she was clinging to. He was at his seat then, and once more she had to wrench herself out of the bubble and into real life.

'You look gorgeous,' he said, and the bubble was back.

They ordered burgers, huge doorstops of coloured buns encasing beef and cheese. The place was well known for it, and the locals were loyal to the place. It wasn't that the tourists didn't love it, half the time it was a struggle trying to get a seat. It was just relaxed, the kind of place families loved in the daytime and the perfect spot for friends to talk and hang out in the evening . . . and eat. They did a lot of both. Sides of fried pickles and tiny chicken sliders, French fries loaded with salt and vinegar. Luke ordered a pitcher of lager, and he raised his glass to her.

'To an accident-free evening.'

'Ha!' She clinked her glass against his, laughing. 'It's not over yet.'

'True,' he said ruefully. 'So far so good though. Not bad for a first date either. This food is amazing.'

Rebecca choked on her pickle. 'Date?'

He passed her a napkin, and she took it to cover her mouth.

'Yeah, well. To practise for Saturday.' *Oh, great. I'm a pity plus one. Nice.* 'So, yes actually, a date.' He waggled his eyebrows at her, and she almost keeled over as butterflies fluttered away in her stomach, followed by a side of nausea as she brushed away what those butterflies might mean.

'I am glad I have someone to carry all that stuff with me,' she deflected. 'A date is a small price to pay for some muscle.' He flexed his arms at her, accidentally sticking the French fry he was holding straight into the ear of a diner at the other table. 'Oh! Sorry mate!' He patted the bloke on the shoulder, and the diner waved him off, seeing the funny side. Next to him, his girlfriend was in hysterics, trying not to spray burger everywhere. Luke looked across at Rebecca, who was trying not to laugh herself. 'What is wrong with me?' he said, aghast. He was genuinely asking, and Rebecca reached for his hand. She could feel her stomach and shoulders tense up with the pressure of not laughing in his face.

'It's fine,' she said, stroking the back of his hand with her fingers. 'They laughed. Just maybe keep the guns away in enclosed spaces.' She flexed her own arm muscle at him, gurning. As she made eye contact with the girlfriend of the chip ear guy, the two women grinned at each other. A shared moment, laughing at their dates. It felt nice. Normal.

'You're a bit of a nutter when you relax, aren't you?' He was stroking his thumb along hers now, eating fries between sentences. 'I bet you've seen some things up here, too.' She had, there was no denying that. She'd also seen and been through some things she wished dearly she hadn't but that was life. It laughed at your plans and threw a stick into the spokes of your passing bike, whilst you were riding off into the sunset, thinking your dreams were about to be achieved. Life was a little shit sometimes.

'I sure have. Some sights to see around here, shame I'll never tell you. You glad you came?'

She let go of him reluctantly to finish her food, and his hand flexed when her touch left his. He left it there a moment, before picking up a piece of burger.

'Well, this burger alone was worth the terrifying plane ride. And freezing my arse off all the way here. Yeah, it's been good. Different. I think I needed to do it. Tomorrow Hans is going to teach me how to ski.'

'Oh?' She acted nonchalant, eating as demurely as she could with her hands, trying not to panic at the thought of Luke being scraped off the side of a mountain with a cat litter pooper scooper size of a shovel. He'd almost taken out a bloke with a chip, so what hope did he have of surviving unscathed, especially with Hans as a teacher? The man could ski, but he was mountain-sized himself. When *Game of Thrones* had come out, people had started asking if he was one of the characters. He'd liked it at first, but it had soon worn thin. He looked like a giant on toothpicks on a pair of skis, and if he fell, which was rare, he bounced – and took a chunk out of whatever had broken his fall, be it snow, wood, or rock. If Luke fell, he would shatter like an ornamental glass unicorn. She shuddered at the thought, and he reached for her hand once more.

'You cold?' he asked, every inch the concerned date. It made her heart swell. 'My coat's pretty good. I am reluctant for you to cover up though, you do look nice.' Even with the lighting, she could see his cheeks redden. She leaned forward, squeezing his hand and pushing herself to be bold enough to hold his eye.

'You don't look so bad yourself. I think this is the best date I've ever had.'

'Wow! That was brutal timing, as always. Must be our thing.' A deep voice startled them both. 'You always did know how to get to me. I do beg to differ though. That night on Whistler Mountain was pretty epic, I thought. And it involved a lot less clothing. And people. Hi, Becks.'

Standing by the table, pushing into their bubble of ignorance, was Robbie Goulding. *Best date ever, Rebecca. You said it. You jinxed it.*

'Canada, eh? Nice,' Luke drawled, his voice neutral. 'We shall have to add it to the list, honey.' He didn't pull his hand away from hers, and she felt his grip tighten a little. He looked Robbie up and down, and Rebecca couldn't do anything but look at Luke. Her throat had completely closed up. She couldn't speak if she wanted to. It felt like seeing him had frozen her whole body. All she could feel was the fast thud of her heart in her ears, her face aflame, and Luke's gentle and comforting touch. He was circling his thumb around her palm, and it was the only thing keeping her in her seat.

'I'm Luke, pleased to meet you.' He didn't move to shake Robbie's hand, and he didn't even look at him. He kept moving his thumb, and his gaze was now set on Rebecca. Robbie's smile dimmed, standing there in his designer clothes and gelled hair. The man didn't know what to do. From the corner of her eye, she saw his feet start to shuffle.

'Er, yeah,' Robbie muttered, visibly trying to gather himself, and Rebecca finally allowed herself to look at him properly. He looked good, but it did nothing for her now. He looked the same as before, and she knew he was still the same man underneath. 'I didn't expect to see you here. You dating him now?'

'Evidently,' Luke said in a bored tone. 'That was the plan. And you are?'

Robbie didn't look at him, but his jaw flexed. He was staring at Rebecca now, his brows knitted together, his fists clenching and unclenching by his sides.

'This is Robbie. Goulding.' Rebecca found her voice, finally. 'Luke is my date, yes. And don't call me Becks.'

Robbie's lip curled at her words. 'Why not? It's how you're known isn't it?'

'No. Not anymore,' she spat. 'Robbie, it's nice to see you, but we are trying to—'

'Not anymore, eh? That apply to everything still? I thought no more dating was your thing.' He made a loud gameshow noise. 'Nuh-nuh, survey said? Incorrect. Lukey boy here is giving me

97

the evil eye. Are you entering the Alpine Challenge? Is that why you're back?'

Luke was looking at Robbie now like he wanted to kill him. It made Rebecca feel oddly protected. Like he had her back. He'd come across all manly from the moment Robbie had rocked up. Rebecca thought he might pee around the table in a minute, mark his territory. That would make people look.

'Becks?' Robbie pressed her again. Same old bullish Robbie, she noticed. No patience. The people around them were already starting to take notice of the tension at their table. Robbie tended to do that wherever he went. She had forgotten what all that attention felt like, and now she had a reminder, she hated it even more.

'Back?' Luke echoed, all caught up and annoyed now. He squeezed her hand and stood up, facing Robbie. Robbie grinned at him, his best fake grin, and Luke's eyes flashed.

'Lovely to meet you, Robert, but—'

'Robbie.'

'Bobby, right.' He took a half step forward, so his chest brushed against Robbie's. 'Well, Nobby, it's nice to meet you, but we are on a date, and I'm sure that you have people waiting on you.' He nodded his head behind them towards the bar, and Rebecca could see some of his old crew, along with a tall, black-haired woman wearing a short white dress who was looking at Rebecca as though she knew exactly who she was to her man. Rebecca stared right back till the other woman looked away. *You can keep him love. I have no designs on the bloke.* Mina walked past, and Rebecca caught the look of horror on her face when she clocked Robbie at their table. She started coming over, making her way through the tables as discreetly as she could.

'Luke . . .' Rebecca went to stand up from the table, and Luke automatically reached for her hand. Moving to her side, he pushed Robbie out of the way with his arm as he passed. Robbie went to grab his shoulder, and Luke grabbed him by the wrist. 'Luke, please. Let's go. Mina's coming.'

Luke was too busy glaring at her ex-fiancé to hear her, but he still kept his grip on both of them. He was eyeball to eyeball with Robbie now, their chests butting up against each other like men did before a fight.

She found Luke's ear and whispered, 'Luke, come on. You do know you're not actually Clark Kent, don't you? What are you trying to do, laser beam him with your eyes?'

'Eh?' Luke asked, his head moving in her direction slightly before returning to glare at Robbie again. 'Clark Kent,' Robbie laughed. 'As if.'

'Shurrup,' Luke growled. 'I don't need lasers for pretty boys like you.'

'Luke,' she whispered again, trying to move them. 'Mina!'

She didn't want to cause a scene and get her friend into trouble.

Mina arrived, and she did not look happy. 'Robbie, knock it off. Go back to your pathetic snow groupies.' Too late, she was standing at the other side of Robbie now. 'You okay, Rebecca?'

Robbie was looking around him as if he was the butt of some big joke.

'The Great Becks Atkins, nothing to say? Mina, what the hell's going on?' He bent his head around Luke, looking right at Rebecca now with a confused look on his face. 'When did you come back?'

He was talking to Rebecca again now, peppering her with questions, and she was trying to take out money from her purse to pay for the food. Luke took her bag, closing it and tucking it under the arm holding hers.

'Becks!' Robbie was shouting now, and the diners closest to them had heard him over the soft music and relaxed chatter. She could see people starting to look, putting things together. She felt hot, her hand clammy in Luke's. She went to pull away, but Luke pulled her closer, pushing some notes into Mina's hand. 'Sorry Mina, we'll be leaving now. It was nice to have met you.' He glared at Robbie, who whooped like a schoolgirl at him.

'Ooooo, you getting mad, are you? Big man, eh? Come on then, let's share Becks stories eh? Can't top Canada, can he Becks?'

Mina was trying to push him out of the back now, Robbie's own security posse standing close by. The guy needed his own security team because he was such a colossal dick. They looked positively fed up, and Rebecca smiled at them apologetically. Lester, Robbie's head security guy, gave her a wink and rolled his eyes. He mouthed 'you look great' at her, and she loved her old friend for it. Lester stepped forward then, his thickset arm easily wrapping around Robbie's waist as he reached where they were all standing.

'Pleasure to see you Rebecca,' he said just low enough to be heard, 'Luke, take care of my friend. Robbie, time to go. Team, extraction in 3. Next location.' The next bar, it meant. Somewhere else for Robbie to make his presence felt. She'd spent enough time in their company to know all their little codes.

The people around him started to shift, moving Robbie and his party back away towards the bar, and the side exit. Robbie was having none of it.

'Come on Becks, what the hell? You got nothing to say to me, eh? You just going to leave me here, standing like a fool?' He was taunting her now, she could feel it and Luke was reading her face, his own getting darker by the minute. He faced her now and made her look at him. He nudged her chin with her finger till she looked at him. He squeezed her hand again.

'You okay?'

Robbie was yelling behind him, Lester telling him to knock it off and Mina telling him to bugger off in her mother tongue. Rebecca knew that Mina knew *all* the worst curse words too. She was furious, the whole night was ruined. 'Just ignore him. I take it you dated?'

'Dated! Ha!' Robbie, bat-eared and wrapped in a bear hug by Lester, was flailing his arms around everywhere. The diners had mostly chosen to ignore him now, though a couple had pulled their phones out. This was bad. Damn the inventor of the smart phone. Nowadays you couldn't have a poo without someone making you into a viral internet star. 'We were more than that, we were partners. Right, Becks? Or is it Ice Rebel? You tell Luke about any of that, eh? About Canada? When I proposed?' The whole room gasped, and the phones were all out now. She felt like Harry Styles in a concert hall, mobbed and filmed from every angle.

She closed her eyes tight when he said those words. She didn't need to look at Luke to know that he'd heard every little detail. Her name, and all the gory secrets she'd tried to hide for five years. Her truly spectacular fall from the top of her sport, and with a messy and very public break-up to boot. Luke had frozen still, his hands still in place. She felt a tear drop down her cheek and into his hand, before his shirt blotted it into the fabric. He started to walk, tucking her into his side as he parted the crowd before him like a messiah. Rebecca kept her eyes to the floor, willing herself not to break down till they got to the front doors. Mina was telling Lester to get Robbie out, that he was barred, but Robbie didn't care. He was loving every minute.

'That's it Becks, run away! It's what you do, right? We'll be seeing each other, don't worry. We have a lot of catching up to do. Enjoy the rest of your whatever that is.'

Luke was there one minute, and gone the next. He turned, growling his head off like a baby tiger, and ran at Robbie with a booming war cry that would make Mel Gibson look like David Brent.

Mina took a step back, Luke swerving around every person effortlessly. *Wow*, thought Rebeca. When he was mad, he was so sure of himself. If he'd have run like that normally, he would have ploughed through them like bowling pins. Lester, still holding Robbie, shrugged at Rebecca, who was looking at him in horror, and dropped him back onto his feet. He tried to back into Lester, but Lester just laughed.

'Sorry boss, breaktime.' He took a step back, motioning for his guys to retreat to the bar. 'Play nice.'

Luke felled Robbie half a second later, flying through the air and slamming him to the floor in a rugby tackle. Robbie grunted as the air was knocked out of him. Mina disappeared and Rebecca ran over to them both; they were now rolling around on the floor. Lester, now drinking a virgin cocktail with the others, was telling Robbie's girl to stay put, whilst she shook her fake nails at him and gestured wildly.

'Luke, get up!' She tried to reach him, smacking him on the bottom as it bobbed past her.

'Hey, don't spank me!' he shouted as he rolled, pinning Robbie to the floor. His knee was digging into Robbie's chest, and Robbie was spluttering, trying to bitch slap Luke, who kept deflecting the blows. He straddled Robbie, one knee right near his crown jewels.

'Say sorry to Rebecca,' he commanded, and Rebecca tried to pull him off. He didn't budge, a button popping off his shirt as he twisted gently away from her. 'Step back Rebecca, I don't want you to get hurt.' He got a slap right across his chops from Robbie, who had seized the opportunity. 'Hey!'

He grabbed at Robbie's hands, and Robbie was stuck. All he could do was wiggle on the floor like a worm, whilst Luke kept slapping him with his own hands.

'What you hitting yourself for, eh?' Slap. Robbie's face was as red as a tomato, and he was shouting for Lester. Some of the guests were laughing into their napkins. A couple of people shouted, 'Yeah, hit him again!' and 'About time someone slapped that guy.' Lester was chuckling too, she could see his shoulders jiggle up and down through his tight black T-shirt. Rebecca ran over to him.

'Lester, come on! Stop this, please!' Lester rolled his eyes and nodded.

'Okay, but that was fun. You have to admit it.' He gestured to the rabble on the floor, Robbie trying to buck Luke off, who was now open-shirted and laughing as he made Robbie move like a marionette.

Lester strode over and put out a hand to Luke. Luke passed Robbie's hand to Lester, and Lester half carried, half lifted him to his feet.

'Show's over folks, don't drink and drive. Have a good night.' A man at the table nearest to him flinched as Lester plucked the phone from his outreached arm and put it in his back pocket. 'Call the office,' Lester said to the dumbstruck man, who just nodded. One of Lester's team was going round the room, giving people holding phones a knowing look. He gave the man a business card.

Lester lifted Robbie into his arms like a father would a weeping baby. 'And if anything goes online, in any form, Robbie's lawyers, and we, will know about it.' The lads behind him, all huge and quite fearsome-looking when they turned it on, nodded to the crowd. Lester winked at Rebecca, and she lifted her shaking hand to say goodbye. Luke was off the floor now, picking up the chairs that Robbie had kicked over and apologising to the diners. He passed her handbag back to her, his face unreadable as he looked her over.

'We need to go.' He placed her coat around her shoulders, throwing his own on and taking her hand to walk her out. No one said anything else, and she felt the atmosphere change as they reached the doors. A second later, they were outside, heading away from the heated area and down the street. They walked till they were out of sight of the place, away from Robbie who would no doubt still be close by. Probably chewing out Lester for making him deal with his own stuff for once. He should do that more often, the look on Robbie's face was almost worth it. Almost. He wouldn't leave it though. They'd had the perfect life, but then she'd crashed out in the competition, and changed overnight. He never got that, never.

She let go of Luke's hand, and started to head to the taxi rank.

She could hear him chuntering to himself as she put her arms through her coat.

'My shirt's shot to shit now,' he muttered, pulling each side apart and exposing his chest as she turned to look at him. He looked so hot, she couldn't help but stop and turn to face him. She didn't feel the cold anymore, but she was still shaking. 'I'm so sorry, I never do that, or act like that.' He bit his lip, striding over to her. She didn't move till he was standing right in front of her. He was close enough to touch now, and she could see that his chest was heaving. He was pumped up from the fight. She felt it too.

'Thank you—'

'I wish I'd knocked him out as soon as he—'

They laughed, their icy breath mingling together in the night air. There was no one around, the businesses here all closed for the night, the houses all lit up. The windows cast glowing shadows over everything.

'I'm sorry I went for him.'

'I know you aren't though.'

'No, I'm not. Sorry for that too. Again. I ruined our date. If you don't want me to come on Saturday, I can stay away.'

She was shaking her head at him.

'Oh God, you don't want me to come, do you? I was bluffing then.'

Rebecca laughed, and took a deep shuddering breath inwards.

'Robbie was my fiancé, for a day or two at least. My boyfriend and ski partner before that. We did go to Canada, but then something happened to me, and I didn't handle it very well.' She thought back to lying in that hospital bed, Robbie bouncing around her room, talking about exclusive interviews, and marriage sponsorship deals. 'Neither did he. I changed. He changed too, I guess.' *Or I just saw more of his flaws, when my own were exposed.* 'He didn't like my choices. He's angry with me.'

'He's a jerk.' Luke frowned when he noticed her shaking. He

pulled her coat tighter around her and rubbed her arms with his own. His coat was a black puffed parka, lined with a faux fur hood that made his bristle look darker against his skin. It made his eyes sparkle. *I'm in shock. This isn't a fairytale. He's not a prince, come to bloody save me.* 'Let's go get warm.'

'I'm fine. I need to get this out.' She wanted him to know. She needed him to. 'I was Ice Rebel, for a long time.'

Luke's head dropped. 'I know.'

Her shields came clanging up, the screech of welded metal ringing in her ears.

'You know?'

'Well, I didn't, till *him.*' Venom dripped from the last word. 'My dad's a bit of a sports nut. It's how the student exchange thing came about. My mother was an ice skater, semi-professional. He loved ice sports. Loves. I thought I recognised you.'

She gave him a sad smile. 'I know you did. It freaked me out. Not many people know I'm here. I wanted to keep it that way.' *Want to. Period.*

'Why is he angry, because you broke off the engagement?'

'Yes and no. The wedding was a bit of a money spinner, back then. We had our own sponsors. Till the accident.'

Luke didn't break eye contact, he moved closer. She could feel his bare chest through her coat, pressed against the fabric. 'Money and fame, eh? I thought as much.' He looked angry again, his eyes turning dark. She reached out and put her arms around his waist. His face softened, the response immediate. She could feel her heart pick up once more. 'I've got to be honest, I can't really see you two. He's all show, you never did the showbiz thing, did you?'

He'd paid more attention to her career than she'd thought.

'No, it was about the sport for me. The snow was what mattered.'

'Well, you are better off without him then. Obviously. If he comes to the café, I am going to spark him straight out.' She laughed at his words, which reminded her of home.

105

'He doesn't know I live here. He thinks I just flew in. I could tell. He doesn't know I work at the café. My friends are loyal. Hans never liked him.' That was the understatement of the year. When she'd come out of hospital, sponsors already onto the next hot thing, Robbie off on his tour as usual, Hans had scooped her up and given her a new life. If Hans ever saw Robbie again, it wouldn't go well. She didn't want that. 'We can't tell Hans about this.' Mina would no doubt tell him or Holly as soon as she got a chance, but it wouldn't come from her. She didn't want to cause them any stress. They were in their own bubble, a baby bubble and given that Robbie was a massive prick, it didn't take a genius to work out it wouldn't be a good day for anyone. Once upon a time, he would have been an uncle to their baby. Amazing how ludicrous things looked in the rear view of your life choices.

'It won't come from me. I would never do that to you, Rebecca. I couldn't. I just want you to be okay.'

His face was lit up by the backdrop of the snow, and Rebecca took a moment to process just what had happened.

'You really went for him. Are you okay?'

She looked down at his shirt, their close quarters causing her forehead to brush down his face. He kissed it, the low rumble in his chest making her breath catch. 'I'm fine, as long as you are.' He moved his lips down to her cheek, kissing her once there, before slowly pulling back, and going in for the other cheek. His stubble brushed against her skin, and she tugged him closer, turning her mouth to meet his. He picked her up off the floor, walking them both backwards till they reached a shop doorway. He turned her to face the doors, pressing her gently against them with his body, deepening the kiss. She was clawing at his back, trying to get a better grip on him, and he huffed, leaning away a little.

'I can't do this.'

His breath came out in hot little mists into the cold air. Her libido went 'wait, what?' as he took her hand and pulled her back onto the street. She went on wobbly legs, her lips still feeling on fire from his delicious mouth. 'We need to get a cab home. Now.' He turned to her, and the look she saw in his eyes had her walking that bit faster. They walked to the nearest taxi rank, standing in a thankfully tiny queue silently, their thumbs rubbing each other's hands. The cab pulled up, Luke sweeping open the door and giving the driver the Fir Tree Lodge address whilst sitting her close to him in the spacious back seat. There was a glass partition between them, and the driver was listening to folk music, humming away to himself. Rebecca's phone rang in her bag, and she reached for it with her free hand. Looking at the screen, she saw Mina's name flash up on the screen. She showed it to Luke. 'Mina.'

Luke nodded, his hand still in hers, and turned to look out of the window. She felt his grip tighten, just a fraction, and she gave it a squeeze.

'Hello Mina, I'm sorry about that. Did Lester get him out? Are you mad?'

'Is Mina mad?' Robbie's cold tones came out of the phone like icy fingers, making her ear prickle. Her grip tightened around Luke's hand, hard and fast. Luke turned to the phone and jabbed at the speakerphone button. 'What about me, eh? What about that? You can't even say anything, can you? It's path—'

Luke's jaw clenched, and he took the phone out of her hands.

'Listen to me, you lycra-wearing little shit stick. Listen carefully, if you have any actual brain matter in that massive head of yours. You don't know who I am, but I sure know who you are. I have a very special set of IT skills, the very best. If you don't leave Rebecca alone, or if you harm her in any way, I will use my special set of skills to end your internet life as you know it. You think you get attention now, wait till I am finished with you. You'll have no need to worry about everyone knowing just who and what you are, because I will show them. Amazing what a bit of Photoshop and an internet connection can do, Dobbie.

107

I will end your little following, and then I will track you down, and smack seven bells of shit out of you. Do you understand?'

Rebecca didn't give Robbie time to stop spluttering, taking the phone she ended the call. The night fell silent once more, the driver humming along to his tunes, muffled by the screen.

'I'm not going to say sorry,' Luke started, and she took the phone from him, turning it off and shoving it back into the bag by her side.

'I don't want you to.'

'Good, cos I'm not.'

They both looked out of their windows, hands on their laps. The music changed to Elton, singing about a rocket. The driver stopped humming and started bobbing his head like a nodding dog. Everyone was an Elton fan. Her mother loved him. Did she know Robbie was here? Were they still in touch? Another reason she knew Robbie was playing the part of the wounded duck. If he really wanted to find her, he would have contacted her mother. And her mother would never have been such a pain in the behind all this time. She was 100 per cent team Robbie. He'd bailed on her in her time of need, and she knew it as well as Rebecca did. Typical mother, choosing to only see what she wanted to see.

'I'm really not you, know.' Luke broke the silence. 'I will absolutely knock his block off if he rings you again.'

'I don't doubt it.'

'Good, cos I will.'

'I know, you said.'

'I mean, what the hell did you see in him anyway?' He puffed his fringe out of his eyes. 'I mean! I know it's not my business, but . . .' He bit his lip. 'Well, his hair for a start. His hair looks like he's been dipped in oil, and his clothes! Well, his clothes were nice, but clothes don't maketh the man, Rebecca. Colin Firth lied. A knobhead in Armani is still a knobhead in my book.'

'Manners,' she muttered.

'What?' He turned back from the window to look at her.

'Manners maketh the man. That was the line. Never mock Colin Firth.'

'Why was he a tailor then?' he asked, genuinely confused.

'He wasn't a tailor, he was a highly trained . . . look, does it matter?'

'Not really no, but I do want to watch that one again now.'

'I have it in the lodge on DVD – oh Luke, what are we going on about?'

'I don't know, you started that one.' He turned his head back to the window. A moment later, she saw him pull his phone out and Google 'Colin Firth film quotes'.

Rebecca pushed her lips together to stop herself from laughing. Thank God she could press her face close to the window so he couldn't see her face. She could see him though, he was still spouting on, first about how confusing *Kingsman* was, and then back to Robbie. Then he kept impersonating Robbie's hairstyle by putting his own hair into ridiculous peaks and patterns. She could see his reflection bouncing back as they parked up by the café. The driver turned and smiled at them jovially.

'Good night?' he asked, as though he was utterly new.

'Great, thanks,' Luke said, back to being Mr Polite to everyone. It was so cute. Robbie treated people like they were all in his entourage, whether they were or not. 'Keep the change.'

He handed the notes to the driver and got out. Rebecca went to open her door, but Luke was there, hand outstretched. She took it without hesitating and the driver went on his Elton-loving way. She fumbled for her keys, using the distraction to push the words out of her throat.

'I didn't see all that, not at first. The hair, sure, but he wore a helmet a lot. Everyone we knew had weird hair. It was good at first. We gelled.'

Luke shuddered. 'Go on.'

She reached into her bag to try to locate her keys again. Her hands were freezing already.

'He was committed to the slopes, just as much as I was. We ended up hanging out with the same people, entering the same competitions, it just evolved from there. He wasn't as bad as he is now. He hates me, so he's only showing his evil side. I broke our dream.'

'You didn't break anything, Rebecca. You had an accident. Was he not there, after?'

She thought back to that day on the slopes. Half delirious with pain, she'd heard him on the phone. Not to her mother back home, or any of their friends. They would have been calling too, given that her fall from grace had been televised for the world to see. They'd have seen it all, in instant replay. Her making the jump, landing, and her ski breaking. Turned out, it had been damaged in flight. Unchecked, the moment her body weight met the snow, she was out for the count.

Robbie was on the slopes, right there with her, but he wasn't calling her mum. He was calling the agent they shared, telling them to make the most out of this 'opportunity'. She couldn't blame her agency, that was what they did. They did their job, controlled the damage, spun the stories, kept the offers rolling in. But when she'd heard him like that, she knew the engagement they'd decided to keep under wraps till after the competition was over. It hadn't even been a week. She'd only worn her ring once, that night he proposed on the Whistler mountainside. The next day, she'd given it back to him for safekeeping whilst they flew to France. The rest? Well, that was bone-shattering history. She'd never seen the ring again, and she'd never asked to.

'He was there when he thought it was a blip. He thought I'd maybe broken a leg, be off the circuit for a season. He was hoping to squeeze a quickie wedding in between. My agent, our agent, he was great. Matt handled my hospital treatment, got me the best. Listened to me when I said I didn't want bedside YouTube videos with updates for my "fans". There was no point to it anymore, I wasn't that person.'

She felt herself weaken, and sniffed.

'Hell, I was never that person. I didn't care about the fancy merchandise, or the money. I just wanted to be the best at what I loved.'

'How bad was it?' Luke's voice was low, caution whispering out of the question.

'I didn't let anyone touch me for the first two weeks. Not when I was awake, anyway. The pain meds were intense.'

She had a flashback of waking in the middle of the night, the pain in her body making her stir. Pushing what she came to call the bye-bye button. You pressed it, you went bye-bye.

'Holly came to see me, and she told me I stank.' She laughed, but it turned into a little sob. 'She washed me, sorted me out and told me to pull myself together.'

'She's a good friend,' said Luke as Rebecca pulled her keys out and unlocked the café door. They walked inside and she breathed in the scent of home, relaxing just a little. She could hear Luke locking the door behind her. 'Are you recovered now?'

She didn't answer for a moment, and he slowly walked closer to her. His footsteps were the only noise now. He put his hands around her, his front pressed tight to her back. She took his hands and wrapped them around herself.

'Yeah, all better. The doctors did an amazing job.' That was true, other than the scars. The roadmap of her crash and burn. 'Few pins and plates here and there.' Not to mention the physical therapy till she was sick, her muscles burning from the effort of keeping her body going. Working half arsed wasn't an option if you wanted to get back to normal. Whatever normal passed for these days. Robbie wasn't there for any of that.

'Do you still ski?'

She didn't give an answer, and he didn't press for one. He dropped a kiss onto her cheek.

'I think we drank all the wine . . .' He whirled her around, dropping one hand so that she twirled around him. 'Or I would suggest a nightcap. For our shot nerves.' He looked down at his wrecked shirt. 'And to celebrate our victory at Fight Club.'

Rebecca put her finger to her lips, looking around the empty café. 'What happens in Fight Club, stays in Fight Club remember?'

He drew her to him, his feet moving into a slow step.

'Dance with me then. Let's shake the night up a bit.'

She laughed, throwing her head back as he picked her up off the floor and spun her around. Slowly releasing his grip on her till their eyes met, he lowered her till her feet were just brushing the floor.

'It's weird Rebecca, but so far, this week with you has been one of the most exciting of my life.'

'From what I've heard, that doesn't take much.' He stuck his tongue out at her. 'Thank you for tonight, for standing up for me.' She patted him on the shoulder. 'It felt nice to have someone there, having my back.'

'Even though I pissed in your bin?'

She laughed like a drain, making him chuckle.

'My new bin is nicer, thanks for that.'

'I haven't seen that yet.' He touched his cheek to hers, dancing to a beat that they both seemed to hear. 'You'll have to show me.'

She pulled back slowly, enjoying the rough touch of his cheek against hers.

'I have new sheets too.' She brushed her lips against his. 'You missed that as well.'

He kissed her till her toes curled, still moving her to the same beat.

Pulling away, just a little, dropping little kisses still as though his lips couldn't bear the separation, he murmured something that made her heart melt.

'Trust me, I have missed so much in my life already. I don't intend to miss anything else. I don't care if we've only known each other for three days. People spend years together, and it still doesn't work out. I say we go with the flow for once. I think a full room inspection might even be required.' He was smirking at her now, and it was her that couldn't wait any longer. He was right! She'd not had sex in *five* years. What was the worst that could happen? He'd be rubbish? She'd be rubbish? He was leaving. It didn't even matter. It was perfect, actually. She wouldn't exactly bump into him, would she? Once the baby came, Hans would be busy, and Luke had whatever he had going on . . .

He was leaving though. The first man she'd liked in five years enough to break her sexual drought, and he was leaving. Soon probably.

'Thinking too much is not part of the new plan, Rebecca.' He smiled at her, giving her the sweetest little kiss. 'I am a gentleman though, and I am sorry for being a bit forward.' He grinned ruefully, looking out at their footprints in the snow. 'Blame the French night air, eh? Or the wine.' He started to pull away just a fraction, and she stopped him. He looked down at her, his hair still at odd angles from the cab ride. Utter sex hair. Wow.

'We take this slow, okay?' She tried to slow her words down. 'I like you, but you're—'

'Leaving, I know.' He dropped his head, and she brushed back his hair. He nuzzled into her hands. 'I didn't plan to do this, but—'

'It's okay. Let's just leave that conversation for another time. The date's not over yet.'

He kissed her again. 'I like you too. When Robbie spoke to you like that, I just lost it. I've never been like this before.' He covered his mouth with hers, teasing her with his tongue. 'I think it's something to do with you.'

She smiled at him, nodding her head in the direction of the display case.

'There's some wine in the bottom of my wardrobe.' He raised a brow, and she kissed it. 'Shut up, it's my emergency stash. I stockpile for winter. It's pretty boring around here when the season's done.' His smile dimmed a little, but she wanted it back. 'You go up, I'll get us some dessert.'

113

His eyes lit up. 'God, woman, you know how to turn a man on.' He grabbed her, making her laugh as he dipped her to the floor. 'Sorry, the song was ending. Big finale.' He ran his stubble along her neck, and she almost felt a bit Austen-like herself. She wasn't as dignified though, and the feeling of his mouth on her collar bone made her want to dry hump his leg like a happy rescue hound. 'Don't be long, okay?'

He lifted her back up, taking the keys and unlocking the interior door with a spring in his step. Rebecca gathered her bag and shrugged her coat off. Dumping it on an upturned chair, she took out her phone, and with a shaky breath, she dialled Mina back.

'Hi! It's me, don't worry.' Mina's voice sprang out of the phone, and Rebecca loosened her grip on the chair leg she had been gripping onto. 'He grabbed my phone in the ruckus out back, the slimy little rat. Are you okay?'

Rebecca could hear Luke upstairs, the radio on as usual. She could hear glasses clinking together.

'I'm fine, thanks. We got back home okay.'

'Wow, the date did go well.'

'Well, he lives with me. It's complicated.'

Mina didn't reply. Rebecca found herself filling the pause in conversation.

'Not Robbie complicated. He's from back home. I didn't know him, but he'll have to leave.'

'Aww, you're screwed then.' Mina, as dry as ever. 'If only the human race could invent something to transport people from country to country.'

'Nice try. I can't leave the café.'

'Why not? Hans can get someone else in. Hell, once the baby comes, Holly will be glad of the break from him. He is going to be a gooey mess when that little one arrives.'

Rebecca laughed. 'I know, but still.'

'Still no excuse,' Mina pressed. 'Ignore Robbie, he's a total mess. He thinks life is defined by sponsors and followers. Lester really went off on him after you left. He got my phone when he stomped off. What did he say?'

'Not a lot,' Rebecca headed over to the counter, picking out some nice treats from the display case. 'Luke took over and went all Liam Neeson on him.'

'Liam Neeson from *Taken*, full on?'

'Yep.' She filled two plates and grabbed two juice bottles too. She'd settle up later. 'Nerd edition. He works in IT.'

'Brains as well as brawn, eh? What the hell are you doing wasting time talking to me? I'm stocktaking, but if I had a hot alpha male brain box in my flat, I wouldn't be calling you about it. I will, however, want a blow by blow tomorrow. And I want every detail. It's been a while. Lester's a bit of a dish, isn't he?' Mina was to the point, as ever.

'Lester, eugh. He's like my brother. And Luke is hardly alpha male. I don't know what got into him tonight.' She dropped her voice to a whisper.

'Yeah, well, he isn't my brother! Don't put Luke down either, he didn't like Robbie, and he stood up to him. That's a good man. You need a good man. You deserve it, after everything you've been through. It was nice seeing you, I mean that.'

'I know, you too. I won't leave it so long next time.'

'Don't let that be the only thing you start doing again, Becks is part of you too. I saw her tonight, just for a second. I saw you when Luke went for Robbie. You care about the guy.'

'Do I, hell!'

'Luke, idiot. You care about Luke.' Mina shouted something in Mandarin to someone in the background, a deep sigh escaping her lips. 'Listen, someone should be getting some. Go get some for both of us.' The phone clicked off as she started to shout at someone again, and Rebecca took everything upstairs.

The radio was off now, and she could see that he'd lit the candles in her lounge. He'd put a new sheet on the sofa, and set the wine out. On the table was an envelope. He'd got changed too. He was barefoot now, his glasses back on. Wearing a pair of cream sweats, he was shirtless.

Holy moly. He looked up as she entered, getting up automatically to take her plates from her.

'These look amazing.'

She watched him pick one and take a bite. 'Hans made them, good, eh? I learned from the best.' He swallowed his mouthful.

'I think I like your buns better though.' The atmosphere changed again, and she realised that she was still standing there in her dress.

'I bet you tell all the girls that. Why don't you pick a movie, and I'll go get changed?'

Closing her bedroom door behind her, she grabbed some clothes, chucking her outfit in her laundry hamper and grabbing a towel and some fresh loungewear she'd picked up in town. Another little thing she'd changed thanks to Luke. Raggy old yoga pants with holes in just didn't cut it for nightcap time.

When she was freshly showered, she walked into the lounge to find him watching *John Wick* under a blanket. He lifted the blanket up for her, and she went to sit next to him. He smushed it around them both, putting his arm up for her to slide under. She did it, resting her head on his chest. He reached forward, taking her with him and picked up two full glasses of wine.

'What's wrong with Keanu?' She took the wine, taking a deep sip.

'His wife died, and then someone killed his dog.'

'So that's why he's mad?'

Luke thought for a moment. 'Essentially yes. It's awesome though, Reeves is the best.' She looked up at him, his glasses reflecting gun fire from the screen.

'Christopher Reeves?' He rolled his eyes, and she turned back to the screen chuckling.

'Ha ha, Clark Kent. Yes, yes. I've heard that before.' He huffed.

'Dean Cain ruined my sex life in high school, and then bloody Tom Welling came in with his sodding underpants over his trousers.'

'Aww, you poor thing.' She watched Keanu take out a room full of bad guys, making enough time to run his hand through his floppy hair. 'I always thought Clark Kent was a bit of a cutie myself. The best part of *Superman*.'

She could feel him smile, and his hand started to rub her shoulder.

'I never thought of it that way before.' He turned to her, and she felt his breath on her cheek. 'I'd give anything for his X-ray vision right now.'

'Cheesy.'

'I know, but it's funny.'

They both put their glasses down, kissing each other slowly.

'Perv.'

He laughed, before kissing her again, his hands moving to her sides.

She shuffled underneath him as he moved over her, their legs and arms ending up wrapped around each other as they lay down on the sofa together.

'Ow! My hair!' He'd pinned a chunk of her black hair to the sofa with his elbow.

'Oops, my bad. These aren't the new sheets, are they?' he checked, suddenly nervous again. She took his glasses off, putting them on the coffee table and taking his face in her hands.

'No, they're in my bedroom, with the new bin.'

'Ooo, someone's in a hurry.'

She laughed, but it was a little hollow. The truth was, her bottle was going. If she didn't do this now, she'd think about all her sca— *don'tthinkaboutitdon'tthinkaboutit—*

'No, I just wanted to show you what a urine free bedroom looks like.'

He grinned, and she pulled him to her again.

'Stop talking, and take me to bed, Luke.'

He jumped to his feet, surprisingly nimble for him. Scooping her into his arms, he flipped her over his shoulder.

'Grab the wine, woman.'

She did as she was told for once, grabbing the bottle and squealing as he carried her off to the bedroom, kicking the door shut behind him as he went.

Chapter 7

'Well, that must have been some burger!'

Rebecca was dreaming of Hans. In her sleep. His annoying voice was talking away to her, and she cursed her brain for making her think of her hairy friend when she'd just spent the most interesting and exciting night of her life since the accident.

'Shut up Hans,' she heard a voice say, and she felt herself nodding. *Good, glad someone said it.*

'Yeah! Shut up Hans,' she shouted out groggily, her eyes still firmly shut. 'So loud.'

Her brain finally caught up. That, and she was pretty sure that a naked man was rubbed up against her. Last night came screaming back. And the fact that Luke was still in her bed.

'Hans! Shit!'

Rebecca sprang up then, covering her bits as she realised that Hans was there, looking like Ned Flanders in skiwear, open-mouthed and laughing at the fact that she was naked, in bed with Luke.

'Hans!'

'Hans!' Rebecca and Luke spoke together again, high-pitched with indignation. They flashed each other a horrified look.

'How the holy hell did you get in?'

'Why are you in my room?'

Hans held up his hands.

'Hey, I came to pick up Luke for his first lesson. The door was unlocked, I shouted to you both. I was worried you'd murdered each other.' He smirked then, his moustache bristling with mirth. 'Evidently, you made friends. How lovely.'

He ducked as Rebecca threw a heel at him, but he didn't dodge the nut-crushing throw of Luke's shoe. He crumpled like a paper bag to the floor, making the ceiling light shake as he hit the deck.

'Bullseye,' Luke shouted, high-fiving Rebecca as they both scrabbled to get their clothes from where they had thrown them to the floor.

'Nice one, ten points for the crown jewels.' Rebecca threw a sock Luke's way. They had tiny little computers printed on them. 'Twenty, surely?'

Pulling on his sweatpants and passing her top to her, he stood over Hans, who was still clutching his nether regions and making a high-pitched keening sound.

'What about a nipple twist, whilst he's down?' Luke suggested.

Rebecca pretended to consider it as she smoothed her hair down.

'Maybe next time.' She'd seen the clock. 'I'm late to get started with work.' She waved her hands over Hans. 'Can you handle this?' Luke yanked his top on and ruffled his hair back. Leaning over his friend, he kissed her on the lips and smiled.

'After last night, I can handle anything. Don't watch me out there, okay? I'll have enough people laughing at me as it is. I left something on the coffee table. Will you read it? It's why I'm here.' He kissed her again before she could ask him anything else. 'Have a good day.'

Domesticated bliss. The thought popped into her head, but she brushed it away. What was in that envelope was going to test that thought.

'You too. Don't break anything, for God's sake.'

120

He rolled his eyes, sticking his tongue out of the side of his mouth, flashing his white teeth. 'Me, never.' Rebecca was just leaving when she heard Hans take Luke down to the floor, and for the second time in as many days, she saw Luke in a floor scrap. This time, laughably tame. Hans had two distinct handicaps. She headed downstairs to get her day started.

Luke was seriously regretting his life choices right about now. At one point last night, Rebecca had flipped him off the bed, and now he had a bruise across his bottom cheeks. Not that it wasn't worth the flip, or the bruised arse, but it did smart on his delicate peach-like skin. Which meant that every time he fell on it, it hurt like being lashed. Hans wasn't helping either. They'd been on the nursery slopes all morning, and some of the toddlers who had started learning with their parents that morning were already better than him. The last time he'd slipped backwards, he'd skied down further still, catching himself between his tight skiwear clad legs, and two of the kids had pointed and laughed.

'I hate kids,' he muttered under his breath.

'No, you don't,' Hans laughed, waving at two of the toddlers, who both stared up at him as though he'd just walked out of Narnia. 'You'll be a great uncle. Hey, I can't wait to tell them stories of how their uncle met their Auntie Rebecca.' Luke used the pole to pull himself up, crab walking till he felt safe enough on his feet to stand upright again. He eyed the toddlers before he tried, giving them the stink eye. They nudged each other, pretending not to look. Their adoring parents were snapping photos of the pair of them.

'They should have devil horns,' he shouted in their direction, placing his goggles back over his eyes again quickly and shuffling away. Hans took a snap himself, his fingers surprisingly nimble in his gloves. 'Put that away, or I'll shove it somewhere so hard you'll never get it out.'

'Wow.' Hans put his phone away, but not before sending it

to Holly and Rebecca. He captioned it to Rebecca 'You've seen this naked', laughing his head off as he looked across to the café. Rebecca was just finishing up serving a customer, and Hans could make out her reaching for her phone. He looked away quickly, and his phone pinged in his hand. She'd replied, 'Yep, and rubbed it on every surface in YOUR lodge. Arse prints are in fashion I hear.'

He guffawed with laughter, Luke looking over his shoulder just in time to read the whole thing. He swatted at Hans, lunging at his throat.

'You total arse! Why did you do that!'

Hans tucked his phone in a zip pocket and pointed up to the first slope.

'Cos it's funny! Come on, grab your lady balls. We're going in the lift up to that.'

Luke paled beneath his goggles.

'No, come on. The joke's over.'

Hans pointed to the family who had just been mocking him, they were headed to the lifts themselves.

'It's still the family slope, it's gentle. Come on, you can't enter the competition without the basic skills. They're not slack on safety here. They're not just going to let you rock up on competition day and break your neck in front of the spectators. It bums people out, you know?'

Luke rolled his eyes at his gargantuan friend, knowing full well he wouldn't be able to see it anyway.

'Okay okay, but no laughing, and no photos. I mean it. I don't want to scare Rebecca off. It's complicated enough as it is.'

Hans grinned, holding his hands to his heart.

'I knew you two would get along. Holly said that Rebecca would hate it, but I knew!' He was waggling his finger now, like a smug dad proving to his teenager that he was still indeed down with the kids. 'I knew you'd be able to help each other.'

'You did not. And she did hate me. I made a total arse of myself, annoyed the hell out of her and then . . .' Luke smiled,

Hans looking at him like a proud parent. 'Well, she's just amazing, isn't she?' His smile faltered then. 'I left her the list. Asked her to read it. I don't want her to realise I'm just a nerd, but I wanted her to know. You know? Even if it doesn't last.' He looked down at the snow. 'Nothing lasts, that's the point. I'm sick of doing the same thing, day after day. Look at Dad! It nearly killed him! I don't want that for him, or for me. I really like her Hans, and I really think I'm going to mess it up. I've no life experience. What have I got to offer a woman like that?'

Hans looked thoughtful for a moment, and patted his friend on the arm, as gently as he could. Over his shoulder, he could see that Rebecca was pretending to work, but her eyes kept flicking to them. She dropped the tea towel she was holding, picking it up and headbutting the counter in the process. A second later, he could see her head bob up, looking at them again.

'I think that you and Becks have a lot more in common than you think. You forget, we've been friends for such a long time now, and the same for me and Becks. I can see it, Luke, even if you can't. All I'm saying is, you're here now. You're doing it. This is not the dress rehearsal my friend. This is it. Your old life ended when you boarded that plane. One event changed the course of everything you knew. Rebecca forgot that too, for a long time. Since the minute you landed, I see a lot more of the old Becks coming through. That's a lot in a few days, especially for a nerd who's supposed to be scared of his own shadow. Your dad protected you all your life, a bit too much maybe, but he loves you. You love him, it's why you're here. Love finds a way, Luke. Just let it.'

Luke bear hugged his friend, who picked him up like he was a toddler.

'I love you man.'

'Love you too,' Hans said, wiping a tear away from his goggles. 'Now get off me, people are staring.'

The two of them pulled away, grunting and patting each other on the back in a manly way.

'One of us should fart or something. Break the moment.' Hans went cross-eyed for a moment, but nothing came out. 'Damn it.'

Luke laughed, heading towards the ski lift.

'If I fart, I'd go up like a balloon in this get up. I've been eating a lot of cake lately.' He blushed under his goggles at the memory of him eating a slice of cake in Rebecca's bed, feeding her little spoonfuls in between kisses. If they kept it up like last night, he'd be able to roll down the hill and win the comp as a snowball. Something told him it would be worth it. 'Come on, we came to ski. Let's get on with it.'

Luke watched his friend grin and walk to catch him up. Looking back at the café, Rebecca was standing at the window now. He waved, and she waved back. He put his fingers to his lips, touched them to his heart, and then blew it to her. For a second, she stared back at him, and his stomach flipped. *Oh God, why did I do that?*

Lifting her hand again, she made a catching motion with her hand, pressed her closed fist to her heart, and turned back to the café. Luke watched her work, taking in the moment when he blew a kiss to a girl in a French mountain café, a girl he liked too much already. The moment when he finally started living, and she liked him right back. It was time to call Dad. He wanted to tell him so much, and this time, he was going to bloody well listen.

Rebecca turned away from the window and looked down at her still closed fist. She felt like she didn't want to open her hand, to let his little token out into the atmosphere, but she had customers. And an envelope that was burning a hole in her apron pocket. She'd been desperate to read it, but Alpe d'Huez was getting busy now. Everyone was starting to gear up for the competition season, and the tourists were here in droves. She didn't even have enough waiting staff to cover everything till next week. They employed seasonal servers, but the rush had hit them a little early. Blindsided. She could relate. This week, she had been through so much, and felt like she was hanging off the back of a carousel horse. Normally, she'd have been screaming for the ride to stop, but now, she wanted to go faster. She wanted to see this out. So he was leaving! They had the time when he was here, and that would be enough. She'd been flip-flopping like this all morning. They were so natural together, even in their collective awkwardness, and she really liked him. Especially now, after that window moment. Last night had been like that too. It had never been like that with Robbie, not that she had compared it in detail. The differences were like night and day between the two, and how they made her feel. Maybe Luke would come and visit Hans again. If the letter wasn't something too earth-shattering. She'd thought of everything, from him being from another planet, to him being a secret journalist wanting to do a scoop on failure and what it looked like.

Or maybe he was actually married, with a whole brood of bespectacled children with washboard abs and an ability to hack into NASA in their nap times. Or fresh out of prison for killing his father, or all his family, down to the pet parrot.

She kept herself busy, her eyes flicking from her work to the windows, trying to keep an eye on them both. She'd not seen any commotion, so he was still in one piece it seemed. He'd looked cute in his skiwear too. The more she looked at him the more she noticed, and the more she fancied him. Noticed little things that someone who was attached might miss when they were no longer present.

Last night, wrapped around each other, they had just lain there, talking, kissing and gazing at each other. It sounded cringe now, and she knew Holly would take the piss, but when he fell asleep, she'd watched him still. Just the sound of him breathing, in her space, felt so unreal. Her mother had always told her that no woman was an island, that she needed people, but till now, she'd always disagreed. She'd fallen asleep that way, lulled by the feel of him there. She'd told him about herself, about Robbie, the whole mess, and he'd not even flinched. The way he'd looked at Robbie, she knew that he hated him for his part. His lashing out at her. Which was what had made her think twice about why she'd never questioned it. Not once. She'd taken the blame really, slunk off. He'd not got his way, but he'd moved on from it. He'd stepped back into his life, and she'd shut herself away. It had taken a man that had never got on a plane before to remind her that she wasn't living life, or moving on. She was stuck. Not making any choices was the same as not trying, letting things pass her by. The envelope in her apron was just as bad as the competition forms in her bedside drawer. They were instruments of bloody torture. Grabbing her phone, she dialled Eloise.

'Hi Eloise, it's Rebecca, from Alpine Bites. Yeah honey, we are busy early. I wondered . . .'

Eloise lived nearby, and currently had a husband who was working from home after an op on his knee. She'd said yes and put her bag on her arm before Rebecca even finished the sentence.

'That's great, you are amazing. Ha ha, yes, still illegal to murder him though. Tell him to ring his mother if he can't work out the washing machine. Don't try to batter him with it! See you soon, give him my love. *Au revoir, ma cherie.*'

She normally put most of the extra staff off as long as she could, her usual Grinch-like tendencies spreading to work colleagues too after a while, but she wanted to read what Luke had to say, and she wanted to ring her mother too. It was time.

Chapter 8

Friday was relatively uneventful in the café. They'd had an injury or two limp in for a shot of sugar and caffeine, to nurse their wounds. A lot of families were on the resort, and the café had been busy with the chatter of kids laughing, falling out over who had the biggest slice of cake, and who was the 'sickest' and 'peng' on a pair of skis. Rebecca laughed as she saw one of the fathers roll his eyes when his seven-year-old called him 'Bro'.

'I swear, when I was a kid I would have been just like them.' Eloise looked to where Rebecca had nodded, laughing herself when she saw the father of the boy take a huge gulp of coffee and roll his eyes at the laughing mother. She patted the kid on the top of his head, ruffling his hair. The boy smiled, hot chocolate and cream all around his beaming mouth. Rebecca remembered the letter, and asked Eloise if she could nip off. Luke had not long ago gone to practise skiing, so the lodge was empty upstairs. Eloise waved her off, holding out a steaming hot mug of coffee as she passed, her apron still on. Rebecca smiled gratefully at her friend and employee, and headed upstairs, closing the door behind her. She headed to her room, just in case Luke nipped back home and saw her in the lounge, and took out the envelope Luke had given her. Taking a deep breath, she pushed her index finger under the flap, and ripped open the paper. Inside, was a photo and a collection of clippings from magazines. She looked closer, and saw the Alps in one. She read the writing and smiled. It was a plan, it seemed, a road map for family life. Luke's family. She frowned, knowing it couldn't quite have gone like that. She turned the page over, and it was empty. The remaining two pages were different to each other. Both were handwritten, but their age difference was evident. One page was crisp, white and covered in Luke's handwriting. Her name was at the top. The other was more delicate, yellowed and the texture of a moth's wing. The writing was different, more sweeping. Feminine.

A list for our life
1. *We must all make time to ski. There is nothing better than the view from the top of a mountain.*
2. *We must be daring. We must always say yes to challenges, enter competitions. Be in it to win it!*
3. *We must protect the things we love, at all costs.*
4. *We must never be too scared to try. Failure is part of life.*
5. *We must always take photos, make videos, and make memories.*
6. *We must make our house a home. Love is where you lay your head.*
7. *We must never be sad, when things don't go our way. Getting back up is what counts.*

Rebecca drew a deep breath when she read that line. If this was Luke's mother writing this, she was not surprised that Luke was such a good guy.

The rest were more specific: days out, camping trips. Luke had mentioned some of them in passing when they'd been talking. They talked a lot now, even if the deeper stuff was still something she pushed down. Inaudible.

It made sense now, why he was coming to do this. How could he not, having seen this? He'd started right at the top. Putting the paper outside, she began to read Luke's letter. Tucking her legs under her, she sat back against the headboard.

Rebecca

I've been trying to tell you why I came here, but we always seem to get interrupted, or I fall over and take half your worldly goods out with me. My mother died when I was born, and my father seemed to watch the film Finding Nemo once and take life lessons from Marlin. He followed that list, the list that he and my mother made before I was a twinkle in their eye. Dad raised me all on his own. I had a great childhood, but I didn't really experience a lot of the things that other kids did. The crap stuff like the dead mum, obviously, but not the fun stuff. Drinking cider in the park with my mates, throwing up behind the slide. All rites of passage type stuff. It never really bothered me that much to be honest, till now. These last few weeks have opened my eyes in more ways than one.

Dad had a stroke. They caught it early, but he still needs to work to get better, to come home. Mobility and fight is needed, and my dear old dad just wants it to be over, I think. I did think that he might find love again, he has a friendship with a woman from the sandwich shop that is basically marriage, without the acknowledgement or funny business. And now I'm thinking about funny business and my dad, and I'd better sign off. I just wanted you to know why I'm here. I want to enter that competition, and even if I break my neck, if it gets my dad off his arse, it's worth it. My dad lost the person he loved most in the world, and so he kept me close, so nothing could happen to me. The only trouble was, by doing this my whole life, nothing did happen to me. None of the lows, or the life lessons. He didn't take risks. Getting better to go home to a lonely isolated life, I think he's realised he doesn't want that, but he'd rather die than try. I really think if I do this, if I show my dad how life CAN change, be better, full of colour, I really think I can save him, or get him to save himself, and that's what brought me here. It's been worth every single awkward moment too.

Especially because I met you. It's corny I know, but I am glad, Becks. So very glad I fell into your café doors that day. Come find me when you've read this. I need to kiss you, and see your face. Don't laugh at me being soppy.

Yours,
Luke

Rebecca read the pages twice, and let the puzzle pieces of Luke form a complete picture in her mind. This was a man who fell over his own shadow, but he was fighting to keep his family together. And his own life, judging by how busy his clients kept him. She put the papers back into the envelope and pushed it back into her apron pocket. Opening the drawer beside her, she pulled out the competition entry for the Alpine Challenge. She'd filled it in, it was ready to go. She tapped her finger on the form, making it bob up and down in her grasp. Luke was going to the offices later to take his entry in, she could go with him. Take hers. Enter. Shut her mother up. She could manage one, surely? Even if she tanked, so what? She wouldn't be trying to beat her own record then, she wouldn't have *that* pressure. No one had failed there yet. It was brand new. Until *she* failed of course, and that would make her the first loser for the comp. Nice.

The door knocked downstairs then, and Eloise shouted out 'Sorry Bec, but we're filling up!'

Damn it. She'd been up here a while. Dropping the form on the bed, she ran downstairs.

'No worries, coming!'

* * *

130

Luke's phone rang, the shrill tones making him jump. He'd just finished a long day with Hans, and he needed to get showered for his date, and get his entry form taken into the competition offices.

'Urggghh,' he moaned when he saw who had called him. One of his best clients. He had to get it, even though he was super pushed for time. The guy was due to open his first business the following month, he was imploding with panic over his website, and Luke leaving had seemingly sent the man over the edge.

'Hello?' He tried to be as professional as he could whilst half naked and still thawing his body parts out. 'No, don't worry about that. Can I help?'

Last night had been another amazing night. The best date. Not that Luke had a wealth of dating history to choose from, but he had been on dates. He wasn't exactly a virgin, but he might as well have been. In Rebecca's bed, he felt like everything was brand new. He stroked her pillow as his client explained his problem, and then stopped himself because it was a bit stalkerish. The perfume sniffing was bad enough. He just loved being here, with her. The client kept chatting in his ear.

'Right, okay,' Luke spoke into the handset. 'Let me get a pen, you tell me what you think you need to change, and we'll get it sorted. Plenty of time before the grand opening.'

He was good at what he did. He always felt confident with work. IT never let him down. His dad used to joke that he was more computer chips than boy growing up, and he wasn't wrong. Luke had loved technology for as long as he could remember. *I think it's how it connects us to people. It makes the world feel a little bit smaller, a little less scary. Dad always said that people were what mattered.*

Looking round at his surroundings right now, he could only agree. Getting out in the world, whether online or in person, was better than not connecting at all.

'Do you have a pen?' the client asked. Luke looked across at the bedside table, but it was empty bar a glass half full of wine from the night before.

The client was already chattering away. Luke looked around for a pen, padding around the room naked and trying to ignore the fact that his toes felt like they were going to shrivel up with the cold and drop off. Along with other parts of his body if he wasn't quick. He shuffled around as quietly as he could, one hand on his wedding tackle and one scrabbling in drawers, on the desk in the corner. Nothing. What kind of person didn't have pens? Luke got his delivered every month for work. He decided not to tell Becks that. She would only take the piss, call him a stationery nerd.

Whirling around, his head bent with the motion of pinning the phone to his ear using his bare shoulder, he saw Rebecca's bedcover was lying half over a piece of paper. Frowning, he lifted the sheet and saw a competition form sitting there. Completed, in Rebecca's name, for the Alpine Challenge. Wow. She was entering! The client hadn't drawn breath yet, and he was forgetting points already. Looking away from the form, he pulled open the drawer and found a biro. He didn't want this job to take all day. Rebecca had told him that she wanted to take him somewhere after work, and he had no ruddy intention of being plugged into the matrix all night.

'Yes!' he shouted, brandishing the pen in victory. The client stopped talking abruptly. 'Sorry about that Steve, just very excited here at the prospect of these changes!' He spied an empty white windowed envelope and wrote across the back of it. They chatted for a few minutes, and placated and happy now, Steve ended the call. Luke dropped the phone onto the bed, taking a deep breath as he waited for his heart rate to return to normal. That was not a nice, easy start to the day, and they'd both stayed up late last night. He was feeling it today. Putting the pen back in the door, he started to put the things back into the drawer, feeling bad for rummaging in Rebecca's things. It was weird how comfortable they had gotten with each other already. He'd never felt so close to someone he was interested in, and he'd had relationships longer than a package holiday before. He knew that this was different somehow. He made sure that the drawer looked untouched, and sat down on her bed. A second later, he got back up, realising he'd just sat naked and cold on her new sheets. She would know, the woman was like a bloodhound. Smiling to himself at the thought of Rebecca, he looked back at the entry form. It was just sitting there on the bed, all filled in. Picking up his phone, he gave the form one last look, and headed for the shower.

When Luke got back from the competition offices later on, she was waiting for him outside Fir Tree Lodge, ready to ski. Boots on. He spotted her immediately, his face lighting up as he walked towards her. It was dusk, the slopes were quietening off, the colder air sending the families indoors for warm baths and early nights.

'Wow,' he said simply. 'Is this your surprise date?' *She really is healing.*

Rebecca shook off the last of her nerves.

'Yep. You put your forms in?'

'Eh?' He looked behind him, as if the offices were standing right there. 'Er yeah, all in. Shall I get changed?'

They headed out and Rebecca didn't say much for a while. He followed her lead, and he could tell that she was being cautious on his behalf, taking an easy route out to where there was space to be alone. They took things really slowly, till she came to a stop at the side, pushing her skis out and sitting down on the snow. Luke followed suit. Well, he aimed himself in that general direction and she caught his legs and pulled him to safety.

'You okay?'

'Yeah, I'm good.'

They took their headgear off, pulling up their fur hoods around them. He shuffled across awkwardly, putting his arm around her. She settled into his side, her head on his shoulder.

133

'Look at the view,' he marvelled. It was great here. Every time he looked around him, he couldn't believe it was real. It looked like a painting.

'Still takes my breath away every time.'

He smiled, holding her that bit closer.

'Back in the bubble,' they said in unison.

'What?' Together again.

They both sat up, looking at the other in shock.

'What did you say?' they said together yet again, before laughing at each other like maniacs for a full five minutes. This led to high-fiving, more laughing, and then a fair bit of kissing. They snogged each other's faces off till they couldn't feel their lips anymore, and they laughed about that, making silly noises with their icy lips.

'It is like we're in a bubble though,' he said eventually. 'Whenever we're together, I feel like we're just on our own, and everyone else just kind of . . .'

'Melts away?' she finished for him. He kissed her again. He couldn't bear not to. 'I read the letter. Was it your mum?' She'd done nothing but think about it all afternoon. She'd barely been able to put her eyeliner on without jabbing her retina before their date. Dates with goggles demanded excellent eye make-up.

He couldn't see her face, so it made it easier to answer her. She'd surprised him. She had a habit of doing that.

'Yeah,' he said. 'She was like you. Loved the snow.'

'Is your dad in a bad way?'

He nodded, and she looked up at him when he didn't speak.

'I'll help you, you know. Hans is great, but another pair of skis won't hurt. When it's quiet.'

Luke felt himself relax for the first time that evening. Properly relax. Having a night like this, a week like this, was amazing. He was loving every moment, but the gnawing knot in the pit of his stomach had still been there. It had been there since the moment he'd gone to change for the offices, and seen Rebecca's entry form on the bed. The drawer was shut, it was filled in, signed. He had literally been about to walk out of the door and take his form to the same office. It had felt so easy. No drama, no stress for Rebecca.

But it was a risk.

'Are you sure you're up to it, giving me lessons? I think we've established I'm not a natural out on the slopes,' he asked her now, dropping a little kiss on her nose. He hoped to God she said yes. It was too late to take back now.

She reached up and put her hand around the nape of his neck, slowly pulling him in. Her eyes were on his.

'Yes.' She touched her lips to his. 'I want to help.' He went to open his mouth, to check she wasn't just toughing it out, but she kissed him again and he forgot his own bloody name for a second. He thought his skis might curl up with his toes at one point. 'And I call bubble. No more talk.'

Luke looked at her and nodded his head.

'Bubble. Now kiss me again.'

Chapter 9

Saturday morning, and Frank was awake as usual. Dante would be coming into his room any moment, to open the curtains and make him get out of bed. Frank lay there, slowly trying to wake his body up. Some parts of his body still felt alien to him, as though someone had removed a limb and replaced it with another. One that didn't connect with his body. His left arm was a dead weight when he'd come to. Dante's face gave him away whenever he looked at it, lying there on a cushion. Frank looked at it himself now. His wedding ring was still on. They'd tried to take it off in the emergency room, worrying about swelling and circulation. He didn't let them near it. His right hand was still strong enough to slap a doctor or two if they got a bit close. That ring had never been off his finger, and he wasn't about to let them take it now. He wanted to be buried with it, with his wife. She was still wearing hers. The funeral home had offered him it, at the time. He'd booked all the appointments for the same day, wanting to confine the misery to one horrible twenty-four hours. He had a son to raise now, and he was not going to let his beloved wife down.

He still remembered sitting there in the draughty old council offices, a tiny bundle in his arms. His son slept on, full to the brim with formula milk and oblivious to the fact that they were there registering his birth, and his mother's death. It was just too sad for words. Even the registrar took a break halfway through. He could hear her sobs in the little side kitchen next door. When he got to the funeral home, and they asked about the ring, he declined. He wanted it with her. To be honest, if he could have got in there with her himself, he would have. In a heartbeat. Anything to avoid the sheer gut-wrenching pain of missing her, and knowing he could never get her back. To just close his eyes and surrender, that would be sweet relief.

Then his son had woken up, with a little chicken squawk as he opened his beautiful blue eyes. When Frank looked at him, he smiled through watery, tear-filled eyes.

'Hello, little man. You awake?' He could hear the registrar pulling herself together, splashing her face in the sink. 'We're having a horrible day, I know, but it will get better.' The little pair of eyes opened a little bit further. Frank leaned in and kissed his son on the top of his head.

'Truth is, the bad days are all we have for now, but it won't always be like that.' He thought of the plans they'd had, and his resolve hardened. 'We will have adventures, you and I. We shall see the world.' His smile dimmed a little. 'Your mother was the wild one, you know. I never quite understood what she saw in me. The adventures were her idea really.' He thought of how carefree his wife had been, how full of life. She'd never showed any fear, on the slopes, in life. Not even in the delivery room, when things started to go bad. She kept her bravery till the end, but then it was snuffed out. Now, looking down at this tiny human, totally dependent on him now, his chest clenched tight. He had to protect his son. That was his new life.

As the registrar click clacked back into the room, giving them both her best professional smile, Frank made his mind up. He would love this little baby enough for the both of them, and never let anything happen to him. Ever.

His leg flinched as he moved in the bed now, feeling frustrated. He wished he could go back, shake the sad little lump that he was out of his melancholy. *It's too late though. My boy is grown, and I'm stuck in this bloody bed.* His memory was much clearer, but his anger was still there. His frustration. It had lessened, but only to conserve energy. Frank had never felt so tired before. Well, he had once. When he'd walked through the doors of his house, the one he still owned, a new father and a widower, all in one day. The weeks and months that had followed that day were one big blur now to Frank, but he remembered the small details. The registrar office. The little white romper his baby son had worn at the funeral. Frank hadn't let him out of his sight that day. The cards, letters and Pyrex dishes of food left on his doorstep, the packs of nappies for the baby. Marilyn, the woman who owned the sandwich shop, and had been their friend for years. His friend for long after. She was the annoying woman who waggled the fake pot at him. She was there at the accident, he felt sure. She was the one that held his hand.

She was raising her boy alone too, and the two had bonded over the years, at the school gates and in the shop. She would be here at the hospital too, after the shop was closed up. She'd come through those doors, smelling of sandwiches and perfume, all smiles and nervous jokes to fill the silence he left around him. He hated talking, he'd been practising on his own, when he could make sure no one would hear. He sounded a little drunk, his mouth still slack on one side. His arms were improving, but only because he did the bare minimum of the treatment they offered him. He knew he was wasting their time, but he just couldn't help it. He wanted them to give up. He'd even flipped them off once, but they all just clapped him for the achievement. The cheek of it!

He had nothing to go back to really. His garden would be too much for him now. He wouldn't even have his trips to the sandwich shop anymore. His car was a write-off, and given his current state, he could imagine the DVLA wouldn't be too pleased to hear he was back on the road. He'd be stuck in the house, and that didn't interest him anymore. When he thought of home he thought of the dread it managed to evoke in him even now. He didn't want that life, so it was time to just shuffle off. He'd done what he said he would. He'd raised their son to adulthood. He would understand, one day. Maybe. Or maybe he would just repeat the pattern. Maybe he'd be in his house all alone one day, wondering why he hadn't said yes to more things. The thought of that made Frank want to cry all over again. Looking down at his hand, he saw that he was half clenching his fist. He focused on it, thinking back to what made his hand curl in reflex. Luke. The thought that he would be alone, like Frank, but worse. He pictured Luke in their house, rotting away with memories of his long dead parents all around him. His fist clenched a bit tighter. There, he could do it. He just didn't want to. They should just discharge him, give the bed to someone who wanted the chance to live.

He heard a commotion outside the door, and for a second thought he'd heard Marilyn. Maybe he wasn't as awake as he thought. *Good, sleep is good. Take me now, Mr Sandman.*

'Dante, come on love, my lad's at the shop, and the new shop girl rocked up in a low-cut top this morning. I want to know that the place will still be standing when I get back. Has he said anything yet?' Dante's voice was deep, but muffled outside the door, and he heard Marilyn huff and tut loudly. 'The stubborn bugger, I tell you. I will deck him one of these days!'

Frank laughed and turned it into a cough. The voices outside stopped, and the door opened.

'Good morning, Mr Sunshine!' Dante trilled, his legs entering the room half a minute before his smiling head. Marilyn trotted him after him, a tablet in a black case in her hands. 'How are we this fine Saturday morning?'

'Not time,' he pushed out, pointing with his finger square at Marilyn. Her eyes widened, and Dante flashed her a warning look.

Yes yes, the old dog learned a new trick. I also know my ABCs. He turned back to the window.

'Well, Marilyn here has special permission. She has brought someone who wants to talk to you.'

Frank turned to the door, but it was closed. 'Not time,' he said, feeling like he was showing them the whites of his eyes. He didn't want any bloody visitors. He wasn't even dressed. It wouldn't be Luke anyway.

'Well, this visitor has a pretty busy schedule these days.' She brought the tablet over, pulling open the case and clicking on an app. 'Just give me a second.' She frowned, and lifting up the sleeve of her top, she squinted at some writing on her arm. *The woman's as nutty as ever.* Frank laughed just once, and she studiously ignored him. Dante left the room, and when Frank looked, there was no one outside. What was this, a pointing game or something? He'd watched enough kids' TV growing up. He wasn't about to follow a C-bloody-beebies phonics program. The app popped up, and she rested the tablet up on its stand, on his overbed tray, facing Frank. Frank looked at the screen, and a call popped up. Quick as a flash, Marilyn pressed the button, and the screen went white. A pure brilliant white, with a bluish hue.

'Are we on?' a voice asked. Frank's eyes welled up. His lips pressed together as best they could now, and his lower one trembled. *My son. My boy. My life.* Marilyn leaned forward into the tablet, and she spoke into it as if she was an air traffic controller.

'We can see you! Go ahead!'

'Dad,' the voice began. 'I know you told me to go away, and carry on with my life, but when I went back to get your paperwork, I found Mum's list, and the plans.' Frank swallowed hard, and his eyes never left the white of the screen. It shook slightly, and he realised that his son was holding the camera. 'I get why you never told me about it. I would have wanted to do it all, obviously, and you were scared. I get that now. I think you're still scared. We both lost Mum, but you gave up too, Dad. I let you give up, in a way, cos I didn't know any better. I never really knew the Frank you were when Mum was here. You've got to fight Dad. Marilyn, he still listening? His blood pressure okay?' Marilyn was tearing up, and her voice broke when she laughed. 'He's okay.' She smoothed Frank's hair, and he flicked his eyes to her. 'Keep watching love.' Her touch was unexpected, unwanted even, but he felt a little jolt when her hand made contact. Maybe she wasn't that irritating. She did smell nice too.

Frank turned his eyes back to the screen, and the white changed. The camera zoomed out, and there, standing right in front of a snow-covered mountain, was his boy, clad in skiwear, a big smile on his flushed happy face. Frank felt a sob block his throat. He looked just like his mother.

'The Sommersbys are in France Dad!' Luke shouted, and a woman laughed in the background. 'I am skiing, the first thing on Mum's list. Second, enter a competition. I entered the newbie challenge today! Hans says hello by the way.'

Frank muttered, 'I'll kill him' slowly under his breath, and Marilyn grabbed him by the chops and landed a quick smacker on him. Frank spluttered, but not for long.

'Keep going Luke, he's moaning!'

Luke laughed, and looked intently at the camera. Making a 'come here' gesture with his hands, he said, 'Come here woman.' The camera shook for a second, Luke standing there with a huge grin on his features.

'Come on!'

The camera moved from side to side again, saying no and he chuckled.

'Chicken,' he challenged the person holding the camera, and the camera shook with laughter.

'He looks happy,' Marilyn whispered in his ear, and Frank nodded, a tear falling down his cheek.

141

'Come on, don't keep me waiting!' Luke said again. His face was lit up, Frank noticed. He'd never seen him looking so full of life.

The camera was still shaking.

'Yes!' he insisted.

The camera repeated the motion. Luke laughed, and put out his arms wide.

'Come to me now, or lose me for ever!' The camerawoman groaned, but the screen showed she was trudging through the snow towards him. She flicked the camera down once and they could see she was wearing a pair of skis and laughing her head off whilst telling Frank's son exactly what she thought of him. Luke was laughing too, and taking the camera, he turned the image till the two of them were standing in the frame. Frank gasped, and Luke nodded his head slowly, his smile broadening as he saw this girl blush.

'Yep Dad, you guessed it. I met a girl.'

'Ice?' Frank asked, and Rebecca laughed.

'Ice Rebel, that's me! Retired of course, apart from teaching your son how to ski with Hans. Hello Mr Sommersby!' Luke was gazing down at her as if he couldn't believe his luck, and Frank recognised the look. It matched the expression on his own wedding photo. The tears fell again, and Frank started to weep. The faces on the screen fell, and Luke turned the camera away, till it was just him. Frank could see that Rebecca was hugging him from behind. He had someone. He wasn't alone, he was out there. He was doing it. Frank couldn't stop crying.

'Sorry Dad, too much? Marilyn, get Dante, get Dante. Shit.'

Marilyn went to run for Dante, but Frank's hand moved. Slowly and shakily, whilst Marilyn watched in awe, he lifted the fingers of his strongest hand, fingers to his lips, and putting them on his heart, he blew his open hand at the screen. Luke started to cry then. Rebecca took the phone and held it in her hand, whilst Luke cried on her shoulder. Catching it, Frank watched as the Ice Rebel placed it over her heart and Luke's.

'Proud,' Frank said, punching his hand against his heart now. 'Proud . . . of you, son.' Luke turned to the screen, Rebecca kissing his cheek as he wiped his tears away.

'If I can do this, Dad,' he motioned around him at the scenery, flashing his dad another view of their ski clad feet, close together, 'you can too. Number two on the list, Dad. That's one that never quite gets done. You remember it?' Frank nodded, pressing his fingers as close to the screen as he could without touching it, toward his son's determined face.

Number two: we must be daring.

'Good. I get why you sent me away too, now. Number three on the list. We must protect the things we love.' Frank's face crumpled a little, but he nodded again, his fingers moving over the screen to be near to his only child, the song of his heart. Luke looked relieved, choked even, but then he pulled himself together and Frank saw a fire in him that he'd not seen before. Another genetic trait from his mother, no doubt. He wanted to see more. 'Now do it. I'll speak to you soon, okay? The tablet is for you, Marilyn picked it up from the shop for me. Ring me any time. Love you, Dad.'

Luke put his arm around Rebecca, and she melted into his side, smiling at Frank. The Ice Rebel, with his son. Who would have thought? At first, Frank had wondered whether his mind was playing tricks.

'Bye Mr Sommersby, pleased to meet you!'

Frank waved at the screen, making Luke laugh. 'He can't believe it's you,' he teased her, and she poked him in the chest.

'Shut up you,' she admonished, rolling her eyes. Just like Luke did. The two of them were like peas in a pod. It made Frank's heart swell in his chest.

'Bye Dad.' Luke smiled, and the screen went off. Frank sat and stared at it for a long moment, touching his fingers to the spot where his son's face had just been.

'Love you,' Frank said, and turning to Marilyn, who was

weeping like a washerwoman, he opened his mouth and said something he'd never said before. It took him a while, and a couple of words were tricky to get out, but Marilyn just waited patiently, her face lighting up with every new word he uttered.

'Get me out of this bed, Marilyn, I need to get out of here.'

Marilyn did a jumping twirl on the spot and running to the door, she yelled for Dante as if she was on fire.

'It worked, Dante, it only friggin' worked! Get me the washcloth too, he stinks to high heavens!'

Frank groaned, and looking at the tablet once more, he smiled. His little Luke, out in the world, just like his mother wanted all along. Now that would be worth sticking around a bit longer for. That was worth getting out of this bed and getting well for. He wanted to stick around. He hadn't broken his son, he hadn't made him a replica of himself. Frank realised that all along, Luke had been a mixture of the best of both parents. He had their work ethic, their love of routine, but more importantly, the same sense of adventure his mother had. Frank could see it now, as plain as day. He'd done his job. He'd raised their son, and now he was out in the world to be enjoyed. Reaching for the paper, he dragged it closer towards him. Flicking it to the sports section with a slow and shaky hand and a fair bit of cursing under his breath, he waited for his meddlesome and annoying friends to come back. He had a lot of work to do, and he'd wasted enough time already. He owed it to his son, and his late wife. Not only that, he owed it to himself.

Marilyn half ran into the room with a bowl and what looked like a car sponge. It was huge. Frank looked across from his paper, right at her, and smiled. It was lopsided, and he felt as though he might dribble a little from the corners, as he sometimes did, but Marilyn's returning smile told him that his attempt wasn't half bad.

'Ready?' she asked cautiously. Frank could see her grip tighten around the sponge.

'Ready,' he said. 'But only Dante washes my dangly bits.'

Marilyn's laughter rang out into the hall, and Dante smiled as he passed, wheeling a patient back to their room. These were the moments, he thought to himself as he went on his way. These were the moments that made his job worth all the struggles.

Rebecca headed to the ski lift after the call had ended, wanting to give Luke a minute to recover. His dad had looked pretty beaten down at the start of the call, but when he'd made that motion, that gesture of love to Luke, her heart had nearly stopped. That was personal to the two of them, she could tell by Luke's reaction. The fact that Luke had done it to her, it meant even more now. She couldn't be reading into it, could she? He didn't seem the type to have 'moves' like that. Robbie moves. She felt a bit panicked at first, that he'd shown that to her after a week of knowing each other, but none of this week was average. She was liking him more and more each day. The whole call she'd had a lump in her throat, a snowball of anxiety in the pit of her stomach. Not for her, but for Luke. She knew how much this call meant to him, how well it needed to go. Luke's dad had given up since the stroke, and sending Luke away was obviously something that he'd struggled with. The love between them made her think of her own mother, and the call she'd been putting off herself. Not all the paper grenades had been detonated yet either. She still had the competition entries to defuse. Luke had entered the day before, and he was so excited about it.

They hadn't spent a night apart since that first night, and today was the baby shower and the party after. Everything was ready, all the gifts had been delivered to the venue. The café was staffed for the day, and Rebecca had the weekend off. A whole weekend of skiing and seeing friends, with her hot new . . . lodgemate. Lover? Bunk buddy? Eugh. They didn't need a label, it was what it was. 'Not even known him a week but can't get enough' didn't have a box to tick next to it on any form. 'It's complicated' sounded like simplification. He'd showed her his list, and his plans, his worries about his dad just giving up. She'd shown him her scars, her emotional ones, and the physical ones. He'd ran his fingers along the surgeons' handiwork, the neat scars that showed how they put her pelvis back together, piece by piece. What he didn't know or hadn't thought of, was that people were waiting for her comeback. Expecting it even. Hell, Robbie assumed she was back on the circuit. The rumour mill was a good one, even if the shit they were peddling had no substance at all.

'Well, that went well!' He'd caught her up, a little less unsteady on his feet since the days with Hans, and the nights with her. She'd had him up on the sofa cushions, whilst she threw things at him. He had to keep his balance, his legs and arms ready. It was hilarious, but it worked. He didn't fall half as much now. It was less funny, but safer. His bum cheeks were still bruised enough. 'Did you see his face? He couldn't believe it. I really think that this is going to be the turning point.'

Rebecca smiled, but she didn't reply. If Frank was really going to fight to recover now, Luke would absolutely want to be beside him to do it. Once the comp was done, so were they. As much as she liked Frank already, she found that she couldn't truly be happy about the thought.

They waited for the lift, holding hands as they walked to the next available one. Sitting down, they both looked out at the view as they headed up.

'Beautiful isn't it?' She was looking out at the scenery around her. Luke looked at her.

'Sure is.' He squeezed her hand, their gloves knitted together as they neared the top. 'Thank you. I think my dad thinks I might be punching above my weight though in the girlfriend department.' He chuckled. 'I'm pretty sure we have a longer conversation coming about that one.'

She didn't refute his wording, she just let it hang there. Girlfriend. She hadn't been anybody's anything in a while. Did he mean to say that?

'And another one, about the fact that I just called you my girlfriend, and you said nothing. You didn't try to stab me, or push me off this thing straight to my death.' He raised his hands around his body when she turned to him. 'Oops, spoke too soon. Tell my dad I tried!'

She pulled his hands down. 'I didn't say anything to give you chance to take it back.'

'Pfft.' He pushed out of his lips. 'Not a chance. I think that's what we are, isn't it? I just wanted to slip it out there, not make it a thing.'

'But a thing is something that comes up and makes people need to have a conversation.'

'That sounds like a penis. Or a molehill.' He jabbed his finger at the mountains, making the chair shake. 'Or a mountain!' He clicked his fingers together, or tried to, at least, whilst gloved up. 'I didn't want to make a mountain out of a molehill. I just wanted to see what you thought.'

'So where does the penis come into all this?'

'Ahh!' He raised one finger. 'Well, that depends on your answer.' He looked down at his groin. 'Doesn't it, little Wilbur?'

Rebecca had no words. He laughed again. 'Don't take the mick. I was raised single handed by a man, he had his ways of getting around awkward words and conversations. He still mutes *Bake Off* when they say "moist".' Rebecca's lip twitched. He'd get on well with Hans and Holly.

'Please tell me,' she asked seriously, 'what part of all this is supposed to make me want to own up to being associated with you?'

They neared the top, and jumped off, skiing off to the side.

'All of it! Did you not hear the little Wilbur part?'

'Please, please, never say that again.'

'I won't, if you'll just say you'll be my girlfriend. I know that sounds like a twelve-year-old thing, but we are going to this baby shower today. People are going to ask me why I keep kissing you.

147

I don't think "I met her through a hairy pen pal" sounds good. I just want to know what to call you when they ask.'

Pulling down her visor, she gave herself a minute. Looking down the slope, she felt the usual thrill she had always felt before her accident. She looked back at him then got ready to push off.

'I tell you what, you make it to the bottom, without falling over.' She blew him a kiss, and off she went. 'And you're on! Catch me if you can!'

She could hear Luke whoop for joy halfway down, and she laughed her head off. If her mother could see her now. Tomorrow, after they'd been skiing, and the party hangover was gone, she'd call her mother. And she might even tell her about Luke. Fair's fair, and a bet was a bet. If she had a boyfriend at the end of this slope, then she should tell her mother. It made a change to say something she might actually be happy to hear.

Slowing at the bottom, she didn't need to turn around. She could hear him coming. At the top of his lungs, whilst coming to a very awkward and rather lucky stop, he was singing a Pussycat Dolls song, the one about having a hot girlfriend. She pulled her visor up, and looked around as the skiers around clapped and laughed. A couple of people took camera shots, she could see camera phones being taken out, and she looked around, but all she could see were people cheering them on. One of them shouted 'go Becks' and Luke came to her side. Rebecca flinched at her name, but tried not to react.

'Take a bow, Becks.' He nudged her arm, and she bowed with him, making them clap harder. 'Come on, let's go get ready for this baby shower. I have a hankering to decorate a onesie after all that hard work.'

He steered her back towards the café, and they took just a little too long to get ready. It was quite hard to get out of all the gear, after all.

* * *

148

'*We are late,*' she whispered to him as they headed to Hans's place. Luke was about to knock at the door when Holly opened it, looking even bigger on her feet now. She was wearing a loose floaty dress, and she looked amazing. 'It's your fault.'

'Whose fault?' Holly asked, hearing. 'This?' She put her hands around her bump laughing. 'This is your fault in a way. Who introduced me to Hans in the first place?'

'You did that?' Luke looked across at her, astonished. 'I never knew that.' He leaned forward, hugging Holly tight to him. 'You have my sympathy. You do look lovely though. Excited for today?' She went to take their coats, but Luke waved her off and took both of them to hang on the rail behind them.

Holly squeezed him tight. 'I am excited! Aww, why didn't you come over before Luke, I need you here. You're so polite and lovely, nothing like those two.'

Luke blew on his nails and polished them on his suit lapel. The suit, well. He looked gorgeous in it as usual, his glasses making him look like an extra from Suits. A hot extra.

'Why, thank you. I had to ski down a mountain to get a nice gesture from Rebecca this morning.' He prodded Rebecca, who was wearing her Eloise dress, the one with the flowers that she loved. She jabbed him right back with her elbow, balancing the nappy cake in her hands. He took it from her. 'I'll take this in, shall I?'

Rebecca glared at him, and he bent down, kissing her like he'd never seen a woman before. A slow, full of promise for later kiss. Pulling away, seeing her lust drunk face, he winked at Holly.

'She loves me really.' He headed in and Holly pulled Rebecca in for a hug.

'I think you do! Look at you!'

'Shut up, I know Hans has been telling you every little detail.'

'I know you know. The tag team beating you gave him was a little harsh I thought, but Hans can take it. And I told you so too! Thanks for all this. You shouldn't have.'

'Luke helped. He's a great ribbon curler.'

'I bet he is,' Holly smirked, waggling her perfectly shaped brows and giggling.

'Shut up, or I'll take my cake back.'

Holly pursed her lips together. It was good cake.

'Okay, I'll button it for now. Come see everyone.'

It all looked great, all set out in their home. People were milling around, plates and glasses in hand, having a go at decorating money boxes and making onesies. Luke was sat making one, chatting to others at the table. The women were eating out of the palm of his hand, and he didn't even realise. Typical Luke. He looked up, winking at Rebecca when he caught her eye. She smirked at him like a schoolgirl.

'You sure you're ready for all these people in your house, and tonight?' she asked her friend. Holly waved her off.

'Listen, it's nice to not be stuck on the couch watching *Friends* reruns on Netflix. I need the company.'

Holly led her over to Luke, saying hello to people as they milled through.

'Listen, the most interesting thing that's happened to me since this baby is Luke coming, so having a party to celebrate it all sounds pretty amazing. Ladies, Rebecca's here!' Rebecca felt a shove, and she fell forward. Luke caught her and pulled her onto his lap.

'Like it?' he said smoothly, showing her his handiwork. On the onesie was the café logo for Alpine Bites. 'Thought the little bugger should earn its keep early on. Bit of free advertising.'

He flipped the material around. In black writing on the back it read *I was conceived here.* He put it onto the pile of finished outfits.

'I'll let them enjoy that later.' He wrapped his arms around her, and she kissed him without even thinking about who might see. His eyebrows shot up. 'Look at you, all nonchalant.'

She kissed him again, and he kissed her back, lifting her up. 'Come on, let's go get a drink. Either that or find the make out station quick.'

'Damn, missed opportunity. Did the cake get here, did you check?'

She still couldn't believe that they'd made it and kept it secret. Luke had got one of Hans's friends to collect it and stash it there earlier. Another thing they'd done together. Luke's competition date was coming closer, but it still seemed a way off. She had plenty of time to enjoy things. Today was about being here and having fun. Tomorrow she could let her mother know she wasn't entering yet again, but at least a new boyfriend might cushion the blow back home. She could at least tell her mother that she filled the forms in this year, and maybe next year would be the one. She was feeling different lately. *That new resolve could get on the plane with Luke though, and fly away from me. Just like him.*

'Yep, all stashed in the back. Stop worrying now. Come on, let's get a drink.'

'Can I just ch—'

'Before you ask to check the c—'

They both laughed. Luke tapped her on the nose with his index finger.

'I knew it. I checked the cake, it's all intact. It looks amazing. Drink?'

Rebecca rolled her eyes at him.

'Drink.' Luke winked at her, and her anxiety just fell away. Today was a good day.

Later that afternoon, when the baby things had been cleared away and the caterers had taken over, Hans and Holly's place looked so different. Lit up, showing off the homely feel of the modern space, the atmosphere was more relaxed. Mina was sitting talking to Holly, and as Rebecca took a drink from Luke, she knew that they were talking about her.

'My ears are burning.'

'Mine too,' Luke came and sat next to her on the sofa. They had a good view of the front door, and the whole room. She was still a little on edge, although everyone had been nothing but happy to see her. A few raised eyebrows and shocked expressions, sure, but after hiding away for so long, she had to expect that a little. Hans had kept to his word, only people she still had in her life were there for the most part, and none of her old Robbie crew.

'No nasties lurking though, eh?' Luke said it as though he'd read her thoughts. 'I had a word with Hans.'

She shook her head. 'No, just friends. A few old acquaintances. What did you say to him? Did you threaten to kick him in the ankle or something?'

Hans was sitting at the other side of Holly, talking to some of his friends. From the movements he was making with his beer bottle, he was telling one of his terribly longwinded and incredibly boring jokes.

'No, I just told him that I didn't want anything to spoil the night. He feels the same anyway. You want any food? The rabbit is gorgeous, and the mini burgers? I've had about twelve of those suckers.' Luke scanned the room. 'I'm pretty sure the waiter's avoiding me.'

'I've had some.' She hadn't, she felt a bit too jippy in the tummy area to trust herself to eat yet. 'I'll eat more later.' That was in response to Hans's raised brow. He knew her too well.

'Listen,' Luke started. 'I actually did something a little stupid the other day, and I wanted to talk to you about it. It's been playing on my mind.'

The front door opened in front of her, and Rebecca choked on her drink.

'It's not that bad, it's totally fixable. I just saw it, and—'

'Robbie.'

Luke frowned, his eyes darkening. 'No, this has nothing to do with him. Not one thing about this to do with him.' He downed his drink grumpily, and Rebecca touched his arm.

'No Luke, Robbie.' She shrank back in her seat behind him, pulling him back with her. 'He's here, at the door.'

Robbie was standing there, talking to one of the partygoers. Evan. He was a nice guy. Rebecca had got the impression before that he wasn't one of Robbie's biggest fans. She wondered idly if they were friends now. She didn't know who Robbie hung out with these days. She hadn't wanted to know either. Evan looked a little uncomfortable, but chatted back to her ex and turned his back to Rebecca, shielding her. She glanced across at Holly and Hans, but they were still laughing with Mina.

'Luke, we need to go.' She went to stand up, and Luke tensed at the side of her. 'Luke, I'm not scared. I don't care about him at all. I just don't want a scene.'

A second later, Luke took her hand in his and they stood up, heading to the back patio doors and the outside. As they pulled the door curtain closed a little and headed out into the night air, Rebecca glanced back. Robbie was still talking to Evan.

'We left our coats inside, you got your bag?' Luke asked as they felt the cold air hit them full in the face.

She shook her head. It was with their coats on Holly's bed now.

'Shit.' He kicked the ground in front of them, crossing his arms in front of himself. His white shirt was long sleeved, and he came and rubbed his hands down her arms, trying to keep her warm.

'We can't stay long out here. Why did he come?' Rebecca kept an ear out, but the place hadn't exploded yet. *Thank God for Evan.* 'Hans would never have invited him.' *The photos.* 'He saw it online, didn't he?' She looked at Luke, and he was already on his phone.

'Nothing I can see online,' he said, scrolling through his notifications. Rebecca took the phone from his hands, and brought up her own Facebook profile. There it was – a photo of the pair of them, bowing on the slopes that morning. Somebody had put it online, and then someone else had tagged her in it.

Luke's eyes narrowed when he saw the screen. 'Nosy calculating bastard.' He glared at the house, as though his laser eyes had come back, and he was trying to pop Robbie through the walls of Hans's home.

That had to be it, the photo. Robbie knew enough people to get wind of Hans's get-together. He still knew her well enough to know that she would be at any party of Hans's. He'd come to fan the flames. Taking the phone from Luke, she scrolled down to the comments. Lots of people commenting on where she'd been, who Luke was. Why she was 'back' in France. They thought Robbie and her were maybe back together. Someone had even asked whether she was involved with both men. 'Where do they get off, talking about a stranger like that? This makes me sound like the village bike.' She removed the tag, deleted it from her timeline and blocked the random poster for good measure. He'd done enough damage with his bloody snapping.

'Mountain bike,' Luke quipped.

'Luke!'

'Sorry, bad joke. It's a defence mechanism. I'm mad too, but we're not standing out here all night freezing to death because of him, or any of those keyboard warriors.' He took his phone back and headed back inside. 'Come on.'

As they neared the doors, Rebecca saw Hans at the other side. He was still talking to Holly and Mina, but she could see that Evan was losing the battle of distracting Robbie. He was alone too, sans whatever girl he was boinking at the moment, which meant he was on a mission.

'Want me to go get our stuff?' Luke asked, pausing by the door. He didn't take his eyes off Robbie. Just as she was going to say, *Yes, please ninja in and sneak back out so we can run back to the café and hide under the covers*, Hans spotted Luke, and clocked what he was scowling about. He must have looked like an angry bear, growling and fogging up the glass with his breath.

'No, we'd better go in.' They walked in just in time to stop Hans from getting up. Luke jumped on him, pinning him to the huge corner sofa. Mina smacked Luke on the behind as he went past. 'Hey, watch the drinks!'

Luke snuck in between Hans and Holly, checking on her like

a midwife. 'You okay, no crowning or anything?' Holly elbowed him, laughing.

'No crowning, gross! What's wrong with you?' Hans tried to stand up, and Luke sat on him again.

'Hans?' Rebecca was barely audible in the room, but Luke heard.

'Bec, come and sit down,' Luke said, breaking into her dazed thoughts. Robbie was on his way, Evan mouthing sorry at them. Rebecca sat down, Mina moving up for her.

'Oh God, not again,' Mina said, clocking Robbie a second before he stood before them. He pulled an envelope from his jacket pocket, smiling at Holly. Hans looked like he wanted to murder him, but he stayed where he was. Luke was clinging to him like a rider would a rodeo bull.

'Congratulations to you both. Evan tells me it's a boy!' That was a bit of a moot statement, given that the 'it's a boy' banner was still up outside, after their announcement that afternoon. No one said anything. Holly was looking at him as if he'd rocked up in a chicken costume to a vegan party.

'This is for you.' Robbie offered the envelope to her, but she didn't move, so he put it down on her leg and left it there. 'So, we all ready for the competition? Becks?'

He addressed her directly now, all small talk gone. Rebecca looked him in the eye, and glared at him.

'This is a private party Robbie, you weren't invited. Don't cause a scene, for once in your life. Just leave it alone.'

Mina made an 'uh-huh' sound in her throat. 'Be nice, given the other night. Give it a rest, Robbie.'

'Right yeah, big bad Robbie. Left his girl all alone in the hospital, whilst he went off on tour. I know, I've heard it all before. Except I didn't leave her, she left me. She checked out of life!' He jabbed in her direction wildly. 'And now you're back, good as ever.'

'Pretty much,' Luke said. 'Now, please just leave it. I don't want to ruin another shirt. And I am not spoiling Hans and Holly's night.'

'And you're here. Perfect.' Robbie rounded on him like a snake would a rodent. Except in this case, Luke wasn't the sly rat. 'Not dumped this one yet then.' He thumbed in Luke's direction, his eyes fixed on his ex. 'Not engaged to him, are you? That's more your style, quickie engagement before the comp and then sack the lot off after.'

The stunned faces around said it all, and Rebecca lost her temper. She could feel her face flushing with the shame of being outed in the room, but looking back now, she wasn't quite sure he was the injured party after all.

'No, no engagement. I'm not that stupid. Once was more than enough. Tell me, how much did you make from *my* accident in the end? Enough to get right back on tour after, eh? We shared the same agent Robbie, don't bother lying. I bet no one can tell the difference with you anymore anyway.' Luke was there, still holding Hans down and supporting Holly, but he was looking at Robbie as if daring him to make a move. His eyes were shark-like and slit almost shut. She touched his leg, and he moved to sit near her. Holly shuffled into Hans's side.

'Don't you dare move,' Holly whispered theatrically to her husband. 'Baby trumps dickhead.'

Hans scowled but put his arm around her and kissed the top of her head.

'Leave, Robbie, you weren't invited for a reason. No one cares.'

'Really?' Robbie still didn't take the hint. 'I think they will, everyone loves a comeback story, eh Becks? Ex-lovers, fighting it out for the title. Not bad, eh? I can hear the merchandise money rattling in the tills already.'

'I told you,' Rebecca spat. 'Not this year.' *Or any year at this rate.*

'Why wait till next?' Robbie jeered. 'Why else are you here? Can't seem to figure that one out yet, but the gossips online soon will. Seen your Facebook lately?' he sneered. 'I won't have to wait till the line-up announcement, I bet.'

Rebecca's eyes flicked to Hans. He nodded at her as if to say, 'take him down.' She glanced at Holly, but she was cuddled up to Hans, looking relaxed.

'You don't need to wait,' she said, pulling herself up off the sofa, and standing in front of him. Luke was right there with her, his hand still in hers as ever. 'I'm—'

'All in,' Luke broke in. 'Competition entries have gone in, she's ready. She's even been teaching me a few things. I entered the novice one. Looking forward to it, aren't we Rebecca? Hans, Holly, it's been lovely but—'

'You entered together? What's the point?' Robbie scoffed. 'You're hardly in her league, are you?'

Luke's jaw clenched.

'Robbie, shut up.' She couldn't feel her face. 'Sorry, Hans, Holly. Ring you tomorrow.'

They got past him unchecked, for some reason he was more interested in eyeballing Luke. The two men shuffled around each other like dogs on a lead, not knowing whether to bark or bite, or both. Rebecca couldn't do anything but walk away, trying not to run. She was waiting for Luke to say something, but he was so quiet. Maybe the ex showing up again was a bit of a mood killer for boyfriends. She wasn't feeling quite so bright and shiny herself.

'I don't get you Becks, I really don't.' Robbie was standing there now, addressing the room, not just her. He was in full influencer celebrity mode, she'd seen enough of his YouTube videos back in the day to realise now that he wasn't addicted to the danger, or the sense of achievement you felt when you went out there and did your best. He was addicted to the byproducts – the fame, the hangers on. If he could film himself now, working up to his big monologue, it would already be livestreaming. They were almost at the door. She could feel Luke almost vibrating with anger at the side of her, and she knew he was holding it in for her. To get her out without causing a huge scene or make her look even more of a spectacle than she felt already. He was so angry with Robbie, had said so many times how he couldn't believe anyone could be that calculating. His anger made her question her own, or lack of it.

'See you soon then, Becks! Looking forward to seeing you on the slopes.'

Stopping at the door, she pulled away from Luke's hand and walked through the rest of the party guests to get to Robbie. His smile faltered a little, and she leaned in, pushing her index finger deep into the middle of his chest. She wanted to poke it all the way through, take that swinging brick of a heart out of his chest and stamp on the bloody thing till it was dust.

'You can tell people what you like, you can play the jilted loving fiancé, but we both know,' She leaned in closer still, 'You were out of this the minute my body hit the deck. You just wouldn't admit it. The fact is Robbie, it took all that for me to see just what a shallow, fame-hungry, little div you are. Luke is three times the man you are, without even trying.' She smiled then, her fears fading as she took in his shocked expression. 'The best thing that ever happened to me was that ski breaking. It took me till now to see that. I'll see you out there. If you can get close enough—' she drew herself tall, making her voice that little bit stronger '—you can eat my snow, Robbie. I'm done with you, and I don't care who knows it anymore. I know the truth, and so does everyone here. Carry on with your childish little stunts, and the rest of the world will too. You're not the only one who had a platform, remember?'

She turned on her heels to walk away, but Robbie grabbed her wrist. She heard Luke suck in his teeth behind her, and she wrenched herself out of Robbie's grip, holding out her hand behind her to stop Luke from coming over. She needed to do this herself. Look him right in the eye.

'Don't you ever touch me again. I'm leaving now. It's over Robbie, it was before Canada.'

Robbie's face fell a little more, and she knew she'd finally hit home. He wasn't a monster, he was just addicted to the buzz. She was addicted herself at one time, to the feel of the snow beneath her feet, the adrenalin when she rushed down the mountain. It had been all she'd cared about for so long.

'I . . .' Even Robbie was stuck for words. The party atmosphere was one of stunned silence, but Rebecca could see that Hans and Holly were both smiling, and when she looked to Mina, she gave Rebecca a thumbs-up, brushing a tear from her face like a proud mama. Christ, she'd even taken Mina down. 'I don't know how we got here,' Robbie muttered. It was the first honest thing he'd said.

'We are where we're meant to be Robbie, moving on.' She looked over her shoulder at Luke, who looked like he was about to burst into tears himself. His eyes were blazing with emotion, and she smiled at him, lifting up her hand.

'Luke, take me home.'

'You were amazing,' Luke marvelled as they lay in her bed, hours later. The lights were dim, one bedside lamp showing off the shadow of her collarbone as he looked down at her. He was propped up on one elbow, their lower limbs wrapped around each other in a complex love knot.

'You weren't so bad yourself,' she grinned sleepily. *God, she's gorgeous. Robbie's right, I'm not good enough for her. I'll never stop trying though.* 'I think we broke the headboard at one point.'

He kissed her, and she touched her hand to his cheek.

'Not that,' he said, reluctantly pulling away. 'Tonight, with him. You put him in his place. I think you made him understand.'

She didn't say anything, just looked up to the ceiling.

'Yeah, but he'll soon have the last laugh, won't he? I'm dreading competition day now. I'll come for you and Hans, of course, but I might skip watching after you. I can watch the rest on the TV in the café. Holly can come down for the day, keep me company.'

She turned on her side and started to open the bedside drawer. Luke couldn't do anything but hold his breath. He'd done it. Just like he said he would. He'd gone and messed everything right up.

Reaching in, she pulled out some papers. The competition entries her mother had sent her. She thumbed through them, frowning and thumbing through them again, a bit faster now. She sat up, looking into the drawer.

'It's not there.'

She turned to look at him, the covers pulled around her, papers spread out on the bed in front of her now, discarded.

'What's not there?' Luke played dumb as long as he could. Maybe she'd give up looking. Maybe they could get through this night before reality hit. All the while he cursed himself to the heavens.

'The Alpine Challenge Entry form. I . . .'

Rebecca was staring at him now, her confusion and trust breaking his heart. He'd done it. He'd gone and fucked everything up.

'After we spoke to Dad, when we came back from the mountain that night. I saw the form filled out.'

He waited and forced himself to watch the moment when the cogs all stopped whirring and she realised what he'd done.

'Luke, tell me you didn't hand it in.' She pulled the sheets around her tighter, closing her body off from him. 'Please, tell me you didn't enter me in the competition.' *Bingo. Survey says, you are going to get royally dumped, you idiot.*

'I'm so sorry. We'd been having such a good time, and when you were skiing, I don't know – I just thought you could get back on the horse.'

'Horse!' she shouted, her voice cracking as she struggled to place which emotion was surging through her with the greatest potency. She angrily brushed a tear away, pulling the covers off the bed and heading towards the bedroom door. Naked, Luke jumped up from the bed and blocked the door.

'Move! It's not a horse, Luke. It's a massive competition, on television, with everyone watching me and remembering the last time I jumped!' She tried to get around him, but he held her tight.

'But you told Robbie!'

'I lied to shut him up!' she shouted back. 'Why would you do this?'

Wrapped in the quilt, she couldn't do anything but kick out at him. She got him with a couple of elbow digs, but he didn't move. He didn't want her to leave. If she left the room, that would be it. He had to make her see.

'I'm sorry, please! Please.' He lifted his arms, letting her go but not moving from the door. She walked backwards, sitting on the edge of a bed like a sad burrito. He slid down the door and spread his legs out in front of him. 'I wasn't thinking about Robbie, I wasn't thinking at all, I suppose. I just thought it might give you a push.'

'This isn't about Robbie.' She didn't take her eyes off the floor. 'I don't need a push Luke, I'm done.'

'But why the entry forms though? I know you haven't competed, but—'

'You don't get it, do you?'

'I get that you're scared, but—'

'You get that, do you? Shattered bones before, have you? Have you hit the ground and realised that you are not going to come out of it in one piece before? No Luke, you haven't. I sat in a bed for weeks, left behind by most of the world. It's not a game, Luke. It's not for a trophy. I'm not scared, I'm just done with it.'

'The woman I saw out on the snow this week isn't done. I've been watching you. You are more alive on a pair of skis than most people are their whole lives. You shouldn't turn your back on that.' He wanted to push her, make her fight back. Why didn't she want this? It worked with his dad, why not with her?

'Turning your back on something is different than giving up. I'm not giving up.'

'Really? Why are you mad then? You just told a whole room full of people that you were entering, you looked for the form. Why are you so mad?' *She was making his head spin.*

161

'Because it was my choice Luke! Not yours! You went through my things, and did it behind my back! Why are you here anyway? For me or for your dad?' She stood up. 'You can't save everyone with a cute gesture and a big plan. I don't need saving. It's you that's lost. Please, just go back to your room.'

'I know I did wrong, Becks. I know that, but I'm an arse with only the best intentions for you. I'm not lost, I'm happy here. With you. I'll sort it out, I'll get the form back. No one will have to know.'

'It's too late, once it's in, people will know. Damn it, Luke. Just go!'

'No, please. Come into the lounge and talk. Just for a little while. I can't leave things like this.' He spied his pants on the floor, and quickly put them on. She didn't move towards the door, so he took a chance and sat next to her on the bed. 'I will never do anything like that again. I just thought that you were doing so well, I thought you'd be happy.' Hans had told him more over the past week, and he knew that she was well enough to ski. Hell, she could still compete. She just never did. 'I know someone who is stuck in a rut. I've felt like that pretty much my whole adult life, till I came here. I'm braver here, I want to do things, try new things. I want to show Dad that life isn't all bacon sandwiches and pottering about in the garden. No more playing it safe.'

Rebecca took her chance and walked out into the hall. Luke stayed right where he was. She went towards the lounge, and Luke waited for the door to slam shut. Hans would probably be here in five to escort him off the premises. He sighed, wishing he could talk to his dad, ask his advice.

'This was my life,' Rebecca started, standing in her bedroom doorway, holding up the photo album he recognised from under the coffee table. She sat next to him on the bed again, pulling an arm out of the sheets to turn the pages. Page after page of Rebecca, Rebecca and Robbie, Rebecca and Hans, Holly and her, Mina and Evan, a few other faces that Luke recognised from the party. Her

162

inner circle. 'Was. I still have the friends, the ones that counted in the first place. I still live here, I ski. You saw me. I'm fine.'

'Exactly! You're better than fine. I did wrong, I'm sorry, but you can do this, Rebecca.'

She threw the album to the floor. It landed with a loud bang on the wooden surface.

'How would you know? You've known me a week, Luke. Have you ever done anything that scared you, before your dad's accident?' He could feel his jaw clench. *She's hurting, don't bite.* 'You never did anything before this Luke, you said it yourself.' She was staring at him now, and he went to stand up. 'You've never watched everything you've ever worked for, all that you have ever been, crash and burn around you. That ski broke, and it might as well have killed me. To be honest, it would have been less painful.'

'Don't you dare say that in front of me. Ever again. Dad had a stroke, and he gave up. I changed that. I changed you, and you changed me. We're all here, trying! Let's do it together! Fuck Robbie, screw the competition! Do it for that! Do it for the girl in those photos. She's part of you Becks, she's a part of you and always will be.' She didn't say anything back to him.

'I'll go to my room, but this isn't over.' He stood up and started to walk to his room. He went to reach for her but she moved out of his grasp. She was just sitting there, still wrapped in the quilt, make-up streaked eyes making her look so beautiful, and broken. He'd really gone and done it now. He needed to let her cool off.

'Luke?'

He stopped and turned to face her. She wiped her face with a shaky hand and stood up tall.

'Yeah?' He held his breath.

'I want you gone when I get up. Don't contact me again. Go home Luke, spend time with your dad. It's where you should be. You never should have left. Some things are just over.'

Striding over to the bedroom door, she slammed it in his face, leaving him standing in the hallway in his pants, wondering what the hell had gone wrong so fast.

Stunned, he stood staring, and reached up to the wood. Putting his hand on the surface, he rested his head on the wood and sighed.

'Rebecca. I might not be perfect, but I am here. I would always be here. My dad sent me away. He made me leave the hospital. He stopped me from seeing him. I didn't leave him, I came here to help him.'

'Luke.' The voice sounded faraway and tired. 'You're leaving soon anyway. The competition is in less than two months. We're just ripping off the band aid early.'

'It was never going to end after two months, don't give me any of that crap.' He knew she was angry, but he'd felt like she wanted this just as much as he did. Didn't she? 'Open the door, talk to me please.'

'No Luke. Leave. I don't want to see you. It's done. The whole thing is done.'

Luke's fingers itched to touch the door handle, but he didn't move. He gave it one last try.

'From one coward to another, you'll have to face it sometime. And me. I'm not leaving, Bec. This isn't over.'

Rebecca didn't answer. He kept talking, telling her that she could do this, that he was sorry, that he was falling for her. She didn't answer again. When the sun started to come out, Luke reluctantly left her doorway, packed his stuff up and headed to Hans's place. Another person's morning he was about to ruin. Lovely.

Chapter 10

'Luke, phone.'

Rebecca pulled her hair away from her face, pushing her leg behind her to wake Luke up.

'Luke, phone!'

She recognised the ringtone. Hers. She scrabbled for it, the events of the previous night coming screaming back into her consciousness. That and the fact that she'd polished off her emergency tequila. The one she hid under the floorboards for emergencies of the Robbie level kind in the old days. Now, it had Luke's name written all over it. Jabbing at the buttons, trying to blow her unruly mop away from her eyes. Eyes that felt like they were glued together with sleep at this precise moment.

'Luke! Luke?'

'Who's Luke? Take your ear away from the camera, dear.'

Looking at her phone in horror, she saw her mother's smiling face. A face that stopped smiling as soon as it clapped eyes on Rebecca.

'What are you doing? Have you been crying?' She could see her face on the little screen in the corner, and she looked like a mad scientist had spent a wild night with Alice Cooper, and she was the resulting offspring.

'Yes. No Mum. What time is it?'

'Time you were up dear girl!' Her mother had her phone propped up on something on the kitchen table. Probably not the boob shakers. She reached for a cup of tea, and Rebecca could see that she was midway through a sandwich. 'You could have been out there this morning, getting all the practice you need!'

Rebecca tried to rub at her make-up, but just managed to smear it across her face. Her tongue felt like a hairbrush. Linty.

'Don't rub at your face like that dear. Use a facial wipe.'

Rebecca looked around her. No facial wipes. Just tissues from her weeping as quietly as she could whilst getting secretly shit-faced. Whilst the boy she liked slept in the next room. For the last time.

'Sorry Mum, my masseur doesn't come till eleven. I usually get rubbed down and spruced up then.'

Her mother snorted down her nose. 'Eleven! You'll be lucky. It's gone two here! Have you really been in bed this whole time?'

She put the phone down on the duvet, looking for the clock by her bedside table. It had been knocked to the floor. It was after three. Where was Luke? Had he gone?

Her mother was still chuntering away as she dived out of bed, covering the screen with her quilt as she ran in her nightshirt out of her room. His bedroom door was open.

'Rebecca, what the hell are you doing? Rebecca?'

Walking slowly into the room, she looked automatically to his suitcase, which he'd put under the bed. There was nothing but space. She didn't bother walking to the wardrobe. She'd told him to go. He'd gone.

Her mother's braying tones kept erupting from the heap of tear- and tequila-soaked bedding that she'd left her in. Walking like a zombie back to her room, she picked up the phone and sat at the end of the bed. Looking her mother square in the face, she listened to her go on.

'Where have you been! I have things to do you know. Mildred

from the paper shop on the corner? She brought me round a printout of your internet page thingy.' She waggled the piece of paper in front of the screen, pushing it closer and further away. *Cheers Mildred, you nosy old bag. You should stick to selling the news, not ruddy spreading it like glitter at a unicorn convention.*

'Can you see it? I can't get this ruddy thing to focus. It's you! You got papped again. Oh, I can't tell you how excited we were. Who's the new chap? Does he compete? He looks handsome in the photos. A bit Cary Grant, I thought. It's finally—'

'Shut up, Mum.'

It took her mother a whole minute to digest what Rebecca had said. Probably because no one had ever said it to her before.

'What did you just say to me?'

'I said, shut up, Mum. I can't take any more. No more. The guy in the photo? That's Luke. I've been shagging him, in my little café flat, for the past week. Yesterday, I told him to bugger off. This morning, he did.'

Her mother gasped like a fish, and for a second Rebecca hoped, nay, prayed that the connection had dropped on the line.

'Shagging? Luke? Week?'

'Yes Mum. Your daughter is a dirty little tramp, a washed-up old ski champion with a penchant for anything in spectacles and a sexy elbow patch. I met him a week ago, and now I'm pretty sure I've fallen for the huge dork, and I cocked it all up.' She looked at the screen, bursting into tears.

'Mum, I just don't want to listen to you talk about what a total loser I am, because I already knoooooow-woooo-woooo-waaa!' She dissolved into a full-on ugly cry, her words just little squeaks and snot bubbles. Her mother's face filled the screen, and she saw that she'd picked it up and was holding it close.

'Rebecca, come on. Don't do that!' Her mum patted the screen with her fingers, making it go haywire for a second. 'These bloody touch screens!' She jabbed at the screen, and Rebecca had stopped crying enough to see her mother come back into view. 'Don't do that. I didn't even know you were seeing anyone! Why didn't you tell me!'

'Because you don't listen Mum! You never do. You never listen to what I actually say. You hear what you want to hear.' She blew her nose on an old tissue from the bed, honking loudly. 'Oh, what's the point.' She flopped back on the bed, her head hitting the pillows. Taking the phone with her, her mother was still staring at her.

'I do listen Rebecca, but I worry about you.' Her face softened. 'This is the first time I've had any emotion but ignorance and pure anger from you in years.' Her mother went to the fridge and Rebecca saw her pull out a corked bottle of Chardonnay.

'Mum, day drinking is going a bit far. I'm not that bad.'

Her mother ignored her, taking a glass from the cabinet on her way back to the table. Putting Rebecca back resting on the prop, she slowly poured the wine to the brim.

'Bugger it, it's good for you now and again.' She took a deep sip and looked at the camera.

'Rebecca Daphne Atkins, I love you, but you are a huge worry for me.'

'Mum, not a lect—'

'I'm talking now, I have the talking glass.' She raised her glass and took another sip. 'When you were a girl, you wanted to walk. So badly, you didn't even wait to crawl. Do you know that? You didn't want to take that middle step, and you were like that your whole life. When my friends' daughters and sons were getting married, having babies, going to university, I used to look at you and think, she knows what she wants.'

Rebecca lay there, listening to her mother speak.

'You always knew what you wanted, till that day. You never needed an audience, you never wanted anyone to notice, you just loved it. When your accident happened, I felt like you died.'

Rebecca was stunned. 'I thought they called you, right after.' She realised that for the first time, she was thinking about how

168

her mother and father must have felt. Her dad never gave her any grief like her mother had, but he had treated her differently than before when they spoke on the phone. She never wanted them to come cheer her on, but they always watched back home. *If I ever had a daughter, and saw her go through that, well.* 'The team had your details, I made sure they called.'

Cecilia Daphne Atkins pulled the screen closer.

'You are my baby, my bright shining star, and you were hurt. Hundreds of miles away, on your own, without us. Your father nearly had kittens on the sofa. You didn't die that day, but I never got my daughter back. The last time we spoke before the accident, you were so happy. Excited for the future, the competition. After, I couldn't even get you to call me back. Robbie went AWOL. The man spent Christmases here, but he was just gone. Unavailable. What did you want me to do? You didn't want me there.'

'Why didn't you tell me how you felt?' Rebecca realised that she had been punishing her mother for trying to get her daughter back.

Cecilia smiled, her eyes filling again. 'Because you were shattered, my darling, I didn't want you to hate me any more than you already did. I just wanted you to try again, to be you. Whatever "you" was. I know I put you under pressure, but you never told me anything! I just wanted you to be happy again.'

'I saw Robbie,' she admitted, and her mother's face was a picture. 'He's come back for the competition. It didn't go well.'

Her mother sat back in her chair, filling her wine glass up.

'Your dad never liked him, you know.'

'Where is Dad?'

Cecilia thumbed behind her to the open patio doors that led out to the garden. 'He's in his man cave, banging about. He's in a mood, the football match didn't go well.'

Rebecca rolled her eyes, wincing at the pain it produced. It felt like a tequila worm was burrowing into her forehead with Doc Martens on.

'Typical Dad.'

'Yeah I know. I should have held out a bit longer before I married him. Could have trained him up a bit more.'

They giggled together, and Rebecca realised that this was the first conversation they had had in forever that didn't end up in an argument.

'I told him off. Robbie, not Luke. Well, I told Luke off too.' She looked towards the door, but he wasn't magically standing there. 'That's why he left. Why didn't Dad like Robbie, anyway? He never showed it.'

Cecilia took another sip.

'He put up with him because you were happy, or we thought you were.'

Rebecca pushed the air out of her lips with a pfff sound.

'He thought my accident was going to be the springboard for a whole new life, a life I never wanted. I just didn't want to anymore.'

'And now?'

Rebecca pursed her lips.

'Luke entered me into the competition. The Alpine Challenge. It's in seven weeks. He's in it too, novice round. He thought I needed a push.'

'Sounds familiar. Have you called him?'

Rebecca shook her head. 'Not yet. You woke me, remember?'

Her mother groaned.

'Again, only teenagers sleep till this time on a weekend.'

Rebecca opened her mouth to say something catty back, an old habit, but her mother placed both hands on the table and leaned in.

'Rebecca, I know it's been hard, God knows I do. I just want you to know, whatever you decide, it's fine with us. If you want to come home, start again, I won't give you any hassle.' Rebecca's snort said it all. 'I mean it love. Your dad and I just want you to be happy, that's it. I don't care if you're a ski champion, or a baker. I just want you to be you again. I miss my daughter.'

Rebecca welled up, and her mother sniffed loudly.

'I know Mum, I'm sorry.' Her mother blew a kiss at her, and it made her think of Frank, and Luke. Parents, they all had their little ways of making you feel connected. Loved. 'I love you. Tell Dad I'll call soon.'

Her mother wiped at her eyes, draining her glass.

'Woo, I needed that.' She grinned, and Rebecca grinned back. 'I love you, chicken. Can I say one thing?' She lifted her pinkie finger comically and made a begging face.

'Go on. One thing. In the spirit of our new mother – daughter friendship.'

Her mother's grin exploded then, bursting all over her face. 'I like that. Okay, here it is. Call Luke.'

Rebecca wasn't expecting that. Picking a man over a comp, and one her mum hadn't even credit-checked and had vetted by the secret service yet? This was new territory.

'You heard me say novice, right? He's entering it for . . . for fun, so he's not another Robbie.'

Her mother shook her head. 'Robbie never made you break down to your mother, dear. Your gran always said to me, "Marry the man who provokes the biggest reaction."'

Rebecca frowned, pulling a face.

'It's true, you know.' She looked behind her furtively. 'When I met your father, he made me so cross sometimes, so mad I could spit. He was my best friend, and my partner. The good bits, the life together, that's why people bother. Call him. You forgave me, right?'

She went to top up her glass once more, but the bottle was empty. She shrugged, reaching across out of reach of the screen, and coming back into frame with another bottle.

'Mum!' Rebecca laughed. 'Do not open that wine!'

She tucked it under her arm, grabbing her glass.

'I'm going to see your dad! I can have another.' Picking the phone up, she made a kissing action at the screen. 'I'm celebrating today. My daughter loves me, and she has a boyfriend.'

Rebecca kissed the screen back.

'Bye Mum.'

When the camera went off, Rebecca dialled Luke's number. It went to voicemail. *Shit.* She dialled Holly, and she answered on the second ring.

'Hi, you okay? I've been waiting for you to call. Hungover?' How did she know? 'Luke said he could hear you in your room, singing the tequila song.' Cringe. No wonder he'd left.

'Oh God. Is he there?'

'Er . . .'

'I was mad Holly, I didn't handle it well. Did you know he'd entered me in the competition?'

'I didn't till this morning. I told him off too, but he's really sorry. He was pretty upset Becks, he thinks you hate him.'

Rebecca jumped out of bed, ignoring the roil of her stomach as she tried to look around for something half decent to wear.

'I don't hate him, I . . .' She pulled a sweater over her head, not bothering to look for a bra. 'Oh look, can you keep him there? I'm on my way over.'

'No!' She had almost rung off but Holly's shout stopped her just as she was reaching for a pair of jeans. 'He's not here. Becks, I'm sorry. His dad had a fall today, doing physiotherapy.'

'Frank?' She shoved one leg through her jeans, and got halfway with the other one before realising that her back pockets were at the front. 'Is he okay?'

'Yeah Becks, Frank's okay. He hurt himself, but . . . Luke left.'

'Left to go where?'

Holly sighed, and Rebecca knew what was coming.

'He left on a flight an hour ago. Hans drove him to the airport. He's gone home.'

Chapter 11

'Luke!' Marilyn ran down the hospital corridor at him. 'What the hell are you doing here?' She grabbed him in a perfume-soaked hug, and he hugged her to him. A second later, he felt a clip around the ear. 'I told you not to come! What about Rebecca?'

She looked behind him as though Rebecca was going to pop out.

'She didn't make the trip. How is he? Dante is in there at the minute. He doesn't quit work, does he?'

'He was there when your dad fell. He blames himself, but he's doing better Luke. He's trying.'

Dante popped his head around the door, looking Luke up and down.

'Lukey boy, you look just like your dad. He's all ready for you.' He pulled a face at one of the nurses walking past, and she stuck her tongue out at him. 'The breakfast is gross here. I'm going to go get him something from the café before I go.'

'No bacon!' Marilyn checked, and Dante laughed.

'Fake stuff only, I know.' He lolloped off. Luke pushed open the door, and there in a room on his own, was Frank.

'Hi Dad,' he said, walking over to the bed. His dad did a double take when he saw who was standing at the door.

'Luke,' he said, clear as a bell. 'Here.'

He motioned for his son to come, and Luke sat on the bed and hugged his father tight. He could feel his dad's arms slowly close around him. He felt different, fragile in his arms. He patted his son on the back with his good arm. Just like he had since he was born.

'What are you doing here?'

Luke sat in front of his dad and checked him over. He had a dressing on, covering his newly stitched-up head, and a bruise on his cheek.

'I came to see you, obviously. You didn't need to headbutt the floor to see me though, you could have just called.'

Frank chuckled.

'Rebecca?'

Marilyn was standing beside Frank now. She nudged him, and he ignored her.

'Is she here?'

Luke kissed his dad on the top of his head and took a seat in one of the chairs next to the bed.

'That's a bit of a long story, Dad.'

'Well,' Frank said, settling down and patting the bed for Marilyn to sit down. 'We are here all day.'

Luke smiled sadly at them both, and started to talk about France, the plans and the girl in the Alpine café.

Chapter 12

Six weeks later – one week till competition day

'Mum, you're dying to ask, so just ask.'

Rebecca dumped the tray of burned croissants into the bin. It has half full of wasted baking. She went over to the oven, frowning at her error. Turning the oven down to the correct temperature, she checked on the fresh batch she'd just sent to a fiery death. Luckily, they might just survive with a bit of a tan. She needed to get some of it right, or she'd have nothing left to serve.

'Have you heard from him?' Her mother was looking at her from her phone, which was propped up on the chicken timer. She could see Dad in the corner, reading in his chair and pretending not to listen. The man had floppy ears that were dog-like, so she could see that he was earwigging. Every now and then, he'd turn the page.

'No. He's spoken to Hans a bit. His dad's getting better all the time, they're even talking about him going home soon. Luke's staying at his dad's I guess, or his place. I dunno.'

We're both alone. I know that. He'd been away from her a lot longer than she'd known him in life, but it felt like forever. On both counts.

'Have you tried to call him?' Her dad looked at the screen as his wife spoke, turning the newspaper page to cover his tracks. Rebecca wiped down the surfaces, clearing away as she went.

'No, and I'm not going to. I don't know what's going on with his dad, and . . . I'm still mad too.'

Her mother tutted loudly.

'Rebecca, if I hear that one more time! You were going to go to Holly's and get him back!'

'He broke my trust!'

'You told me you were already going to apply! You were going to send it in, weren't you?'

'No.' She crossed her arms, pouting like a teenager. 'Was not.'

'Yes you were, you told that bloody flash Herbert ex of yours you were! You could have corrected Luke at that party, you didn't for a reason.'

Rebecca stamped her foot.

'So!'

Her dad turned the page again and huffed, blowing the pages out. Rebecca rolled her eyes.

'The jig's up Dad, I can tell you're listening. Do you have something to say?'

He ignored her, turning the page again and suddenly looking very absorbed in reading.

'Dad, it's upside down.'

Cecilia turned to look at him, laughing her head off.

'You're such a berk, Mick! Come here!'

Mick, who was still in his dressing gown, put the paper down and came to sit next to his wife. She giggled, and he stuck his bottom lip out.

'It nearly worked. You're a berk,' he said this to his wife, who just laughed in his face.

'Oh, so you are listening. Tell your stubborn daughter to ring Luke!'

'Do as your mother says.'

'Not like that!'

176

'I did what you said!'

'You're a total berk Dad, but I love you. I can't call him, I don't want to bother him.'

'The poor boy is probably feeling very alone right now, sat at the hospital all those hours,' her dad retorted.

'Frank's not in a coma, Mum, he had a stroke. He's in recovery.'

'Still, it's not nice. You know that.' She bit her lip. Progress like that had been gradual all month, but now she was on a somewhat normal level with her parents. They even spoke every day, or rather she and Mum did. Dad was usually pretending to screw something into a wall, or grouting tiles in the background. Now, he sat right next to her. Progress.

'Hospitals are strange places. They hold so many emotions.' Her mum's voice went a bit floaty.

Mick looked at her, his face aghast.

'That line was on *Grey's Anatomy* last night!'

'Shut up, Mick! It was not!'

'Yes, it was! Her that was married to Derek what's-his-face said it to the other one.'

'It was not! Go back to your paper! You are no help!'

'No help! I'm here, aren't I?'

'Guys, I really need to get cracking. The café's due to open and I need to get changed.'

'Okay love, well ring him, okay?'

Her dad said something else, but the door opened and Hans came running into the café. He nearly took the door off and was halfway across the café before he managed to stop himself. He looked at her, startled, his beard and hair all over the place. He looked like a lion with serious bed head.

'Hans?'

Wild-eyed, he tried to speak. 'Bay! Bay!'

'What? Listen guys, Hans is here. Better go. Love you!'

She clicked off the call, shoving her phone in her apron pocket.

'Hans? What the hell are you talking about?'

'Bay! Bay!'

His needle was stuck. All he needed was a set of cymbals to bang together monotonously and the look was complete.

'Bay-beee! Car! Holly!' He jabbed his hands in the direction of the windows, and she could see Holly taking deep breaths on the back seat.

'Shit! Baby!' Rebecca said, twigging on.

Hans nodded, jumping and pointing at her. 'Baby! Fuck! Baby!'

'Okay, okay!' Switching everything off, she grabbed her coat and keys, running out of the door. A second later, she realised that Hans wasn't with her. She ran back in and dragged him out outside.

'Go to the car, I'll lock up!'

'Okay! Baby! Coming!' He dashed to the car, and she locked up, flicking the sign closed. She'd text for cover from the car. She ran around the far side of the vehicle, and jumping in, she reached for her friend's hand. Holly looked as gorgeous as always, relatively unruffled, if a little sweaty.

'You okay?' Rebecca asked. 'How bad is it, from walnut to watermelon?'

Holly squeezed her hand tight, making her nails dig into Rebecca's skin. From the look she was giving her, Rebecca wasn't quite sure that she didn't mean it.

'If I ever have sex,' she said vehemently, pointing to the back of Hans's head as he navigated their drive to the hospital, 'with that man ever again, shoot me. Please.'

Rebecca laughed, but it turned into a shriek of pain when Holly's grip tightened.

'Laugh again, and I'll rip them right off. You'll never bake or ski again.'

Rebecca sat meekly for a second. The car fell silent.

'Jesus,' Hans said. 'I'm going to be a father.'

They all smiled at each other then, catching Hans's reflection in the central mirror. Holly's contraction started to kick in again, and Rebecca lost feeling in her fingers.

'Yeah,' Holly said. 'Well, you're on nappy duty till he's twenty-five, so good luck with that! It'll give you something to do with all the sex we WON'T BE HAVING! Arrggghhh!'

Hans put his foot down, just a touch. He had to navigate down the mountainside and keep on the road with his nerves jangling, and Holly screaming for his testicles as tribute. It felt like another five years passed on that drive. When the medical centre finally loomed in the windshield, even the baby surely sighed with relief.

'That's my girl! Nearly there!' Hans said, being as supportive as he could.

'Shut up!'

'I love you!'

'Naff off!'

They took the side road, and the car park came into view.

Rebecca tapped out a couple of texts to cover the café and stop people worrying, and Hans drove straight into the car park.

'We'll never get a space Hans, drive to the entrance. I'll park up for you.'

Hans turned the corner. Luke was standing in front of an empty parking space. When he saw Hans, he waved him in, passing him a ticket through the open window.

'Thanks mate,' Hans parked up and scooping Holly up into his arms, he strode off to reception.

'Hans, don't you drop me on this floor!'

Holly had her arms around his neck, and he stopped for a second to kiss her on the lips.

'Not a chance,' he said softly, striding off once more as if she weighed nothing. 'Let's go have a baby!'

'Baby!' Holly shouted, pumping her fist up in the air as they left Luke and Rebecca standing alone. He looked behind him at the waiting wheelchair.

'I thought she might have needed this.' He took hold of the handles. 'Are you okay?'

'I have to go.' She was blindsided again. Luke was right here, being all knight in shining labour.

'Rebecca.'

'I'm Holly's birth partner. I have to go.' She headed inside, feeling her cheeks explode like a tomato. She felt like everyone was looking at her. *Why is he here?* She headed straight to where Holly was getting booked in. Hans was rubbing her back whilst she leaned against the counter. He saw her come up and gave her a sheepish look.

'Don't kill me yet, I want to see my son first. He came back yesterday. Mina put him up.' *Wow.* Mina hated everyone. She'd had him as a houseguest, even after bin-gate? Rebecca smirked. *Typical Luke. Lovely Luke. Lost to me Luke.*

'Here Holly,' Luke pushed the chair towards Holly, appearing at Rebecca's side, and he and Hans settled her in. A midwife came to speak to them, and before Rebecca knew it, she was walking away from Luke again, into the delivery suite with a nervous Hans. Just before the doors closed, she turned to look at him, but the corridor was empty.

It was a very different woman that emerged from that delivery suite. Rebecca felt like she'd been there a week, but everything had happened at warp speed. She'd seen things that she could never un-see, and she had a whole new respect for her own pelvic floor. She'd left the happy new family in their own little baby bubble and caught a cab back to Fir Tree Lodge.

Pulling up outside, she saw that the café lights were still on. Getting out of the cab, she dragged herself inside to see what the carnage was. Unlocking the door, she saw that everything had been squared away.

'Thank you, Eloise,' she said to the ceiling as she tried to uncrick her neck. Holly had a lethal headlock.

Heading to the flat door, flicking off the lights as she went, she heard the radio and felt a pang for Luke. He'd only lived here a week but this past month she'd felt like he was everywhere. She'd thrown herself into work, spent time with her friends, done more skiing than she had ever done. She couldn't get off the slopes these days, it calmed her. It was the only place where her heart didn't feel like it was being slowly crushed.

Locking up, she went into the kitchen. Flicking the music off, she took a bottle of wine from the fridge and poured herself a good measure.

'To you, little one,' she toasted, clinking her glass against the right boob shaker.

'Everything went well with the baby?'

She jumped, splashing half her glass down herself.

Luke was standing in the doorway. 'I didn't mean to surprise you. Eloise was pretty busy, I came to help. I told her I could finish clearing up, so she could get back to the kids.'

'You scared the hell out of me!'

'Sorry. Again. I'll go now. I made you a sandwich, in the fridge. I thought you might be hungry.'

She opened the fridge. He'd bought her some snacks too, the stuff she liked. She'd not even seen it before.

'Luke?'

He appeared again.

'Yeah?'

'Where are you staying?'

Luke shook his head. 'Not sure yet, to be honest, I was going to go to Mina's but—'

'She's a lot, isn't she?'

Luke looked relieved that he wasn't digging her out. 'A bit. She's not a fan of houseguests. Hans did say I could stay there, but with the baby, I don't know.'

'You can stay here.' She took a gulp of wine. 'It's Hans's place. They need their space, new family and all. It's just for a week or so right, till the comp?' Hans had filled her in post crowning.

Luke nodded slowly. 'Yes, I'm flying home the day after.'

181

That was that then. He was here for the comp. To finish what he and his parents had started. She couldn't find fault with that, as much as it saddened her heart.

'That's settled then.' She went to head to the bathroom, wanting to shower off the day and gather her thoughts behind the closed door.

'Are you sure? I wasn't—'

'I know you weren't asking, but Hans did say he would put you up till the competition. I'm sure we can manage to get through a week.'

'The first one was pretty good. With the baby and everything, I guess it will be awkward at Hans's.'

'Yeah, you wouldn't want that.'

'Yeah, nothing worse than feeling awkward around someone you care about.' He put his head down, and she took the opportunity to walk away.

'You off to bed already?'

It was only early, but she was exhausted.

'It's been a hell of a day Luke.'

'I know, I just . . .'

'You're here for the competition, right? That's what matters. Doing it for your dad. Night Luke.'

She heard him sigh as she walked past him, but she kept walking. All she could focus on was getting to the other side of the door before she broke and begged him to stay. There was no point. He'd betrayed her trust, just like Robbie did, thinking he knew what was best for her. Everyone thought they knew best. Just because he was right on this occasion didn't mean that it was forgotten. She wanted him, but she'd gone a month without him. She could live without him again. If she had to.

Seeing Hans and Holly together, cooing over their little bundle, that's what she should be focusing on. They would have their hands full now, and she needed to focus too. On the café, on her parents, on taking the next steps in her own life. The trouble was, the man currently sighing outside her bathroom door keep popping into her head, making her plans feel pathetic and one dimensional. Now he was back, it hurt even more. It was going to be a hell of a long week. The competition was looming, and she was fast running out of places to hide.

'She let me stay here, sure, but only because she loves you and Holly. She knows you need your space.'

Hans yawned into the phone. Luke was working on his laptop, debugging the website of a new client. The new sofa in the lodge looked really nice, but Luke found himself missing the old wine- and steak-stained one, and the sheets they'd draped over it. They owned furniture together, lived together again but this morning she had gone by the time he had woken up, and Eloise was working the café with a server he'd not seen before. No note, not that she had to tell him where she was. At this point, they weren't even friends. It made his heart ache. When Frank had suggested he go back, finish the competition, he'd said no. He didn't want to leave his side again, even if it was to see Rebecca. She hadn't called, but she'd asked about Frank. She cared, just not about him anymore. He'd let her down, and she had cut him out of her life. She was quite good at that, it seemed.

'I have had two hours' sleep, my friend, but you are still slower on the uptake.'

'What?' Luke scratched his head.

'Holly, tell him. Have . . . to . . .' There was a rustling noise, and Holly came on the line.

'Hi Luke, Hans is out cold. His son has a set of lungs on him.'

'Our . . . son, our son . . .?'

'Go to sleep. Did you speak to her yet?'

'No. She's gone off somewhere. Do you know where?'

Holly didn't answer.

'Holly?'

'Wha . . .? Sorry, dozed off. What did you say?'

'Do you know where Becks went, she's been gone all day.'

No answer.

'Holly, did you fall asleep again?'

The line was quiet for a beat, and then Holly spoke again.

'No, I just don't know whether to tell you or not. I just gave birth, my girl code radar's busted up.'

'Please, Holly! I will babysit whenever you like. Whenever!'

'You go home in a week!'

'So, FedEx the little guy over. He'll love it!'

'That sounds awful. And actually quite tempting, which tells me my instincts are definitely off. I can't do it Luke. Have you tried calling her?'

'Yeah, but I'm pretty sure she blocked me.'

'Typical Rebecca. Give her time, Luke. She's working through some stuff.'

'Did she say anything about me?'

'BOOP BOOP BOOP BOOP! Girl code radar's working again. I *definitely* can't tell you that. Talk to her Luke! You live together. Write her a note on the bathroom mirror for God's sake.' The baby started crying in the background, and Luke could hear a man-sized baby start to sob too. 'Listen, I have to go. Please, talk to each other. Try with Luke. No gestures, just talk! Hans, where are you going? Hans? HANS, THAT'S NOT THE TOILET! What the f—'

The line went dead, and Luke cringed. Thank God his ex-girlfriend had put him up. Awkward and heartbreaking as it was to be near her, it knocked spots off living anywhere else. It meant a chance, at least.

He tried to concentrate on his work again, before giving up and pulling some sticky notes out of his work bag. He picked up a pen and started to write. It was worth a shot. He was on his twentieth attempt when Hans sent him a text that had him running to the door.

* * *

184

'My question is also to you, Becks,' began Andy McNabb, the sports reporter for the *Post*. He gave her a courteous nod, and she nodded back. Andy was a good guy, she remembered him. Tough but fair. 'Given that Alpine Challenge is a brand new event on the resort's calendar, why this one? Why not one of the others, the ones you have already competed in, and won?' She could see Robbie flinch from the corner of her eye.

'Twice, in some cases,' she said into the microphone. She always did have the slight edge on Robbie. Andy and a few of the others in the room chuckled. They were in the main conference room of the hub of the competition centre, giving their press conference ahead of the event.

'Exactly,' Andy continued. 'Why this challenge, and why this year?'

A couple of latecomers came in at the back, and Rebecca took the moment of distraction to find her voice.

'The Alpine Challenge is fresh, it's new, and it has no winners and no losers. It's a clean blanket of snow for every single one of us.' She looked down the table at her competitors, making eye contact with each one, and leaving Robbie till last. 'What went on before is irrelevant. The past is the past.' She addressed the reporters once more, the clicks from cameras audible in the space.

'I'm doing this competition because it's time. I have had enough rest, and it's time for the next chapter. For a long time, I sat in the shadows, but that's done now.' She eyed Robbie again. 'I'm here to win.'

Andy nodded, smiling. 'Thanks Rebecca, and the next question is to you, Robbie, if I may?'

Robbie's head perked up, and he made a finger gun at him. 'Shoot.'

Andy raised a brow but didn't miss a beat. 'Thank you. Tell us please, how does it feel to be competing against the Ice Rebel?'

Robbie's smiling lips froze in place and Rebecca resisted the urge to smirk. Only just. Looking away, she scanned the crowd, and then she was staring into Luke's eyes. He didn't look away.

'It feels great, I'm looking forward to it. Like Rebecca says, it's all to play for now.' He gave her a sneering look disguised as a friendly little nod. She rolled her eyes, making a couple of reporters on the front row titter. She looked back to Luke and he was rolling his. Heidi Erskin was getting questioned now, and she took the chance to take him in. He looked tired, but his eyes were sparkling at her from across the room.

She had rather hoped that in the last month he might have gone to seed a bit, like any decent ex should. Nothing major, she wouldn't have liked him to just waste away to a husk without her or anything. They might be from Yorkshire, but this wasn't *Wuthering Heights*. She just wanted a little jowl, or a clump of grey hair perhaps. A sign that he felt as utterly lovesick as she was. She'd been baking, crying and skiing like a madwoman all month. The fact that she had eaten half of what she made was a given. She'd even started making her own ice cream after she got sick of eating the low-fat stuff. The café customers loved it luckily. Between all the hand churning and the skiing, she'd managed to stay trim. Her hip didn't ache any more. Being back on the slopes, trying to ski away her rage and heartbreak, she'd gotten her groove back. Her body responded to her better than ever before, and she felt herself smiling when she woke every morning. She was back. Those first ten glorious seconds when she woke, and she was a ski champion, living her life in the mountains. Then Luke puffed into her head, and she was back to crying, baking, eating and skiing. Sniffing the after-shave he left in the bathroom, and trying not to cry. Pathetic. The least he could do is look like he'd been mauled by a tiger or something.

'Any more questions for me?' she asked, when the conversation lulled. 'I am so grateful to you guys for coming out, but I have a prior engagement.' She went to stand, and most of the room stood with her. Waving them away, she gave a cheery wave to the cameras and headed off the stage. She headed towards the back, but Luke wasn't where he was standing just a second before. Had he left?

She said hello to the guys on the door, walking out of the room and hearing the doors close behind her. The corridor was empty.

'Looking for someone?'

She whirled back to the door, and there he was.

'Yes. No.'

'I don't know anyone called No, sorry. Have you tried the front desk?' His lip twitched. 'Was it me?'

'Who told you to come?'

'No one told me to come, Becks. I came because I wanted to. Was it me, that you were looking for?'

'Hans told you. Holly would never break the girl code, even with baby brain. I'm going to set his bloody beard on fire when my nephew is of age.'

'Our nephew,' he corrected softly.

'Our nephew.' She gave him that one.

'And we own a sofa together. I like it.'

'It is nice. How's your dad?'

They could hear clapping behind them, and the shuffle of chairs and papers being moved around.

'He's not in hospital now. We'd better go.'

He held out his hand just as the doors opened, and Rebecca stopped as half the journalists in the room clocked the moment. She could see Andy give her a discreet thumbs-up behind his clipboard, and she turned and put her hand firmly in Luke's. He squeezed it tight, his thumb stroking hers like two reunited swans.

'Rebecca? Ice Rebel? Who's the guy? A new ski partner? Can we have a name?' A murmur was starting to buzz, they'd recognised Luke too.

'A name, Rebecca?'

'Is this your new man?'

'Is he competing too?'

Luke was trying to walk her as briskly as possible out of the centre. 'I'm sorry, oh I shouldn't have come. I shouldn't have left in the first place, but Dad . . . and I cocked it all up again. Jesus . . .'

He was looking at her as if she was going to go stellar on him again, and he was still trying to shield her from the reporters and rabble. Robbie would be there somewhere, enjoying every minute. Just feeling his hand in hers wasn't doing enough to calm him down this time.

'Let's get out of here, we can get a cab and drive somewhere. Ditch them. I'll fix it. Let me.'

Rebecca stood near the door, and turned around to face him, the small crowd slowing and surrounding them.

She grabbed his cheeks between her hands, and pulled him in for a kiss. He was still babbling away, but the second their lips met, he threw his arms around her, lifting her off the floor and kissing her with everything he had. When they finally came up for air, the crowd now loving every minute, clapping and whooping. The noise deafened them both.

'Bubble,' they said together, touching their foreheads together and laughing.

'I'm sorry, Bec. And for leaving.'

'You had to.'

'Not like that. Never again.'

'Till next week.' He pulled his face away a little bit, but she kissed him again. 'I've been talking to Mum. I'm due a visit.'

He grinned broadly, kissing her again. 'Let's get out of here.'

'One minute. I want to introduce you. Can I?'

He flashed his white teeth at her. 'Go for it.'

Turning to the crowd, Rebecca took Luke's hand in hers, and he stood right with her. 'I'd like to introduce to you the hot new competitor on the novice challenge, Luke Sommersby. My boyfriend.'

Andy started to clap, and the interviews that Robbie was conducting came to a grinding halt as the reporters all wandered over now. When the clapping finally finished, all eyes were on them.

'Say hello Luke,' she laughed when his face went white.

'Hello,' he stammered, pushing his glasses up his nose. Rebecca saw that he'd seen Robbie. His next words were loud, and as clear as a bell. 'I'm Luke Sommersby. Mr Ice Rebel to my friends.' The crowd laughed. 'I am entering the competition for my father, Frank Sommersby, who is a huge fan of the sport, and my late mother Mariella Sommersby, who loved the snow too.' He threw his arm around Rebecca. 'And my girl, of course. Who is going to kick arse too, by the way. In the unlikely event that I win my challenge, I will be donating my prize money to a local centre in my hometown, who specialise in stroke care and rehabilitation. Their care of my father has been second to none.' The reporters loved that, but she could tell Luke didn't care.

'As will I,' she declared, laughing at Luke's horrified face. The reporters were lapping it up, dancing around like little excited monkeys. Well, some of them did throw poo about for a living.

'No Becks!' he whispered, and she tapped him on the nose.

'Oh, shut up, I love your dad. It's not about the money, is it?'

'I love you.' His eyes bulged. 'I didn't mean that. I meant to say, er. No, sod it. I love you. I do.' He pushed his glasses back up his nose. One of the reporters made an aww sound, and he looked across at them sheepishly. 'Er, a minute, please?'

Andy took charge. 'Come on, let's give them a minute. We've got plenty here. Good to see you back, Becks,' he waved, collaring a couple of the pushier ones and corralling them all towards the press lunch.

They headed away from there, Rebecca pushing Luke into the disabled toilet just around the corner. Locking the door behind them, they both listened outside.

'Okay, coast's clear.'

He reached for her, but she pushed him back a little.

'Just let me get this out, okay?'

'Right here? Kinky.'

'Luuuke!'

They both shushed each other, and then shushed each other for shushing.

'Sorry.' He pressed his lips together tight, and pretended to zip it.

'I'm a bit stubborn.' His eyebrows hit the roof. 'No, I am.' He rolled his eyes. 'I'm stubborn, and awkward. Or I thought I was, till I met you. You are a super dork.' He nodded proudly. 'When you entered that competition for me, you reminded me of Robbie. Of everything I had walked away from. I got mad. And you're leaving, and I just thought well, good, that saves a conversation—'

He started to reach for the zipper.

'Then I told you to go, and then I got hammered, and you were gone. I was mad at that too, even though I told you to go but still—'

He unzipped another couple of teeth, and she sped up.

'Anyway, I got mad, and you weren't here. And then you were here, and Mum said I was an idiot, but she was right, and—'

Another couple of teeth came unstuck, and Luke opened the corner of his mouth. He looked like a wonky duck.

'And ... and ... and ... I love you, and I want to win the competition. You were right, I can do this. All of it. I'm not going to hide anymore. Screw being scared. The best thing about it is, I love you. I said that, right? Before the ski monologue? Because that matters too Luke, just as much. More even.' She took a deep breath, bending over at the stitch she had given herself. It felt like her stomach had just unknotted itself and was doing a victory dance. The ball of dread and worry dissolved. 'Oh God!' She jumped back up, slapping herself on the forehead. 'I forgot to tell you, Hans wants to call the baby Thor. Please stop him before he tells Holly his idea.' She panted again, catching her breath. 'You can unzip now.'

Luke unzipped his mouth. 'You love me.' His big daft grin melted her on the spot.

'I love you, yes.'

'No more spare room?'

'No more spare room.'

'Good, I missed your bed this past month. The sheets back home just aren't the same.'

'Full of pee, probably.'

'Ha. Probably.' He reached behind her, turning the lock. 'Let's go home and test that theory.'

Heading out of the centre, arm in arm, Luke suddenly stopped dead.

'What?'

'Thor, really? Did he tell you that?'

Rebecca pulled him along, eager to get home. 'No, I saw his baby name list.'

Luke giggled. 'That was me.'

She slapped him on the shoulder. 'You didn't! I thought that was his idea!'

'I did, but I doubt Holly will focus on that one. He had some weird ones himself. Eggbert was on there too.'

'I know.' She laughed again. 'I added a few myself.'

Chapter 13

Frank squinted at the screen.

'I can't see him, can you?'

The line of competitors were there out in the snow. The camera panned around to the organiser, who was presenting third place.

'Congratulations again, Serena Valentino!' Serena waved at the camera, her huge goggles obscuring most of her tiny frame.

'Look at her. Tiny. She went like a rocket, but her legs are like toothpicks. It's the aerodynamics you know.'

Marilyn sat on his bed, moving the pot of fresh flowers she'd brought in that morning so she could get a better look. She was knitting away, her eyes focused on the screen. Frank put his good arm around her, pulling her in to his side. She kissed him on the cheek.

'Next time, do that with the other arm.' He rolled his eyes at her, but nodded along.

'I'll do it for a bacon butty.'

'In second place, with an impressive round, and all obstacles successfully navigated, Luke Sommersby!'

They both jumped up, bouncing up and down on the bed. Marilyn threw her knitting into the chair and shouted out to Dante, who was stood with the nurse at the medication trolley just outside.

'Second place! He got second place! Fifteen thousand euros for this place!'

Dante whooped, hugging the nurse and totally taking her off her feet.

'Yes! Hear that, Pam?' Pam was twerking her head off.

'I hear new equipment, Dante, and I like it!'

Marilyn left them boogying around the trolley and dashed back to Frank's room. He was looking at the screen, watching his son take a trophy and a huge cheque. He'd looked so confident out there, Rebecca and Hans either had remote control skis, or Luke was a very fast learner. The whole time his son had been on that screen, Frank had waited for the usual constricting fear to take him over. The feeling he had had since the day he'd driven home from the hospital with a baby in the back of his car, and his life in tatters around him. He waited for it to kick in, but when Luke finally came to a stop and had crossed that finish line, all he could remember thinking the whole time was one word. WOW.

'You okay?' Marilyn asked him, a she dabbed at a tear he didn't know he'd shed. Turning to look at her, he slowly manoeuvred his arm off the pillow it was resting on, and putting it around Marilyn's middle, he gave her a tiny little squeeze.

'Oh Frank!' Marilyn looked at his arm as if it was made of solid gold, and to be honest, Frank felt like a millionaire at that moment. 'You did it! I knew you could do it.'

He didn't tell her he'd been practising extra hard. He'd had enough of waiting for life to end. That's what he had been doing, really. Just waiting till it ended, and he'd done his job. Kept his son safe. Now, he was a man who wanted out of this bed. He was a man with plans too. He looked at his son on the screen again, Rebecca running into his arms the second he stood off the podium. He was safe, and happy.

'I did, but my terms have changed.'

'You don't want my baps now?' she quipped, and he laughed,

concentrating hard on his arm around her waist as he moved her that bit closer. 'Go on then, what's the new deal?'

'A bacon butty, and a date.'

Marilyn blushed.

'Frank, I would love to, but I do have to say one thing.' She brushed a bit of pillow-ruffled hair back behind his ear, and he waited. This was something that he'd been waiting a long time for. It's just took a bit of drama to help him figure it out. Marilyn had always been the one he'd talk to, call when he was feeling blue. They'd put flowers down together for their lost loved ones, and she'd never once asked him for anything.

'Go on,' he said. 'Be nice though, my courtship rituals are a bit rusty.'

'I was just going to say, it's about bloody time!'

His phone rang, and Luke's name came up on the screen. They reached for it together.

This is it. This is it. Rebecca waited to head to the top, whilst Robbie stood at the bottom. The Alpine challenge was an obstacle course on the main slope that stood here. She'd been here before so many times, but this was her first time down it since the accident. The qualifiers had been different, on the lesser slopes. Alpine Gins wanted nothing to dull down the tension of the day to come. They wanted people to salivate for the event, and that they were. The stands were packed, the café full of people, so full they spilled out onto the street.

'You okay?' Hans stood beside her. He looked knackered.

'I should be asking you that. Little Thor still not sleeping?'

'No. He might as well have a hammer. It would be less annoying. I can hear him now.' He shoved a gloved finger into his ear, waggling it.

'I can't believe Holly liked the name.'

'Luke's dead to me now. I've told him,' Hans quipped.

She grinned, thinking of Luke who was basically like Tigger

waiting for her to take her shot. Hans had physically restrained him, telling him to go watch in the café with Holly and Thor. They were in the flat so they didn't scare the customers off. They all knew he wouldn't.

'He did well, didn't he?' She had felt the dread when Luke's turn had come. She'd gripped Hans tight the whole time, not even minding when he squashed her to him. He'd looked amazing. Hans was right, he could do anything. 'Don't be too mad about the name.'

'Wait until you have kids,' he grumbled. 'I'm going to pick the worst name ever.'

He nodded to someone behind her, and she heard the Tannoy of the announcer come to life.

'It's time, you can do this,' he urged quickly. 'You just need to beat him.'

Hans had bowed out of the competition with his baby coming a little bit early, but he'd dragged himself out to support her.

'Thanks Hans, for everything.'

'Please welcome our next and final Alpine Challenge Champion Slalom competitor, Rebecca Atkins. The Ice Rebel, with a time to beat from our current frontrunner, Robbie Goulding, of 1:42:46!'

Rebecca went through the motions, getting into position, readying herself. Alpe d'Huez stretched out beneath her, and she could feel the crisp air being sucked into her lungs. She nodded at the crew next to her, and the signal was sent that she was ready. She could hear the buzz in the crowd, see people with banners. They looked like ants waggling confetti. She always used to tell herself that, when she was up here, in this moment. They can't see my fear up here. I look ready, coiled. Looking at the lights, she waited for the signal.

Ready . . .

She took a deep breath. She wanted this, but it didn't define her anymore. She was a ski champion, and she would always love that, but she was more than that. She was a baker, and a lover. A daughter and a friend. An auntie to the future King of Asgard.

Set . . .

Another breath, and she focused on the poles laid out in front of her like a runway.

'Come on Ice Rebel, let's show them what we've got,' she whispered to herself, and the light changed. *Go . . .*

She pushed off, her feet leaving the floor and her skis flying through the air, snow flicking off in all directions as she took flight. She listened to the wind, and her body, and braced, getting her feet and body into the perfect alignment to connect with the snow once more. She felt a flash of panic as she looked down at the people below her. She felt like she was soaring down the slope in slow motion, everything slowing down but her heartbeat.

'Don't panic, don't panic, keep it together!' she said out loud, her hands gripping the handles of her ski poles. 'You are going to land. You are going to be fine.'

She got a flash of something, the memory of how she felt when she'd landed the last time. How her feet had fallen out from under her. Her ski had snapped, detaching the boot and sending her half cartwheeling and half crashing to the snow. The panic she'd felt when her body finally came to a stop was something that she would never forget. She wouldn't survive that again.

'So don't fall,' Luke's voice came into her head. She thought of him down there, how scared he must feel too. It helped, to think of him, waiting for her. Win or lose, she'd be fine. She'd recover.

As she began the final descent to the slope, a calm washed over her with that new nugget of information, and she took a deep breath, dipped her knees and watched the ground come up to meet her. Contact. Her skis stood fast, and everything worked as it should.

'Still on my feet!' she crowed, taking a second to pump the air with a pole-clutching fist. She landed perfectly and headed towards the first set of poles. Traversing them easily, she ignored the crowd whizzing past, the cameras that would be focused on her determined face, the fact that the man she loved was down there watching. She just flew.

Before she had a chance to blink, she was at the bottom. The snow was spraying up from her feet, and she could feel the crowd erupt around her. Pulling off her goggles, she turned to look at the huge clock display, and saw her dad. He was waving at her like a maniac, dressed like a camping shop had exploded all over him. Her mother was standing next to him, waving a banner saying THAT'S OUR GIRL! GO BECKS! whilst drinking out of a pocket flask.

The announcer sprang to life, and Rebecca pushed her fingers to her lips quickly, putting it over her heart. Her mother burst into overwrought tears, and her dad blew her a big smacker back. I'm so glad they came. It's how it always should have been.

'The official time for Rebecca Atkins, The Ice Rebel, is . . .'

The Tannoy went all Charlie Brown in her head when the screen display sprang to life. Wuh-wuh-wuh-wuh.

1:37:18. Oh my God. That says 1:37:18.

The announcer popped back into her bubble of shock.

'Alpine Gins has a new champion ladies and gentlemen! Rebecca Atkins, the Ice Rebel, and now, the Alpine Champion!'

'Noooooooo!' Robbie exploded behind her. His whiny voice was unmistakable. She watched as two women danced around him like little yappy chihuahuas in snow suits, trying to soothe his ego.

The place was going wild, and before she had much chance to process anything, she was in the thick of the crowd. She looked for her parents, but they were making out with each other against the barrier, so she gave them a moment. She wanted Luke. She kept scanning the crowd, talking to people, smiling for photos, letting the crew behind the scenes take her out of the ruckus, to get ready for the ceremony. Her poles were whisked off by a crew member, and she had autograph books and microphones shoved in her face. She saw a flash of something ginger and suddenly Luke was in front of her, basically being used as a shield by Hans, who was weaving through the crowd with surprising ease.

'Hans! When I said get me to Rebecca, I didn't mean as a battering ram!'

Hans ignored him, fist bumping Rebecca.

'My friend, you were better than ever. Congratulations!' He hugged her, pushing Luke's face away with one hand as he tried to wiggle in.

'Hans, bugger off!'

Hans gave him a dead arm, laughing hysterically as Luke span like a top.

'Ha ha, that will cheer me up for a bit. You still owe me.'

'Whatever Odin, let me kiss my girl.'

Hans formed a human shield for them to hide behind from the masses.

'Bubble,' they said together. Luke kissed her, pulling her tight to him.

'Hey, do you think you could wear the skis later? That was HOT!' He fanned himself theatrically. 'You were amazing. I don't think I took one breath or blinked the whole time. Your mother gave me a tot of whisky though, saw me through.' He met her eye. 'How do you feel?'

Looking around at the place she had called home for so long, feeling Luke wrapped around her, she smiled.

'I feel like I'm still standing right there.'

She pointed to the tip of the slope.

'In a good way?' Luke frowned.

She looked at her parents, who were now standing next to Hans, pretending not to watch them. Hans looked like he was asleep. He kept wobbling a little, his eyes fluttering.

'In the best way. I have all that.' She nodded to the view. 'But the best stuff is found right here, at the bottom.'

Luke pulled her to him and kissed her till they were pulled apart by the excited revellers.

Chapter 14

Pocklington, Yorkshire

Frank pulled the comb through his hair for the fiftieth time, tutting into the hall mirror. His face still didn't look the same. It looked a lot better, but the last few months had taken their toll. He was a little slower, but he'd get there. He wondered why Marilyn didn't seem to mind. She looked amazing, had always kept herself well. He thought back to how they had been over the years, why he was such a blind idiot. She'd always been there, right there. God, he couldn't wait another blessed minute. He was going to take life and give it a good squeeze, get the juice out of it. No more someday. He gave his reflection another look and winked at himself in the mirror. *Go get em' Tiger.*

He turned to the sound of a snigger behind him, and he jabbed his cane out. 'Oww! Dad!'

'Serves you right, mocking him.' Rebecca straightened Frank's tie, smoothing the hair at the back of his head. Luke had the same fluffy hair. 'You look great Frank. All set?' Frank tapped his pockets, picking up the small bunch of flowers he'd hand-picked from his garden up and tucking them under his arm. She dropped a kiss on his cheek, smoothing the lip gloss off. 'Go and have fun. No pressure.'

'Top of the mountain,' he said, winking.

'Top of the mountain,' she beamed.

'Home by twelve, or we lock the doors.' Luke dodged the cane swipe this time, but Frank got faster with every mock. 'Missed me.'

The taxi beeped outside, and Frank stood to attention like an army cadet.

'Come on, Dad, Marilyn's here.' Marilyn was sitting in the cab. They were headed out to dinner, their first official date. Luke went to help his dad, but he stopped him with a steady hand.

'No son, it's okay. I can do this.' He stood out onto the path, cane in his hand, flowers in the other and off he went. Luke and Rebecca watched from the door, watching Marilyn's face as Frank walked towards her down the front path. He got to the taxi, and Marilyn got out.

'He's done it! Knew he would.' He pulled Rebecca into his arms as they watched the two say hello.

'Of course he did! He's bloody stubborn, like you. He wanted to go on this date on his own steam. He's been waiting a long time for this.'

She felt Luke nod behind her. 'Months, bless him. I never thought he'd ever leave the hospital that first week. Oh, she likes the flowers.' Marilyn had pulled Frank in for a hug, and the next minute, Frank was kissing her. His stick fell to the floor, forgotten.

'Something tells me that he's been waiting a lot longer than months.' Rebecca closed the door, pulling Luke away from the lovebirds. 'You Sommersby men are not naturally great with the ladies, are you?'

Luke huffed, bending to lift her into a fireman's carry. She squealed as he took her into the lounge, twirling her around in front of the tree. They'd had such a laugh, the three of them. Decorating the house, seeing the Yorkshire sights, meeting Luke's friends . . . She was a world away from Alpine Bites and dinners for one, but she felt so connected now. To home, and here. They were heading to her parents next week, before heading back home.

'I think we do alright. I'll have you know, my girlfriend is the current Alpine Ice Queen, and word is, she's going to beat her personal best next year.'

'The word's out, eh?' The two of them sat together in front of the fire. 'Well, must be true then. Hans thinks he can take me on, he's still wounded he slept through most of last time.'

'What a baby. The marker pen genitalia rubbed off eventually. You looking forward to going home?'

Rebecca thought of their lodge above the café. Luke's old room was now his office, and he worked all over the world from right in that spot, whilst she baked downstairs. *The skiing baker.* Their trophies stood behind the counter on a shelf, along with a photo of them from that day, standing with their friends and families – Luke holding up a phone screen, Frank and Marilyn's little faces in the frame. She thought of the upcoming season, and the thrill of standing on the top of that mountain again, with the world beneath her feet and people to share it with.

'Mr Alpine Ice Queen.' She kissed his neck, making him shiver. 'Wherever we are, I'm home.'

He took her into his arms, and they sat watching the fire.

'Bubble,' they said in unison.

Acknowledgements

Every book is special, and the people involved make it special too. Big thanks to Belinda Toor and the HQ team, I love working with you guys. Here's to many more books. Thanks to Lina Langlee for being my agent on this book, and thanks to the Kate Nash Agency.

A big shout out to the RNA and my writer friends, there are too many to name and I always worry about leaving someone out, but you know who you are. Thanks for being such great mates. You make the words flow and inspire me every day.

Thanks as ever to my wonderful family and friends for their support and love, and the biggest thanks of all go to my readers. Thank you for sticking with me, I love you all. Here's to many more book boyfriends being taken (dragged) on adventures by kick ass women who are not afraid to show their heart AND their teeth.

Never let anyone tell you romance is just fluff, it's the gravy of life. We need it in our lives, so thank you for reading my stories and enabling me to write even more. Bookworms rule.

Keep reading for an excerpt from
The Second Chance Hotel . . .

To You

If I was writing this letter under better circumstances, I could have written a much better opening. I'm sitting here on my bunk trying to think of what to say. I don't even know what to call you. I know we have to be careful. If I could, I would say your name over and over for the rest of my life. How lucky people who see you every day are, for they get to say it willy-nilly.

For you, nothing seems appropriate, or enough, so I decided that You will have to do. My You. My one and only You.

I have the shell you pressed into my hand that night, and I haven't stopped looking at it. It smells of you, of home, and it makes me feel like my recurring nightmare was just that, and that my real life is still there, at Shady Pines with you.

How long do we have left, till the letters have to stop? I fear the day, yet I know it must come. You must live your life, and I should at least try to start mine. Even with the huge You-shaped hole in my soul. Don't tell me, not till you have to. While you're free, let's pretend, just you and Me.

G

Chapter 1

April Statham sat as close to the steering wheel as she could get, nudging herself and her clapped-out brown Ford Escort along the road, turning slowly into the entrance to the chalet park. Unfortunately, a few seconds earlier, a horse rider had passed, and now his steed was going to the toilet in the middle of the road, leaving a huge steaming pile of horse plop right in the entranceway. April wasn't really one to believe in signs, but this was kind of hard to miss.

'Er . . .' She wound her window down. 'Excuse me?' The horse, and the rider, a thin man whose long features mirrored that of his thoroughbred, dipped their heads to look at her. 'Could you possibly move your horse? I need to pass.'

The horse snorted loudly. Or was it the rider? Both parties looked equally nonplussed, but the man nodded once and the horse trotted away, leaving his . . . offerings. April turned the car into the lane, avoiding the pile, and headed for the large wooden hut marked 'Reception'.

'Bloody great pile of steaming poo in the entrance, great advert for the place,' she muttered under her breath, her eyes flicking down to her petrol gauge, which was pointed straight at zero. Past zero, truth be told. She could feel the change in the engine, the car chugging along on petrol fumes. She pulled into the space marked 'Management' in between the reception hut and a small chalet. She yanked up the handbrake and turned the key in the ignition to off. She could swear that her car breathed a sigh of relief as the engine cut out. They had made it, her and her little car, all the way from Yorkshire to the tip of the Cornish coast. She sat back in her seat, her limbs and back stiff and wizened, as though she had been tied in a knot somewhere along the A38 and had driven bunched up like a pretzel ever since.

She was just easing the knots out of her neck when a sharp tap on her window made her jump. A woman stood there, her face pinched up tight, her dark hair tied into curling rollers on her head. She was wearing a pink dressing gown and dark green wellies, and looked more than a little crazy, even at 8 a.m. on a Monday morning. April wound her window down wearily, plastering a patient smile on her face.

'Are you lost?' the woman said pointedly, looking from inside the car to the boxes and suitcases strapped to a roof rack that April had nabbed from a Freecycle site. Her suitcases came from there too, with her not wanting to take the monogrammed luggage set she had been given as a wedding present. His and hers. She'd left it next to Duncan's in the detached garage. Camped out in her late mother's house. They'd looked so pathetic sitting there together, never to be used again, as they once were on honeymoon, and on their exotic holidays and horrifying business trips he'd dragged her along on.

'No,' said April. *Yes, I am a bit. I think I've made a big mistake.* 'I'm not lost.'

The woman looked again at the worldly belongings strapped to the roof and sighed, a small unsympathetic sigh that made April feel about an inch tall.

'Well—' the woman raised her eyebrows again '—you look lost. Can I call someone for you? We're expecting the hotshot new owner at some point today.'

'I'm the new owner,' April tried, her voice a faint whisper. 'I own this place.'

The woman, having caught the gist now, looked at her with wide eyes.

'You?' She leaned into the car window, her head floating there like a balloon. 'You—' punctuated by a jab of the finger in her direction '—actually bought this place?'

April nodded slowly. The woman began to laugh.

'Pull the other one, love, it's got bells on.' She guffawed, her face looming in April's window like an animal in a safari park now. A camel sprang to mind. Something that could spit at you from ten paces if it saw fit. Yanking her head back out, the woman tapped twice on the top of April's car and carried on her way, disappearing as quickly as she had appeared.

April was suddenly alone again, wondering what the hell she had gotten herself into. *Hotshot new owner? What had the camel . . . er . . . the woman heard?* April didn't want to ruffle any feathers here before she had even unpacked so much as a solitary toilet roll. Why did she think April was a hotshot? *Oh God.* She'd said 'we'. 'We have been waiting for the new owner.' Who were 'we'? The woman had obviously found her lacking, and once more, April's eyes turned to her phone, sitting there innocently in her handbag. It looked so normal, but April felt as though the damn thing was a ticking time bomb waiting to explode on her frazzled brain with an influx of messages. Posts on social media of 'You okay, hon?' People commenting on her life, strangers and people who didn't know her well at all. Not the real her, and nothing like the post-divorce her. Emails from old acquaintances. Purchase reminders for occasions she didn't need to be reminded of at all. Ever. It would all be in there, lurking.

It had been bad enough already, without her sudden departure from everything and everyone. Divorce was a great vehicle for gossip, her mum had told her. Boy, was she right, as ever. April had turned all her notifications off. If she didn't need to use the damn thing to navigate, she would probably have pitched it into the nearest and deepest river she could find.

Soon, news of her escape would spread around her hometown, and the gossip would start again. *She couldn't have kids, you know. Tried for years, they did. Broke them apart. Still, his new girlfriend seems lovely. Child-bearing hips, that one. Shame about April, though. She never did quite fit in.* They chatted on social media as if they were in the hairdresser's or in the Post Office queue. *What was it that Gran used to tell me? Oh yeah. Loose lips sink ships. No wonder I feel like a crap second-hand dinghy with a Hello Kitty plaster holding in my deflated soul.*

They'd be feasting soon, beaks sharply stuck in everyone else's business. Just like the buzzards to return to a carcass in the hope they'd missed a piece of flesh, a strip of soft underbelly to rip from the bones of her failed life. She had failed as a wife, as a—

April stopped that train of thought by grabbing her phone and jabbing the off button hard, till the screen powered down. She didn't need her map app now, so why would she leave it on to tick away like a tell-tale heart? She felt instantly better. She was gone, out of their reach. She'd rather thought that being 'off grid' would make her feel a tad edgy or a bit hippyish, but instead, she just felt relief. Bone-deep relief. Un-contactable. Freeeeeee! Relief that she wouldn't have to endure their pitying stares and sympathetic nods, complete with the 'little rub'. People thought that rubbing your arm or your shoulder was comforting, but it was just a bit too condescending for April. She hated it more than anything. She felt like a simpleton half the time after they had descended on her. What a joy life could be After Duncan. AD. Life after husband.

Zipping up her oversized handbag, she looked once more out of the window at the corner of the world she would now call home. It looked a little like how she felt: neglected, empty, peeling at the corners. Muted against the blue of the sky above. She pulled herself out of the car, her bones popping and cracking as her body unfurled itself. She could feel the shale beneath her feet, her black and white sneakers crunching as she looked around her. The Shady Pines Chalet Park was perched on a beautiful strip of land near Lizard Point, Kynance Cove a short distance away. From the park, April knew from memory that there was a direct walkway to the beach area, for the use of her guests. It had been there for many years and was one of the biggest selling points to her, the thought of waking up and having her toes in the water to start her day right.

Stretching her legs, she walked slowly to the reception hut, brand-new keys in hand. She'd picked them up from a key safe at the estate agent's that morning, and now here she was, about to start her new life. Taking a gulp of the sharp sea air deep into her lungs, she unlocked the door. The key slotted into the metal housing like a glove. There was a slight resistance, salt in the old locks making the mechanisms stick, but then she felt it turn, and the lock click open. It was times like this, right now, that April felt like she had done something right, for once. She'd done this; she was here. It was all hers, a new life for the taking. If she hadn't sworn off social media, she would have snapped a photo of the moment for Instagram with a witty hashtag like #divorcerules or #suckonthatduncanyouutterwan—

Maybe not. Not like she threw herself a divorce party, was it? She'd spent half the day crying, the rest feeling completely out of her depth. She obviously wasn't feeling #blessed quite yet, but she could fake it for now. This was her new life; it was time to get cracking. Pushing open the door, she took a step forward . . . and hit the deck with a very loud and dusty bang.

'Ouch! Broken boobs!' April shouted, or tried to shout. Since her face was smushed into the now broken wooden door, it came out as a muffled humming sound. Prising her lips off the peeling paint, she pushed herself up on her arms and inspected the damage. The whole door had collapsed, the hinges still attached to the door beneath her. Standing, she inspected the wooden frames and saw that the wood was old, brittle to the touch. It crumbled to dust and fell through her fingers.

'Great,' she grumbled under her breath. 'Better find a carpenter pretty sharpish, before the rest of my life turns into the bottom of a rabbit hutch.' She heaved up the door, resting it on her face at one point to get a better handle on the heavy wood. Placing it to one side of the room with a loud bang, she looked at the dust on her plain black T-shirt and old blue jeans and sighed. She brushed herself down, gingerly around the already bruising chest area.

'Well,' she said to the room, looking around. 'Cheers for the excellent welcome, new home. Be careful, or I will use the last of my money to have a wood chipper party, right here.' She pointed her finger to the centre of the floor and braced herself, but the ceiling didn't fall in. Phew.

The reception hut was deceptively large, a square room with a desk off to the left-hand side, complete with a counter in the same faded white-painted wood as the rest of the place. Off to the right, against the wall, were rows of shelving, all empty and filled with dust. The floor was the same white wood, giving the whole room a cube-like effect, and making April feel a bit hemmed in for a second.

There were windows behind the desk on the left, and on the back wall opposite the door was a large set of glass-panelled doors, leading out to a grassed area out of the back. The chalet park ran on the green grass like a horseshoe, twenty blue-and-white trimmed identical chalets, all with their own porches and back patio areas for dining out and sunbathing. Where the ends of the horseshoe met, on the left was the sign indicating the park, with a rack that must have once been used for bicycles alongside it. It was metal and had been painted cream at one point, with pretty shell details around the lettering. Currently, it looked a little worse for wear, the paint peeling and rust-coloured. There was a lone rubber tyre and a dented shopping basket using the facilities, and the sign was tilted to one side, looking as though it was hanging on with the one rusty protruding nail that was still attached. To the right of this was the reception, and on the other side of this, her chalet. It matched the others and looked just as dilapidated. Through the dusty doors, she could see the blue sky and the grass expanse beneath, leading off to the track to the beach. The beach where her mother had taken her, that first night here all that time ago.

It had nearly been dark, the sun setting slowly on their first long day in Cornwall. April had been tired. She remembered how cloudy her head had felt, how she'd moaned when her mother wanted them to see the sunset together.

'When are we going home?' She could hear her little voice now, remembered how her mother ignored her at first. Her back to her, facing the fading sun, head tilted up like a flower head. Her mother's fists clenched when she asked again, her voice whinier, higher. It sounded at odds to the crashing of the waves, the laugh-like call of the birds ahead.

The clenched fists were only there a second, but April thought of her father and shrank back. Her mother turned, but her face was kind.

'April, come here, petal.' April went to her mother, and she turned them back to face the chalet park. Other families were in the chalets, or out on their patios. Playing cards, having a glass of wine. Laughing as the kids played. They passed them on the way to the shore, and the happy noises of life filtered down to the beach.

Hands on her daughter's shoulders behind her, her mother spoke. Her voice sounded different. Louder, somehow.

'You hear that?' she asked, gentler now.

'The sea?'

'The people, April. You hear the people up there?'

April looked past the dunes, where the lights from the park could be seen. She could hear the sounds of people talking, laughing, kids screeching with joy as they played and ran about.

'Yes,' she said, her mouth curving into a smile.

'That's what life is supposed to be like, April. I want you to look around you, my girl, soak it in. I want this for you, all of this. We're not going home, April. It's just going to be me and you from now on, and we'll be just fine.' Her mother squeezed her shoulders, a loving gesture that warmed April through as the words washed over her like the waves behind her. 'This is our second chance hotel, sweetheart. New life starts right here.'

Dear Reader,

We hope you enjoyed reading this book. If you did, we'd be so appreciative if you left a review. It really helps us and the author to bring more books like this to you.

Here at HQ Digital we are dedicated to publishing fiction that will keep you turning the pages into the early hours. Don't want to miss a thing? To find out more about our books, promotions, discover exclusive content and enter competitions you can keep in touch in the following ways:

JOIN OUR COMMUNITY:

Sign up to our new email newsletter: hyperurl.co/hqnewsletter

Read our new blog www.hqstories.co.uk

🐦 https://twitter.com/HQStories

📘 www.facebook.com/HQStories

BUDDING WRITER?

We're also looking for authors to join the HQ Digital family! Find out more here:

https://www.hqstories.co.uk/want-to-write-for-us/

Thanks for reading, from the HQ Digital team

ONE PLACE. MANY STORIES

If you enjoyed *Meet Me at Fir Tree Lodge*,
then why not try another delightfully
uplifting romance from HQ Digital?